# SHATTERED

OTHER BOOKS AND AUDIO BOOKS
BY C. K. BAILEY:

*Whisperings*

# SHATTERED

A Novel

# C.K. Bailey

Covenant Communications, Inc.

Published by Covenant Communications, Inc.
American Fork, Utah

Printed in United States
First Printing: June 2006

11 10 09 08 07 06   10 9 8 7 6 5 4 3 2 1

ISBN 1-59811-067-5

*Dedicated to Susan for her unwavering strength
in holding to the truth.*

*And to those who have suffered loss and
are searching for peace.*

## ACKNOWLEDGEMENTS

Thank you to Lane, my husband and best friend, and to our children for their incredible support and patience.

Also, many thanks to Gerald for his willingness in answering all my questions, and to Betty and Duane for encouraging me to fulfill my dreams.

I would also like to express my appreciation to my editor, Angela. Without her diligence, enthusiasm, and talent, I would not be published.

# PROLOGUE

Despite the below-freezing temperature, sweat poured through Kenny's shirt beneath his coat. Was he getting sick or was it just nerves? he wondered. He couldn't think clearly, not with Greg goading him. "C'mon, you gotta do it! You can't back out now!"

Kenny sank deeper into the snow-filled ditch beneath the hill. "How come there's so many of them? It's only been one guy before. I bet they have guns."

Greg stuck his head above their shelter, glancing at the black sedans and the dozen men in dark coats. They were smoking cigarettes and laughing. "Doesn't matter how many there are. You back out now and it's both our necks!" Greg said.

"You got my money? I haven't seen the money!" Kenny snapped.

"You get the money *after* the delivery. You know that. Now go!"

Kenny drew in a deep breath and stood up slowly. He climbed out of the ditch and worked his way through a hole in the chain-link fence. He concentrated on his breathing as the men began to take notice of him. Each of them simultaneously unbuttoned his coat and placed one hand gently inside and rested it there. *They've got guns all right. I should've gone to school. This is the last delivery I do for this guy. I should never've gotten into this mess.* Kenny took in his surroundings as he continued reluctantly toward the group. He'd watched enough movies to know that somewhere there had to be men on the lookout for cops. The railroad yard had been closed for years. Kenny spied several rust-covered trash cans in the distance. There were bodies huddled around them. A spark of light could be seen every few seconds, no doubt the homeless trying to start a fire in an effort to keep warm. *Don't they see these guys here? I'd be gone if I were them.*

"Hey, kid—you lost?"

Kenny wasn't sure which dark coat the voice came from, so he just stared straight ahead. "Nope. Got a delivery to make."

"Well, then, get on with it. We're gettin' tired of bein' in this miserable weather." Sleet began its descent as he waved Kenny on.

Kenny maneuvered past two men standing at the rear of the car. There was an unexpected jerking from inside the car, drawing Kenny's eyes to the movement. The brawny man who appeared to be Kenny's contact directed Kenny's face back to him, but not before Kenny had taken a look inside. Wide, frightened eyes and a duct-taped mouth stared back until another man in the car moved forward.

"Hey, you mind your business now, boy. If you got something for me, you'd better be getting to it." Kenny's contact placed his muscular frame in front of the window.

Kenny removed a small pouch from inside his layers. It was moist now from sweat. He tossed it to the man and turned around, slowly making his way back to the fence.

The large man leaned in as the passenger window was rolled down. Kenny could hear muffled voices, and then someone called him. He kept moving; he knew that was the rule—no matter what, keep moving.

"Hey, kid! I'm talkin' to you. Now get back here!"

Kenny picked up his pace. He was certain that he could outrun most of them if he could just get through that fence and into the woods. His eyes barely focused on the waving arms before him. What was Greg saying? Kenny couldn't hear him over his own breathing. His heart was racing. Then the sound of a shot pierced his ears. He'd heard gunshots on TV before, but never in real life. The sound surprised him; it was nothing like on TV. Were the shots directed at him? Kenny ran as fast as he could on the snow-covered ground. He could hear engines roaring behind him. *Where is Greg? Did he leave me?* He decided not to look back and focused on the fence instead. *Don't freeze up. Just keep moving,* he warned himself. He repeated those words all through the woods and into town.

# CHAPTER 1

Beth Moon said good-bye to her son as he left for school. It had been several weeks since they'd had a real conversation. Something was wrong, well, something *else* was wrong, she amended. He'd never been the same since his brother's death, but lately it was more. Fear at remembering Patrick's death filled her, and she decided to confront Kenny as soon as he came home from school. She passed the day in anxiety, but Kenny wouldn't have anything to do with talking when he got home from school. He walked past his mother, ignoring her request, and went straight to his room. Shutting the door, he dropped his backpack on the floor and sat at his computer. He flipped it on, opened a file, and began to write:

12-18-2004
Greg's missing. I found out Dad's on the missing-persons case for him and that guy I saw in the car. He was some kind of accountant. I've thought about telling Dad what I've been doing, but he'd kill me. I'd be ratting Greg out, too. He's got to be hiding somewhere. Why doesn't he call me? I'd go with him. I saw Thornton's cars around school today. Are they after me?

"Kenny? Are you coming to dinner?" Beth called up the stairs.

"No, Mom. I'm not hungry. Ate a lot at school," Kenny called back.

"I rented that movie you've been wanting to watch. Thought we could do that tonight."

"I'm really tired, Mom. Maybe another time."

When his mother didn't insist, Kenny spent the next few hours locked in his room. He fell asleep leaning against his headboard, thinking about what he'd gotten himself into.

\* \* \*

12-19-2004

Still no Greg. Jen says he's dead since he hasn't shown up. But what does she know? She never liked him anyway. She doesn't always understand me. He can't be dead. He said those guys weren't dangerous, just greedy. Why would they kill Greg anyway? Doesn't make sense. It's Christmas break now. I don't want to leave the house. I lost the one car following me on my way to Jen's today. I don't know how long I can dodge them. Why are they after me?

\* \* \*

12-20-2004

They found Greg's body in the river. The other guy's too. They were found by ice fishermen. Those shots I heard—it was Greg! I can't believe he's dead. He said they weren't dangerous! They know I saw that guy in the car. I can't tell Mom or Dad. Dad'll just say I'm making it up to get attention. And if he did believe me, he'll say I don't have enough evidence. And Mom will just freak. I have to get out of here earlier than planned.

\* \* \*

"I'm not going anywhere, and you can't make me!" Kenny barked at his mother.

Beth remained calm. "We've been over this. You haven't been speaking to me. You won't leave your room. You won't see your friends. You need to get out, son."

"Don't have any friends."

"You've canceled with your dad three times, Kenny. It's almost Christmas. You've got to go this time."

"No."

"Is it the boy that died at school? Did you know him?"

"Leave it alone, Mom. I'm not going with Dad, and you can't make me. I don't want to see him!" Kenny spun on his heels and darted from the small, antiquated kitchenette. Beth heard the door to his room slam. She turned off the flame under the half-done pancakes and slumped into the nearest chair.

The shrill sound of a siren disturbed the momentary silence. *Here we go,* she thought irritably.

"Hey Beth, you in there?"

"Yes, Michael, it's open."

"Where's Kenny? Didn't you hear the siren?"

"Do you think you could honk like normal people?"

Before he retorted, she quickly changed direction. "Sorry, he's in his room. He's not . . . he's hesitant, Michael."

"Oh, that's b—"

Beth cut him off. "You may not—"

"Swear in this house. Yeah, yeah, I know." Michael's face reflected the agitation that had become a common expression of late. "That kid's always hesitant. I'll go get him," he said, pounding his way up to the second floor.

Beth's eyes followed Michael up the stairs. Michael Moon was a large man, six feet and two hundred fifty-five pounds. There was no mistaking his Italian heritage. He had a head of thick, wavy black hair and a showy mustache. His hard, unapproachable look kept most people at bay.

"Hey, son, open up. Got the car runnin'." Michael waited, listening at the door for signs of life. None came.

"Aw, come on, son. Look, it'll be better this time. I promise. Janice and the girls are with their grandma, like I promised. It's just you and me this weekend."

The lack of response came loud at his ears. "Open this door now, boy, or I'll be swearin' so loud your mom'll pop us both!" Michael pushed at the door, immediately noticing at least a week's worth of dirty clothes on the floor.

His visual search switched to "cop mode" as he made a slower and more complete assessment of the room. "Beth? He ain't in here!" Perplexity twisted his voice.

"*Isn't,* Michael. *Ain't* isn't the best . . . What? What do you mean he's not in there?" Beth raced up the stairs, which was definitely out of character for her since the addition of an extra fifty pounds—her answer to dealing with the divorce two years earlier. "Well, where is he?"

"If I knew that, I wouldn't be yellin' for ya."

"Oh stop it. Did you look in the bathroom? Or are you

just standing there waiting for him to jump out at you?"

Michael bit his lip. He would not lose control. He'd already received three warnings this month from his police chief regarding his temper. He knew a fourth could get him suspended, even if it was just his ex-wife complaining.

"Kenny? Kenny?" Michael and Beth began calling throughout the house.

"His bike is gone," Beth yelled up from the back porch moments later.

"His bike's gone? It's snowing like snot out there," said Michael.

Beth sighed. Michael's gift for metaphors certainly wasn't what she'd been attracted to.

\* \* \*

"What in the Sam Hill?" The older man's vision was blurred by the swirling powder, but he was certain he had seen a red bundle of something off to the side of the road. And then there was that feeling of unease. He had learned over his many years to trust that feeling. He eased off the accelerator, letting the truck roll to a stop. Gently he set the vehicle into reverse, knowing full well that if he got stuck he wouldn't be getting out anytime soon. He hadn't rolled back ten feet when he again spotted the anomaly. Nothing red belonged here on this road, especially in snow this deep. He set the brake and climbed out into a wall of white, his hand sheltering his squinting eyes.

"Stupid blizzard. Weatherman said it wasn't comin' till after Christmas. Not sure why they even have such people. Half the time they're wrong, and the other half they're just plain lucky."

Gramps had always had an excellent sense of direction, and he figured it was a good thing right now because he couldn't see anything. For a split second he considered getting down on all fours and going by feel. But just as he did, a noise stirred his senses. He turned his head slightly, listening. It came again, this time sounding more like a moan. He quickened his pace. It wasn't far.

Moments later he'd pulled the red clump out of the snowdrift. "All right, now I gotcha." Gramps's eyelids were already frozen. He carried his find over his shoulder and slowly made his way back to the truck. Intuition told him another few minutes and he wouldn't have been able to get out. The drifts were piling high.

\* \* \*

"Ryan, you're soaked!" Jessie Winston said as she guided her drenched friend into the front room of his grandfather's cabin.

"The weatherman said a *few* flakes," Ryan Blake said, slamming the door and shutting the blizzard out.

"Where's your truck?" Jessie asked, looking through the snow-frosted front window.

"It's about a half mile back. I don't even know if I was still driving on the road. Couldn't see a thing, so I started walking. It's a wonder I found you. If I hadn't plowed my face into the mailbox, looked up, and seen light, I doubt I'd be here. Where's Gramps?"

"He was gone when I got here. We had a date to play cards. When I couldn't find him, I called your place. He was there. The connection died after a few seconds, but he managed to get out that he was checking on the horses and was planning on bedding down for the night. I'd better find you something dry to put on. I'm not sure if your grandfather owns anything other than overalls, but I'll see what I can dig up." Jessie disappeared down the hall.

Ryan took off his coat and gloves and draped them over a chair close to the fireplace.

With Christmas less than a week away, wreaths and greenery with red bows outlined the walls of the country home that used to be his great-aunt's and was now his grandfather's. Red, white, and green stuffed animals of all assortments and sizes were nestled into every corner. Cinnamon-smelling pinecones in baskets had been placed on the hearth. *Jessie's been busy,* he mused. *This is obviously not Gramps's work. All that's missing is a tree and some mistletoe.*

"Here, these ought to work." Jessie handed Ryan a bath towel and a pair of large gray sweatpants and a sweat-shirt. "Leave your things in the bathroom and I'll throw them in the dryer. I'll be in the kitchen finishing my hot chocolate. You want some? I found marshmallows."

"Sounds great."

Jessie returned with two mugs of mint-flavored hot chocolate. Ryan was bent over, adding logs to the fire. "Here you go," she said, allowing herself only a brief glance at his six-foot-plus muscular frame. She'd tried, but finally realized she couldn't keep up with his daily regimen of working out in an indoor gym and running five miles a day. She considered herself lucky if she didn't faint after two push-ups.

"Thanks," Ryan replied.

"I tried Gramps again. The line was fuzzy, but he knows you're here. He wanted to know if I needed a chaperone. I assured him you'd be a perfect gentleman." Jessie's eyebrows rose slightly. "He said if you weren't, he'd rough you up so bad no one would recognize you!"

"Yeah, he would. I'll be a good boy," Ryan teased.

"How come you're here a day early? Not that it's any of my business, really. It's just that, well, you are here, and it seems like the logical thing to ask." She quickly filled her mouth with the hot liquid, embarrassed by her obvious nervousness.

Ryan's lips formed a slight smile as he looked down at the steam rising from his cup. He figured that, after all these months, Jessie had to know how much she meant to him and that everything concerning him *was* her business. But she was still holding back. Unlike him, she hadn't brought herself to verbalize her love—and he didn't want to push her. He tried to give her the space she felt she needed. "I decided it was time to be 'home for the holidays.' I worked through the last few years of Christmases. I knew you'd come out here to take care of Gramps, but it isn't actually your responsibility, now is it?" Ryan held Jessie's gaze before her eyes fell to her cradled cup.

"Well, we'd have managed. But I know that your being here will mean a lot. He's missing Ruth. He's putting up a good front after all these months, but he sits so forlornly in her old rocker, staring off into the fields."

Jessie, too, had grown fond of Gramps's sister, and missed her terribly. She'd only known the woman a few weeks before she'd died from a stroke. But in those few weeks, she'd learned a great deal from her. Ruth had invited Jessie to stay with her last summer while the home Jessie had bought was being remodeled. Ruth welcomed her, a stranger, into her home without judgment. It was at

Ruth's that Jessie had discovered what she wanted out of life, and it was at Ruth's that she'd found the Book of Mormon.

* * *

"Look, Lieutenant, no disrespect or nothin', but fifteen-year-old kids get mad and take off all the time, you know? He's probably just at some neighbor's or friend's. Who's he hang out with? Have you called them?"

The expression on Michael Moon's face suggested this newbie didn't understand that asking his lieutenant an ignorant question would not earn him a quick promotion. "Well garsh darn, Beth." Michael's drawl was overly pronounced. "There you go. Why didn't we think of that? Call his friends. Now there's an idea." His hands were waving in the air in mock concern.

"Calm down, Michael. He's only trying to help." Beth returned to her position at the kitchenette.

"Calm down? My son is missing! I call the chief and give him the scenario, and he sends out Dudley Do-Right! What am I supposed to do?"

"He's my son too, Michael."

"Then how come you're just sittin' there like he's playing ball or somethin'? He's been gone hours. It's pitch black out there, not to mention freezing!"

"He always comes home. Sorry you had to come out, Officer Sanders." Beth's narrow brown eyes looked up at the young police officer. He looked about fifteen himself. His purple braces didn't help matters.

"Does he have a computer?" Officer Sanders asked.

"Yes. Why?" asked Beth.

"Have you looked through his e-mail for anything unusual? We should take a look at it anyway. Even if he's trashed his messages, we have ways of getting them back."

"We don't have the Internet," Beth replied. "He only has games."

"Okay. Well then, I'll file the report, ma'am. We'll find him if he's out there—won't get too far in this storm. Are you headed back to the station, Lieutenant?"

"Yeah, suppose I'll check in. Then I'll be drivin' around town myself. You'll call my cell if he comes home?" This he directed at Beth.

"Of course."

The young officer followed Michael out the door. Beth watched as both backed their snow-covered cars slowly out of the driveway, then she put her face in her work-worn hands and softly cried.

# CHAPTER 2

Jessie was swallowing her last marshmallow when the electricity went out. "Oh, great."

"Hey, where's the flashlight that's always been in this drawer?" Ryan called from the kitchen moments later.

"I moved it to the cupboard above the sink. I'll get it. I know right where it is." The glow of the fire created a flickering path toward the kitchen. Jessie pushed open the door to the kitchen and peered inside. "Okay, where are you? You jump out at me, and I swear I'll beat the daylights out of you."

"You have no sense of humor." Ryan's voice startled her as it came just two feet behind her.

"Yeah well, that's me—sense-of-humorless. Besides, you know I hate it when you do that." Jessie reached in a cabinet and pulled out a large metal flashlight. She shined it directly in Ryan's face. "Oh. Well, now that's a pleasant pose." Ryan's cheeks were scrunched up and his eyes were shut tight.

He grabbed the light from her hands. "All right, so maybe you do have a sense of humor. You've got to stop rearranging everything in here. It's gotta be driving Gramps crazy. Changing things in your home is one thing, but Gramps's and my place ought to be off-limits."

Jessie reached into the cabinet where she had stored the candles. "It doesn't appear to bother Gramps, but I'll leave your cabin alone." Jessie glanced at Ryan. He was using the flashlight to guide him in stirring his hot chocolate. "You know, I'd reach these candles a lot quicker if you'd shine that thing over here instead of using it to illuminate your cup of cocoa. I realize that's a tough job with you being challenged as you are—"

The light instantly flashed into the cabinet. "I got it. I got it. I may be slow but I'm not stupid."

"Here they are. Grab the pie tins from that cabinet above your head? I'll need four."

They lit the scented candles and set them strategically throughout the home. Ryan placed a couple more logs on the fire while Jessie went to her room to change. Jessie had taken up lodging in the guest room on the weekends since Gramps had moved into his sister's home. She didn't like seeing Gramps so alone, and he enjoyed the company.

"Well now, that certainly gives the air a refreshing scent," Jessie said playfully, entering the family room. She was glad she had her long flannel nightshirt and large, furry, Christmas-green bathrobe. She didn't like showing off her figure, especially around Ryan.

"Kind of a cinnamon-vanilla-lilac thing going," Ryan answered lightheartedly from his spot on the rug.

"Ruth had them for different seasons. I don't think she planned on anyone using them all at the same time." Jessie nestled onto the rug and leaned her back into the love seat. "How was your week?" She glanced momentarily at his alluring blue eyes and assessed how he'd cut his hair. The black and previously shoulder-length hair now rested neatly at his collar.

"Not too bad. Wrapped everything up. The buyers from New Mexico are coming up after the holidays to pick up Odin, and . . ." Ryan said the next words slowly. "They've also offered to buy Joanie."

Jessie didn't respond immediately. She didn't mind Odin being sold. He was a noble horse—an Appaloosa Ryan named after the mythological Norse god of war, knowledge, wisdom, and poetry—but she hadn't bonded with him. Over the summer, however, she had grown entirely attached to Joanie, an Oldenburg. She was mother to the foal Ryan had given her. *Surely he wouldn't sell Rebecca's horse?* Jessie took a deep breath, reminding herself that if Ryan wanted Joanie—*Joan-of-Arc*—to be sold, whether his late wife's horse or not, it was clearly none of her business.

"Jessie, did you hear me?"

"Yes. I thought you decided against the sale."

"They've increased their offer considerably."

"What do they plan on doing with her?"

"They'll breed her, I suppose."

"Oh. So, how's Jill?"

Raising a question about his secretary assured Ryan that Jessie was disappointed at the thought of losing Joanie. He valued her thoughts and opinions and wished she was more willing to share them honestly. But for whatever reason, she'd decided that it wasn't her place.

"Jill's been thinking about going back to college in Missouri. She'll be able to stay on long enough to help me pack and transfer everything to my office at the cabin after the new year. After today's commute, I can't wait to be here permanently. She's considering becoming a therapist herself. Said if I could be one, then she could certainly make a career of it."

"That's for sure," Jessie snickered. Then her tone became matter-of-fact. "It's going to be cold tonight. I'll find you some extra blankets. Gramps only has the comforter in his room." She stood with a simultaneous stretch and disappeared down the hall. She returned with an armful of blankets. "Here you go. That should keep you warm enough," Jessie said. "Well, I'm exhausted. Good night." Jessie checked the front door to make sure it was locked, then headed down the hall toward the back door.

"Good night—and thanks," Ryan replied.

Jessie shut the door to her room. Ryan smiled as he heard the lock turn. He'd grown to respect her over the past few months. He would no more enter her room at night than swim in a crocodile-infested swamp. While her trust in him was building, it had a ways to go.

* * *

"No, No! Please, don't. Stop it!" Jessie's screams echoed through the silence of the night.

Ryan called to her gently from the hall. He waited. Jessie's pleadings continued. "JESSIE, WAKE UP!" he finally shouted.

Jessie's body jerked as it woke. She quickly focused on her surroundings.

Ryan pounded on the door. "Jessie, are you okay?" he called loudly.

"Yes, Ryan, I'm fine," she replied calmly. "I'm sorry I woke you. Please go back to bed."

Jessie lit the candle on the small, round table next to her and retrieved the roll of tissue out of its drawer. She wiped her eyes and patted the sweat on her forehead.

"You've been upset for a while, so I figured I ought to snap you out of it."

"I appreciate it. Now please, I'm fine. Go back to bed."

Ryan rubbed his eyes. "Want to talk about it?" His voice was soothing.

"No."

"You *need* to talk about this."

"I don't want to do this now, Ryan."

"You haven't talked to me in weeks, Jessie. You've cancelled four appointments."

"So? Bill me anyway!"

"I've never billed you, Jessie. We're friends, remember? Not client and patient. And as your friend, I want to help."

"Ryan, Christmas is less than a week away. Can't you just put a sock in it already?" She was out of bed now, frantically pulling on her robe and heading toward the door. "I need some hot chocolate," she said, her long auburn hair smacking Ryan in the face as she flew past him.

"Uh, Jessie?"

"Oh, what now? For crying out loud! Are you going to analyze the fact that I want sugar at two thirty in the morning?"

"No—I thought you'd maybe want to leave the roll of tissue behind."

"What?" Jessie looked down to find the end of the toilet paper stuck to her flannel nightshirt, the rest trailing off behind her to the roll at her bedside. "This is precisely the reason I don't like company." She yanked the tissue off her body and tossed it at the bed, then headed toward the kitchen.

Ryan followed her down the hall, but at a slower pace.

Jessie was standing at the kitchen sink with her back toward Ryan when he walked in. "Since you're obviously not going to go away and leave me alone, do you want something to drink?" she asked brusquely.

"Coffee would be fine, but I can make it."

Jessie slammed the cupboard door shut after retrieving two mugs. "I got it," she snapped. She turned on the kettle and located the hot chocolate and the coffee she'd just bought. "This is all I have."

Ryan sat at the table. "Since when did you start buying decaffeinated coffee?"

Ignoring the question, Jessie stirred at least fifty miniature marshmallows into a mug in which she had yet to add water. She wasn't about to tell him that she was working up to the Word of Wisdom challenge from the Mormon missionaries. There was no love lost between Ryan and the Mormons, and while she hadn't come to understand completely why he resented them, she knew it was deepseated. She had resolved to remain silent about her own discoveries. Besides, the Word of Wisdom hadn't all made sense to her yet, and she could probably be talked out of it at the moment. "I want to enjoy Christmas, Blake. I don't want any psychoanalyzing messing it up."

Ryan reflected carefully about his next line of strategy. Jessie only used his last name when she was headed in the direction of severe wrath. "I just figured since we're stuck here, it was a good time to talk."

"Well, you figured wrong," she said, tapping her fingernails on the table. "I need to get through this *my* way, not the way *you* feel I should," she clarified.

"I'm not without common sense, Jessie. But you've been more distant than usual lately—avoiding my calls, breaking dates, and the nightmares have obviously resurfaced."

"We've never had a 'date.' Well, except that one time after Ruth passed away, and that wasn't really a date—"

"You know what I mean."

The newly lit candles flickered against the whistle of the blowing snow. Jessie stared out the back window at the billowing swirls of white, thankful for the warmth of the cabin. She let out a soft sigh. "I've already promised you that I would come and find you when I needed to bounce something around. I just haven't wanted to bounce anything for a while."

The teakettle burst slowly into song, delaying Ryan's response. As Jessie retrieved the sputtering kettle, Barkley, a red mackerel tabby with the encircling pencil markings of an exotic jungle cat, jumped on the table. He was apparently intent on a thorough examination of the candle's flickering flame.

"No, kitty. Tables are for people, not for furry animals." Jessie placed Barkley in her lap and began stroking him. The cat was more than a companion to Jessie. He was a constant reminder of Ruth. Barkley had originally been her pet, and since Ruth's passing, Jessie and the tabby had adopted each other.

The once-fluffy marshmallows were now mashed together as the hot water streamed into the cup. Ryan retrieved the reindeer-shaped kettle from her hands and refilled his mug. He was amazed at the large assortment of decorations Jessie had for the holiday. The thought brought instant memories of Rebecca. She too had loved to decorate for Christmas. Their cabin had held no fewer than four trees each year. The usual live, festive green fir had adorned their family room. This displayed all sorts of decorations. She'd called it their "hodgepodge" tree. Then there was a tree in the kitchen. This was filled with treats, yards of popcorn, and brightly colored cereal shapes. Added to it was a myriad of candy canes in all sizes and colors; thus, it was rightfully named the "goodie" tree. Their bedroom was home to the "heirloom" tree, filled with both of their childhood memories. The ornaments were trinkets made in their youth and small toys that could easily sit on the branches or around the trunk. Rebecca's favorite tree, however, had always been in the loft. It was a white-flocked fir, hung with white glass ornaments and tiny blue lights. Their "peace" tree brought a sense of calm to the space, and Ryan remembered sharing many nights together next to it, just holding each other.

Ryan figured if they'd ever had kids, they would have exhausted themselves running from tree to tree in an effort to locate the one Santa had left the gifts under.

"I know I've been avoiding you, and yes, I do have reasons. Reasons I'm not ready to share. Please, Ryan, can I have Christmas?"

Jessie's question brought him back to the present. "What? Oh, yeah, understandable. I'll back off until after the new year, but then you're going to have to face some things. It's time."

A relieved Jessie placed Barkley on the floor and began rummaging through the cupboard for more marshmallows. "Where'd you go? You had that glazed look on your face for a minute."

"All the decorations around here got me thinking about Brecca. She loved Christmas. She could hardly wait for Thanksgiving to get over with. The day after was the official day to begin decorating. I wouldn't see or hear anything from her till Monday morning. It was absolutely forbidden to bother her till then."

"You didn't get to help?"

"Oh, no. It wasn't my place. And if I tried, she would shoo me away." Ryan's lips began to curve up in a smile.

"Are you going to put a tree up this year, maybe in the family room?"

"Haven't given it any thought."

"Well, I've been neglectful. That's another reason I came to Gramps's tonight. He and I were going to look for a tree for his place." Jessie let out a yawn. "Okay, well, I think I can sleep now." She placed her mug in the sink and headed out of the kitchen. Before leaving she turned in Ryan's direction, keeping her chin down. "Thanks, you know, for . . . well, you know."

For a moment Ryan considered the several times he had awakened her from tormenting dreams. As a favor for Jessie's employer, he'd returned from early retirement the previous summer; Jessie wasn't sleeping, and it was affecting her work. Her employer knew she would never seek the necessary help she needed to overcome her childhood issues, so he sought help for her. Over the years, many clients had stayed at Ryan's cabin on the weekends with him and his late wife and Gramps. Jessie was angered by her employer's demands that she receive counseling, and had only stayed a couple nights with Ryan and Gramps on threat of losing her job. She didn't want either of them to be involved in her nightmares. But slowly, over time, she'd learned to open up little by little until she saw the benefit of Ryan's help and Gramps's unassuming way of making friends.

"Not a problem," he answered. "Never a problem."

# CHAPTER 3

It was dawn, and all was quiet at Ryan's cabin. The unkempt form on the couch hadn't moved during the night, even when Gramps had removed the parka, wet jeans, and sweatshirt. The boy was in his early teens, Gramps guessed. He had an unusually pimple-free complexion, fiery orange hair, which Gramps assumed was naturally blond, due to the roots that peeked through, and light eyebrows. "Now Nelly, quit being a pest and get on outta here," Gramps said, waving Ryan's large rottweiler away from the boy.

Less than an hour later, the boy began to move. His hair was plastered to his forehead as he sat up. His misty green eyes grew wider as Nelly put her jaw in his lap.

Gramps smiled as he picked up his pipe. "She won't hurt you any. She may have a fierce growl and a mouth full of very effective teeth, but she's a baby. She'd work her way completely in your lap if you'd let her."

The boy just stared, first at Gramps, then back at Nelly. What little tail Nelly had was wagging violently. Gramps set his crossword puzzle down on an end table. "You can call me Gramps—most people do. You got a name, boy?"

Nothing.

"What in blazes were you doin' out in that blizzard?" Gramps waited, expecting a break in the deepening silence. But none came. "Hmm, so that's how it's gonna be, eh? Well, okay. You hungry? Just a slight nod will do." Nothing came from the boy. "I'm not a fancy cook, but I got a pretty good-tastin' ham-and-cheese omelet goin' in the kitchen. It'll be done in just a bit. Why don'tcha go and see if your clothes are dry, and I'll get the table set. They're in the dryer at the end of the hall on the right."

Gramps walked out of the great room and into the kitchen to check the progress of their breakfast. Out of the corner of his eye he followed the boy's slow progression to the hallway. As he disappeared from view, Gramps shook his head slowly, wondering at the boy's plight.

A minute later, Gramps heard an ill-at-ease whine from the normally quiet Nelly. He poked his head around the corner of the kitchen, peered down the hall, and was met with a cold blast of wind from the hall entrance. He darted down the hall and threw open the door to find the boy feeling his way down the second step. The snow pounded furiously in the boy's face, his eyes fighting to stay open. Within seconds the boy found himself being yanked off his feet and placed back in the semiwarmth of the hallway.

"Now, you just hold on there, young man. You aren't goin' to get anywhere in that mess. I don't know what's happened, and it ain't my place to pry, but while you're under this roof, you'll be havin' a few manners. First, you'll be stayin' put till I say so. Second, you'll be takin' that coat off and hangin' it back up on that hook. And then you're gonna sit down in there," he pointed toward the kitchen, "and eat a good meal. You got that?"

The boy simply stared back. He hadn't expected the old man to be so strong.

"All right then," Gramps said, pointing toward the utility room.

The boy slowly unzipped his coat and reluctantly hung it on the hook inside the utility-room door, taking a good look at Gramps. He was a big man, over six feet tall, and quite agile. The boy guessed him to be over seventy. The boy inched his way up the hallway toward the kitchen with Nelly close behind.

"Thatta boy," Gramps said as the lad slumped down in a chair at the kitchen table. Gramps wanted to tell him to straighten up and sit properly, but he figured he'd probably demanded enough for the time being. Both remained silent as they ate. The boy finished his first helping quickly and stared at the empty plate.

"Want some more?" Gramps asked. The boy gave a quick nod to the affirmative. "Well then, pass your plate on over." Gramps was beaming. He enjoyed cooking, especially when those doing the eating were appreciative of his efforts. He wouldn't admit it to the boy, but he was also enjoying the company. It was better than the alternative— being snowed in and alone at the cabin.

* * *

Beth Moon stared into the blizzard from her front room window. Her weary eyes were red and her cheeks were tear-streaked. She hadn't changed her clothes from the day before.

The sudden ringing ripped her gaze from the blizzard's hold. "Kenny?" she cried into the receiver.

"No, ma'am, this is Officer Miller."

Several officers had been put on the case, since her husband was on the force, but she couldn't remember one from the other. "Oh. Sorry. You have news?"

"A lady said that someone rode by her place yesterday on his bike. She remembered because she thought it was rather stupid."

Beth winced at the unkind remark but maintained her composure. "Where was that, please?"

"It was over at Stella's Bakery."

*He's headed north,* thought Beth. *But there's nothing north.* "No one has seen him since?"

"No, ma'am. But he couldn't have gone much farther. We'll go looking as soon as this weather lets up."

"I'll wait for news." Beth hung up the receiver and stared again out the front window at the falling snow.

\* \* \*

Gramps was wiping the counter when Nelly broke into a thunderous bark and pranced excitedly at the front door. "Pipe down already! Let's see what's out there." Gramps opened the door, filling the entry with a frigid mass of blowing snow. Two crystal-covered bodies marched past. "Come on in, why don'tcha," Gramps called, forcing the door closed.

Ryan and Jessie took several minutes removing their layers of protection. Gramps brought in a couple of towels, and the dryer was put to use.

"You guys walked from my place?" Gramps asked incredulously as they entered the kitchen.

Ryan cracked a smile through still-moistened lips. "Remember that snowmobile old man Henry sold Ruth a few years ago?"

"Yeah?"

"Well, it broke down about half a mile back."

"We'll find it when it clears. Did you stick a marker on it?"

"Yes, he did," Jessie replied disgustedly.

Ryan blew into his fists and smiled. "I used Jessie's Christmas scarf."

"That wasn't an ordinary Christmas scarf. It cost me forty-five dollars!"

"Forty-five dollars for a scarf?" Gramps gawked.

"It was deep gray, hand-spun wool with the tiniest white snowflakes all over it," Jessie pronounced as if she had raised her right hand and been told to tell the truth, the whole truth, and nothing but the truth.

"Well then, it'll feel right at home out there!" Ryan jested.

"You two hungry?" Gramps asked. "I can reheat breakfast."

"No, we've eaten," Ryan answered.

"That's if you can actually call burnt pancakes food," Jessie retorted. She unzipped the pack she'd been wearing, and out pounced Barkley. He quickly slithered under the couch. "That big brown dog is around somewhere and he knows it," Jessie laughed.

"The cat could have survived at home, you know," Ryan teased.

"You have your pet, and I have mine. Now if you two will excuse me, I think I'll go and at least decorate the room I'll be staying in, since you're being Mr. Scrooge this year." Jessie threw Ryan a final disapproving look as she turned from the kitchen and headed down the hall to the guest room.

When Jessie had first arrived in June, she'd been silently astonished at the immensity of Ryan's cabin and the grounds outside. The immense log construction was surrounded by bushes and trees, and a miniature hedge encircled the front deck and the porch that held an antique swing and chair which had been put away for the winter. Oval-shaped windows decorated the architecture, and a vaulted roof with skylights added one more unique touch to the three stories of grandeur.

But it was the space inside which overwhelmed Jessie. The kitchen was large enough to house a small apartment. It was U-shaped and opened on its long side to the great room. There were windows running from the solid granite countertop to the ceiling. The appliances were restaurant-style stainless steel. Six black-leather barstools stood perched at an island in the center. The entire back wall and portions of the side walls were made of glass. On the other side of the glass wall was one of Ryan's favorite rooms—the solarium. A waterfall fell from a protrusion of volcanic rock built up in the center. Set off to one corner stood a Jacuzzi, with a sauna built into the wall behind it.

The cabin's decor was simple, sporting contemporary off-white leather with glass-and-chrome accents. Assorted throw pillows and a few knickknacks added color. The great room held an overly large fireplace on one side and a large glass wall on the other, both of which reached all the way up to the three-story vaulted ceiling. A spiral staircase led to the two open floors above. Even as familiar with her surroundings as she now was, Jessie admired the views before her as she headed to the guest room.

"Apparently you found your way out here last night through that maze," Gramps said to Ryan, glancing through the frosted window.

"Lost visibility. I left the truck about a mile or so from your place. Rammed my face into the top of your mailbox. Good thing, or I'd be frozen goods by now."

Gramps slid his glasses down to the top of his nose and picked up his crossword puzzle. "Hmm, truck *and* a snowmobile? Remind me not to let you drive anything of mine when there's snow on the ground. I could have survived just fine here on my own, you know. You didn't have to risk a life out there this morning."

"Wasn't my idea. Jessie was worried about you. I'm sure the prospect of being snowed in with me bothered her to some degree, too."

"Seems Nelly has found a new friend?" Jessie probed as she reentered the room.

"Ah, I see you've met our guest."

"Huh?" Ryan asked, confused.

"Go take a look," Gramps muttered. "By the way, sorry he landed in the room you usually use," he said to Jessie.

"No big deal. I can use the room upstairs."

Ryan returned a few seconds later. "There's a kid in there."

"Very perceptive, Ryan," Jessie said.

"Gramps, why is there a kid with orange hair in my guest room?" Ryan asked after narrowing his eyes at Jessie.

"Didn't think I ought to leave him out in the storm."

"Who is he?" Ryan asked.

"Dunno."

"What's his name?"

"Dunno."

"Where's he from?"

"Dunno."

"Is there anything you *do* know?"

"Yep." Gramps filled in the remaining squares of his puzzle. "*Annoy* is a five-letter word meaning to harass repeatedly."

"Gramps!" Ryan yelled.

"What?" Gramps lifted his eyebrows, peering over his glasses.

"Let's start over. There's a kid—"

"Okay, we've been there. It didn't go so well the first time. Let's try a different approach. Now, you two behave while I'm gone," Jessie said.

Moments later Jessie stood at the doorway of the boy's room. "Hey there."

The boy was sitting in the rocker, staring out the window. He shifted his eyes away long enough to give Jessie the once-over, then back to the falling snow.

"Don't blame you. If I were here, I wouldn't want to talk to three people I didn't know." Jessie leaned on the edge of the bed. "One thing is for sure, though. You're a good kid or Nelly wouldn't be drooling all over you."

The boy turned his head toward the dog draped over his feet, asleep.

"I'm sure Gramps has fed you and you've slept?"

There was no response.

"You have your own private shower in there." Jessie pointed toward the closed door next to the closet. "And the hot water never seems to run out. You're safe here." Jessie's words offered the genuine warmth and acceptance she felt as she went forward and gently placed her hand on his wrist in assurance.

* * *

"You've got to contact someone," Ryan said, staring at Gramps.

"I'm open for suggestions. Phones are dead and power's out. Tucker's supposed to be by this afternoon, though. I'll get him to take us into Summitville. It may take us longer than the usual hour to get there, but at least it's something."

"Uh, Tucker you say? Tucker Hansen?" Jessie queried, reentering the kitchen.

"Yeah, that's right, I almost forgot. It's his scheduled day to plow our road," replied Ryan.

"Whoops," Jessie's response was barely audible as she walked over to search for the hot-chocolate mix.

*"Whoops?"* Ryan echoed, his brows raised with piqued interest as he walked toward her.

Gramps continued to peer over his glasses.

"Well, you weren't around when he called." This whine was directed to Gramps, as though somehow her error should be considered his fault. "And, well, the storm didn't look that bad to me, and . . . his daughter Cammie went into labor early, and his wife wanted to leave right away for Virginia. He asked if you'd mind him taking off. He said he'd be home on Christmas and could come the day after to bail us out if necessary."

Before she braved facing their stunned faces, she frantically ripped open the pouch of chocolate mix and poured it into a cup of lukewarm tap water.

"Jessie, are you out of your mind? Look at it out there." The pitch of Ryan's voice rose ever so slightly, but the tone was unmistakable.

"I didn't know it was going to get this bad. I'm from the city, remember?" Her cheeks were flushed.

"All right, you two. That's enough." Gramps laid the crossword puzzle down on the table with his glasses, then lowered his voice slightly. "You're gonna scare that kid in there. I figure he's got enough problems as it is. Doesn't need to hear you yelling. Besides, I remember a time when you made a similar mistake, son."

"I was ten!"

"No matter. Not gonna help any to be all upset over it. What's done is done. Besides it's not like you to get so upset, son."

Ryan wiped at the small beads of sweat building at the back of his neck. He *wasn't* one to lose control so easily. He let out the breath he'd been holding but said nothing. Now wasn't the time.

Gramps continued. "We got enough food here to last till spring. Hey, what about that cell phone of yours?"

"I didn't have it when I reached your place last night," answered Ryan. "I figure it must have fallen somewhere between the truck and the house."

"Mine's dead. I haven't needed it for a while," Jessie added.

"Well, might as well look on the bright side. You've wanted to get that program for kids started. Maybe the good Lord wants you two to start with that one in there."

"It's a *summer* program, Gramps. He's a little early," Ryan grumped.

Jessie pulled out a chair from the table and sat down. "I'm betting he's fourteen or fifteen. It's obvious he's run away. He was in a hurry, too. Things must be really bad if he rode his bike in that storm."

"You got him to talk?" Gramps asked, surprised.

"No. Uh-uh."

"Then how did you get all that?" Ryan asked.

"Ryan, you do big people. I do little ones, remember?" Jessie responded.

"Yes, okay. The age is easy to guess. But 'running away in a hurry,' and the bike? How did you get that?"

"The bike is near where you buried the snowmobile," Jessie said. "I smashed my leg into it. You didn't see me because you were too busy yanking the scarf off from around my neck. I could have been buried alive out there and you wouldn't have even noticed. Hey Gramps, you have those miniature marshmallows I bought last week?"

"Yep. They're in the cupboard behind Ryan."

Ryan retrieved a bag of red and green marshmallows and laid them on the counter. "I knew where you were the whole time," he smiled, attempting to diffuse the remaining tension.

"And if he's on a bike in this weather," Jessie continued, "with only a backpack—which, by the way, is hanging in the utility room along with his parka—then it's fairly obvious he's run away in a hurry."

"There's a backpack?" asked Ryan.

"Yep," responded Gramps.

"Have you looked through it? Was there any identification?"

"It's not my place to be searchin' somethin' that ain't mine."

"Gramps, someone's most likely missing this kid. That backpack could give us the information we need to get him home."

"So what if it does? How we gonna get him anywhere?"

"And how did he get *here* exactly?" Ryan asked Gramps.

"Was pickin' up some supplies in town last night. And it's a good thing I did, by the way. Spotted somethin' red on my way home. He was out cold—pardon the pun— and slept the whole night on the couch. He tried to leave this mornin'."

\* \* \*

"Kid couldn't've got too far in this storm," the man said through the smoke-filled room. He carefully looked down, avoiding the eyes of his employer, Randolph Thornton.

"What I'm trying to figure out is how an inept, teenage boy can avoid getting picked up by you people," Thornton replied. He looked up from his leather chair and met the eyes of the three men he'd put in charge of killing Ken.

"He's never alone. Couldn't get him at the school, and with his dad bein' a cop—"

Before the man could finish, Thornton raised his hand and the room fell silent.

"In the event that anyone in here is confused, I'll spell it out one more time. This kid has got to be found and silenced. He hasn't been missing for long; he can't have gotten too far."

"But the storm—"

Thornton interrupted the protest. "I don't care about the storm—I don't care if half of you die out there. Those bodies were found because you were too lazy to do the job right. That kid wasn't going to say a word. He was too scared. Between his messed-up past and psycho family, nobody would've believed him anyway. But now there are bodies and he's on the run. The cops are looking for him. When they find him, he'll talk. So if you don't bury that kid, you'll wish you *had* died in the blizzard."

\* \* \*

Beth opened the door to her best friend and neighbor. "Trudy, thanks for coming over."

"No place I'd rather be." Trudy sat at the kitchen table, asking all the pertinent questions.

"Is there any money missing?"

"No. That's the strange thing," Beth said. "We have that cash set aside for our trip to Hawaii, and it's all there. His backpack is gone, along with a couple pairs of jeans, and I'm sure he took some shirts and stuff, but I can't be sure. Can you believe he actually took his toothbrush and toothpaste? He's never cared about hygiene before." Beth forced a faint smile as she wiped a tear. "He's taken the cell phone, too. I've tried to call, but he's not answering."

"Well, it's not like it's the first time he's done this. He's been missing up to two days before."

"There is one other thing that's missing, Trudy." This came as a whisper.

Trudy raised her eyebrows, waiting.

"He took the gun."

"WHAT?" Trudy's large frame slid back abruptly from the dining room table.

"I hate guns, you know that, but Michael insisted, *demanded,* that there be one, since it was just Kenny and me. It's been locked in that cabinet." Beth pointed to an old walnut china cabinet.

"Kenny knew where the key was?"

"Yes, he's fifteen for heaven's sake—it's not like he's two!" Beth clenched her fists at her side as she turned her gaze to the all-too-familiar view out the front window. "Oh, Trudy, what am I going to do?"

# CHAPTER 4

The old rocker creaked as Kenny stared at the dropping snow. It could snow for days, he thought, at least that's what he was hoping. He didn't mind it here. It wasn't where he'd intended on ending up, but it wasn't so bad. The old man, while a bit ornery, was tolerable, and the woman was nice. But from the conversation he'd been listening to, it was the other guy he had to worry about. He sounded willing to shovel his way through to the nearest city or hire an airplane to write a message in the sky: "ANNOYING BOY FOUND. COME AND GET HIM!" Kenny's eyes remained fixed on the snow for several seconds as he pictured his mother doing the same thing, her eyes bloodshot from lack of sleep. But in the end, she'd understand and forgive him. He'd had to leave.

"Hey, there." A voice interrupted his thoughts. "You've probably heard my name already, but in case you missed it, it's Jessie." Kenny continued his stare out the window. "I'm not sure how long you're going to go speechless, but you may want to keep one thing in mind. It doesn't matter if we find out who you are. We have no way of getting you anywhere in that storm. You must have wanted to get somewhere awfully bad, or maybe away from somewhere. Either way, there's most likely someone worried about you. The phones are out and we don't have a cell phone that works. We're wondering if you have one in your backpack?" Jessie laid the weathered pack by his side. "You wouldn't have to say where you are, because you probably don't even know. But you could at least let your family know you're safe."

Nelly rolled over on her back, all four paws hanging limply in the air. Her eyes were shut and her tongue hung heavily out of one side of her mouth. Kenny smiled at the comical sight. He had always wanted a dog, but his dad believed dogs were strictly farm animals, not pets.

"Gramps made spaghetti for tonight's dinner. I'm sure it's been simmering since early morning. It's going to be absolutely delicious—tastes even better than it smells. Nelly there and Ryan eat like pigs, so if you're even remotely hungry, I wouldn't waste much time when dinner is called." Jessie left, shutting the door behind her. She quietly crossed the hall to the utility room, leaving the door ajar and listening intently. She peeked through the slit and watched the boy as he quietly opened the bedroom door, looked around curiously, and then closed it just as softly.

\* \* \*

"Kenny?" Beth rasped into the receiver. "Kenny? Please Kenny, if this is you, just say something—anything!"

"I can't talk long, and you can't tell Dad."

Beth's lungs were contracting at an escalated rate. "Where are you! Are you all right? I'll come—"

"NO!" Kenny said sharply, trying to keep his voice down. "Mom, I don't want you to come. I'm okay. An old guy found me and I'm at his house. He's okay and there's this cool dog. She's huge."

"Kenny . . . please, tell me where you are. I'll come get you, and we can take that trip to Hawaii. We'll just get away, and you can have all the space you need. We don't have to talk about anything."

"You can't get to me. The roads are all closed off. I'm stuck here, but I'm safe, so don't worry. I got food and everything. This battery's dying. I don't want you to tell Dad. You promise?"

"Oh, Kenny. Please don't put me in that position."

"Mom, you promise?"

"All right."

Kenny could hear the cracking of her voice. He knew she was crying. "Mom, I'm fine. There's a present for you under my bed. It's wrapped and everything. It's gonna be okay, Mom, you'll see. With me gone, things will be okay."

"Things are fine with you *here,* Kenny. Please . . ." The sobs were uncontrollable now.

"Gotta go, Mom. I'll call again when it's safe."

Just outside the door, Jessie only heard one side of the conversation, but it was enough to know there was a mother somewhere and she was heartbroken.

* * *

"I was thinking, gentlemen," Jessie said as she returned again to the kitchen, "that it's time to be getting a Christmas tree in here, don't you think?"

"A tree? Hadn't noticed. But you're right—Ryan doesn't have one. Not sure how you're gonna find one in that, though." Gramps nodded toward the kitchen window where the now-familiar scene of swirling white met their gaze.

"Well, I wasn't thinking right this minute. Of course we'll have to wait till the storm lets up." This roused a chuckle from both Ryan and Gramps. "It will let up soon, right?" Concern set in on Jessie's face when neither man spoke up. This was her first winter in Stone Ridge, Colorado, and she didn't want to spend the bulk of it locked up with two grown men, a teenager, and a dog. "Well, anyway, we need a tree."

"Think I'll go check on the horses," Ryan said, pushing back his chair. "No phone, I take it?"

"I'll go with," Jessie offered.

"Better get Nelly to go too," Gramps said. "She ain't been out since last night."

"Uh-huh," said Ryan, wondering if Gramps noticed, as he had, that Jessie skirted his inquiry regarding the phone. "And just how do you figure we're going to get her outside?"

"How 'bout taking that kid with you? I'm bettin' Nelly will follow him."

Ryan let out a huge sigh. "And when he tries to run off?"

Gramps pulled at his suspenders and smiled. "Gee, Ryan, let's see. Grown man . . . snip of a boy . . ."

Ryan pinched his lips. "I meant, are we sure we want to stir things up? He's at least staying put and not being hostile."

"Not all teenage boys are hostile, Ryan," Jessie corrected calmly, looking him in the eye.

\* \* \*

Beth walked in solitude to Kenny's room. It was time to clean. With Kenny gone, she wouldn't have to listen to "this is *my* room," or "you can't tell me what to do." *Why is it that kids enter into this world completely dependent, and then at fifteen want nothing to do with you?* Beth sat on Kenny's bed. She stared at all the piles, wondering where to start.

The howling wind intruded on her thoughts, but just as quickly it was swallowed up by the slam of the front door. For a second, Beth prayed it was a miracle and her son was home.

"Hey, Beth, where are ya?"

The rough voice shattered any remaining hope. *If I kept quiet, would he go away?*

"Beth? Beth!" The voice was harsh—not kind, not worried. Michael pushed Kenny's bedroom door over a pile of clothing. "What in the—?"

"Uh—stop there," Beth interrupted. *And he wonders where Kenny gets his anger.*

"I'm a cop. Four-letter words are part of my vocabulary. And I'm not changin'." The snow clung to the blue wool of his uniform and obscured the usual spit-and-polish shine of his shoes.

"Yeah, well, there was a time when you had a *better* vocabulary. And if you want to have a conversation with me, then you'd better cut the street talk. And I don't suppose you'd be so kind as to stand on that rug out there and wipe your shoes off?" The snow had begun to melt, forming little streamlets that quickly made their escape to the growing puddle at his feet.

"Not stayin' that long. Heard anything?"

Beth sighed. "No." She leaned over and began her task at hand by picking up a pile of school papers from off the floor. The lie came hard to Beth, but Michael would believe her because she had always lived by the self-imposed house rules, "no swearing" and "there's never a good reason to lie."

"Don't understand that boy. Got a good home, food, good parents, friends. What's he runnin' away for all the time?" Michael walked tentatively across the piles, working his way to the window. He opened the curtains and looked down at his car. The exhaust from the belching tailpipe was carving a hole in the deepening snow. "He's probably gonna miss Christmas, too, just to spite us."

"He hasn't gone to counseling for several weeks now," Beth said quietly.

"How come?"

"I don't know. What happened on his birthday weekend when he stayed with you and Janice?"

"Oh, don't go there, Beth. This isn't my fault!"

"I'm not saying it's your fault. I'm just saying that's when he stopped going to counseling. He's been cold and moody and not wanting to do anything. He's been sleeping at school, and, well, just look at this room. He used to play basketball and eat everything in sight. I couldn't keep up. Now all he does is sit in front of that stupid computer." Beth tried to keep her voice even. "He doesn't even *talk* to me anymore. He's got all the signs that Patrick was supposed to have." The tears were building.

Michael's head dropped briefly, and his voice faltered slightly before taking on its normal hard steel. "If you hear anything, you call me on my radio."

* * *

The typical jaunt to the stables felt more like a quest to scale a winter-dressed peak as Ryan, Jessie, and Kenny plowed their way through the nearly waist-deep snow.

Trying to run again was only a brief thought through Kenny's mind. It would not be an easy getaway.

Once inside the stable, Ryan set about checking the horses while Jessie headed for Joanie and her now six-month-old foal. Kenny had expected to find a typical barn with the usual equipment. He stood just inside the doorway, his jaw getting a little closer to his shoes as he took it all in. He had entered a huge open arena eighty feet across and fifty-four feet deep. To his immediate right was what looked like a shower, but for someone, or something, a lot bigger than he was. The next cubicle held a variety of tools that he didn't recognize, along with the more typical brushes and such that were obviously used for animal grooming. Next he found a circular staircase that led to an enclosed loft, populated with several windows that looked out over the arena. As he shuffled along what looked like a pebble path, he took in the richness of the polished woods that had been used to construct the stalls and the fencing on his right. Onto the four-foot fencing was placed a stout work of black iron that raised the fence's height and kept the several milling horses safe and comfortable. The stalls were constructed in a similar fashion, except that much of each stall was taken up by matching Dutch doors. There were three horses of differing size and coloring in the fenced area in addition to the ones that occupied the stalls lining the wall before him and to his far right.

He wandered to the end of the path where Ryan had entered the first stall and was checking the feed and water containers, the entire time talking softly to what sounded like his best buddy. The path turned to his right, and he started down the length of the arena checking out the stalls on his left for occupants of interest. His pace slowed to check out a few, but when he saw they were empty, he took to watching the first three animals he'd seen.

Kenny reached the end of the path and could now see to the end of the barn. He counted three more stalls on this wall, making a total of seven, not counting the big open space in the middle. He was about to turn and continue, curious as to whether these last three would hold any more horses, when the door to the corner stall that he was standing in front of swung open. Jessie stepped out. Ryan had moved to the stall immediately to his left. Jessie stood before him, looking like she had something unpleasant for him to do.

"Could you give me a hand?" Jessie asked the boy. He stared at her large Christmas-green eyes, then stuck his hands in his pockets and looked away.

"Look," said an agitated Ryan, appearing magically at the open stall. "If you want to continue staying warm and getting food, you'll give her a hand." Kenny rolled his eyes, then started toward Jessie, dragging his feet as if they were attached to a ball and chain.

Joanie took a step back and neighed fitfully as he approached. "Easy there, girl," Jessie started. "He means you no harm. I just need a little help in mucking out this area. Don't want Buddy filthy, now do you?" Joanie was a brilliant brown, standing sixteen hands high, with a trace of white on her rear ankles. Buddy mirrored his mother except for his ankles, which were completely white, and a small triangle of white that lay between his eyes.

The soothing sound of Jessie's voice gave Joanie the necessary courage to allow the boy closer. "Thank you," added Jessie quietly. Kenny wasn't sure if the appreciation was meant for him or the huge beast before him.

"Here, you take this shovel and scoop up everything on the floor in here, while I take these two into another stall," Jessie said. "Everything goes into that brown bucket."

Kenny held the shovel in one hand and put the back of his other hand up to his nose.

"It's not as bad as all that," Jessie chuckled. "You get used to it after a while."

Kenny made no comment as he turned a slow circle in the stall, unsure of where to begin.

Ryan smiled as Jessie leaned over him and reached into a grooming box. She picked up a brush and began working Joanie. "I don't dare guess at how much it's costing you to heat this place."

Ryan followed suit and began brushing his riding horse, Steel, in the next stall. Steel was a coal-black Morgan. He was intimidating in appearance, but he was gentle in nature, with eyes full of expression.

"It's all solar, same as the cabin, so it's not that big of a deal. Besides, it's worth it," replied Ryan. "The horses are comfortable. But if the kid doesn't shape up over there, he's going to be joining them."

"And *you* want to start a program to help wayward kids," scoffed Jessie.

"That's different."

"How?"

"They'll want to be here."

"Excuse me? You're kidding, right? Not one of them will *want* to be here. They will be here because their parents or guardians have run out of options. You have absolutely no idea of what you're getting into, do you?" Jessie stopped brushing Joanie and leaned over the stall.

"Apparently not."

"Are you sure you want to start such a program, then?"

"Yes. Why?"

"Why? You've been rude to that boy since you first laid eyes on him. And what has he done? Gramps had no other choice. You know that. And you would have done the same thing. This isn't like you, Ryan. Not at all. What's up?"

"Did he have a phone?"

"You didn't answer my question."

"And you're not answering mine."

"Yes, he had a phone," she whispered.

"And?"

"He called his mother. Only he doesn't know that I know."

"So tonight, after he falls asleep, we can find the last number called and talk to his mother."

"Why?"

"What?" Ryan asked, surprised.

"Why?" Jessie repeated.

Ryan was standing now and facing her, trying to keep his voice down. "That should be easy enough to figure out."

"We're not calling, Ryan. And if you can't come up with the reason why on your own, then you have no business starting any kind of retreat for kids." Jessie turned away and walked back toward the boy. She wondered how much of their conversation he'd overheard.

"Good job," Jessie said when she got to him. "Now I'll show you how to feed them. Pull that cart over there to each stall and take the scoop and fill the red feeder, there," she said, pointing to the side of the stall. "The blue one is for water and has a tap right above it. Don't fill it clear to the top though, or it will spill out and make a mess when they first drink. That's all there is to it. I'm going to start clearing out the rest of the stalls on this side, and Ryan will get the ones over there. If you get done before we do, you can help us finish—so you may want to take your time!" Jessie smiled, and the boy turned away quickly, but not quickly enough—Jessie saw the slight upward curve of his lower lip.

\* \* \*

Ryan slid into the chair closest to Jessie. "Smells mighty good, Gramps."

"Well, it ain't too bad, that's for sure," Gramps replied. "The boy gonna come?"

"He'll come when he's hungry enough," said Jessie. "I think he's scared of big bad Ryan here."

"Now what did you do?" Gramps winced.

"I didn't do anything. He was . . . *reluctant* . . . to help in the barn, so I encouraged him a little."

"It was more like a threat than an encouragement," Jessie corrected, looking at Gramps. She folded her napkin in her lap and then blurted, "Do either of you mind if we say grace?" She was as shocked as they were.

"Nope, I don't mind at all. Been a while since I've heard a decent prayer. Ruth always did the prayin' round here."

"I'm certainly not going to stop you." Ryan's surprise was apparent in his voice. It had been only a few months ago that she had given a long recitation on why she despised God, the result of a lifelong festering of the traumatic and misunderstood wounds of her childhood.

Jessie began, "Dear God. We thank You for this wonderful dinner. We thank You, too, for the beautiful snow that is falling, but it would be nice if it could let up just a bit so that we could go look for a tree in which to use in the celebration of the birth of Your Son. Not to mention that it would be great if we could find a way to get this boy home in time for Christmas. But he *is* here, so we'll do the best we can. Oh, and please bless this food that it will sustain us. Thank You. Amen." Jessie didn't want to give herself away, so she had been careful not to open and close her prayer the way that Bishop Grant and Ruth's friend Milly had taught her. Ryan still had no idea that she had been meeting with them and the missionaries to discuss the questions that arose from her reading of the Book of Mormon.

Jessie's thoughts turned to the first time she'd met the bishop. He had come to the hospital to give Ryan's aunt a blessing after her stroke. That had been Jessie's introduction to the gospel. When she had a question about God a few weeks later, and knowing Ryan's reluctance to discuss anything related to the Mormons, she'd telephoned the bishop. He'd been kind to her, and even after he'd introduced her to the missionaries, he still willingly guided her when she asked.

Gramps and Ryan echoed an amen. A fourth amen was offered timidly from the boy who had chosen to sit at the bar. A chair had been set at the table, just in case, but it was evident that he didn't want to close ranks just yet.

"It's not a bad meal considering we can't use the oven," Jessie said to their guest. "There's only one backup power outlet in each room to plug odds and ends into, and you have to be careful how you use them. You'll find an outlet in your room too. You can tell them apart from the others by the little red square on the cover, like that one over there. I put a few candles on your night table, in case you need them." Jessie placed a plate full of spaghetti, green beans, and whole-wheat bread in front of him. "Would you like a soda or some water?"

He didn't respond quickly, so she said, "Good choice. Water goes nicely with this meal."

"Don't use the candles," Ryan said to him after he scooped a spoonful of beans into his mouth.

"It's fine, we have lots of candles," Jessie remarked, placing a glass of water in front of the boy.

"He may forget they're lit."

"Wouldn't the flickering light and sweet fragrance of cinnamon give it away?" Jessie's deadpan expression made Gramps snicker.

"You stay out of this," Ryan said tersely to Gramps. "We know nothing about this kid, except that he's stupid enough to ride a bike in a blizzard. He's not talking, and for all we know he could have a knife or gun or whatever in that backpack. We surely don't need to give him access to matches, too."

"Ryan! That's enough. This may be your home, but you have no right to speak that way in front of him. I don't know what's gotten into you! Just because you had issues with matches when you were his age doesn't mean he does." Jessie stopped short. Even she knew she'd gone too far. She'd brought up a piece of Ryan's past that should have been left there. "I . . . I'm sorry. That was—"

"I don't have a knife," the boy interrupted softly, his head bowed, eyes fixed on the plate of spaghetti. "And my name is—" He paused. He hated being called *Kenny*. "Ken," he continued. "The spaghetti's good. I know how to wash dishes. I'll do whatever else. I'm sorry to be a bother. I wouldn't stay if I didn't have to." His head rose slightly as his eyes snapped to fix Ryan in a stare. "I *can't* use the candles because you took the matches off the dresser earlier. I'll talk about the weather, movies, dogs, or computers, but nothing about me or where I'm from. When that plow guy comes around, I'll take what I came with and leave you guys alone."

"Do you have a cell phone?" Ryan asked, his tone even and controlled.

"Yes, but the battery died when I was . . . the battery's dead."

"Wouldn't his phone charge in your charger?" Gramps asked.

"Probably not, unless he has the same model. Yours a Motorola?" Ryan turned to see his response.

"No, sir."

"Well, at least your manners have improved."

Jessie felt her insides burning. Ryan was overtly calm by nature, not rude. *What is up with him? I haven't seen this side of him since Ruth's funeral.* She remembered his resentment when Gramps had asked the Mormons to be in charge of the service. He'd refused to go to the church building, so Gramps compromised with a graveside service. *Losing Ruth and having a houseful of Mormons explains that day's behavior, but what is going on now?*

"May I have some more spaghetti, please?" asked Ken.

"Of course," replied Jessie. She stood and filled his plate.

"Jessie? Would you and Ken go to the wood bin and bring in a few logs after supper?" Gramps asked.

*I think Ryan's in for a lecture.* "You bet—" she began.

"I can do it. I'm almost finished," Ryan cut in.

"Nope, need your help in here," Gramps replied.

Jessie had read Gramps's mind correctly. And now, so had Ryan.

# CHAPTER 5

Gramps filled the large sink with dishes. "You wanna tell me what's goin' on?"

"What do you mean?" Ryan replied resistantly.

"Have you met that kid out there before? Seems to me like you're tryin' to git back at him for somethin'."

"Never saw him before."

"Then if *he's* not the problem, you wanna talk about what is?" Gramps's voice held an air of concern through the gruffness.

"I saw something in his room."

"Yeah, I know. The matches."

"It's not about the matches."

"Then what?"

Ryan knew this wasn't a discussion to be having with Gramps. It was Jessie to whom he needed to vent this frustration. "You're right, it's not the kid's fault. I'll quit playing bad cop, okay?"

"Okay. How the horses doin'?"

"Fine. It's warmer out there than it is in here."

"Well, it's early, but I'm headed upstairs. Listen, I'm gonna grab that portable TV from your office and see if there's any information on Ken comin' through. Could be somethin' on the news."

The snowy air entered the cabin with Jessie and Ken. After dropping the wood on the hearth, they extricated themselves from the warmth of their coats and placed them on hooks by the fireplace.

"Do you like to play cards?" Jessie asked Ken as they made their way back to the kitchen.

Ken began to clear the table. "I'd like to just go to my room when we're done here."

"Sure," Jessie replied kindly.

The kitchen was cleaned in silence. Jessie had learned long ago when to be quiet around someone who was struggling.

Ken folded the dish towel and placed it on top of the counter, then left.

"I'll walk with you," Jessie said, coming up behind Ken. "I've stayed in that room from time to time, and there are a few of my things I'd like to shift to another room." Ken held back, politely allowing her the lead.

They entered the room and Jessie went through some drawers. "Thanks, Ken, it's all yours now," she said, carrying her things. "Apparently Nelly has taken up residence in here, so it would be best if you kept your door open a few inches. You don't want her having an accident in here. If she needs to go out during the night, she'll go in and bother Ryan.

"There are extra blankets in that top drawer over there." She pointed to a set of drawers built into the wall between the dual closets. "It's going to get cold tonight. Also, two floors up is a great reading loft and a game room. I doubt you'd want to venture up there in the dark, but you're welcome to look around tomorrow. Ryan's room is across the hall, and Gramps and I are upstairs, in case you need anything. Good night, Ken."

He responded with a slight wave of one hand as he stroked Nelly's head.

Jessie headed upstairs and placed her things in her new room, which had the same layout and design as Ken's. The second floor was as just as spacious as the first. Her room was just to the left of an open sitting area to which the circular stairway opened, and just beyond hers was the second guest room. Jessie had learned that the bedrooms on this level were originally designed as suites for clients during the time Ryan worked out of his home.

Ryan leaned on the wall across from Jessie's open door. He watched her hair sway from one side to the other as she arranged items in her dresser drawer. Jessie was the kind of woman who turned heads when she entered a room. The broken nose from an unstable childhood—her father's mark—was her only visible flaw. "Setting up camp far away from me, eh?"

Jessie glanced toward Ryan. "Yep."

"Don't suppose you'd like to have a long, meaningful conversation tonight?"

"Nope."

"We haven't talked in a while, you know," Ryan pushed.

"You said you'd give me till after the holidays, *remember?*"

"Ah—yes, I did. But this conversation wouldn't have anything to do with *your* issues."

Jessie turned her face away from his view. "If it's about Ken, could it wait till morning? I'm exhausted." She wasn't tired at all, but she didn't feel that Ryan was ready to hear why all his instincts about this boy were wrong.

"Tomorrow, then."

\* \* \*

"All things considered, it could be worse," Beth said to Trudy.

Trudy placed a small sack of groceries on the table as she removed her coat. "I suppose. Are you going to call him again?"

"No. I tried just before you got here. There's no answer. Our conversation was scratchy anyway."

"Are you going to tell Michael?"

"I couldn't even if I wanted to, which I don't. I made a promise not to."

"He's going to be outraged if he finds out."

"Yep, and since you're the only one who knows . . ."

"I'm not going to squeal! I've seen his temper." Trudy began sorting the store-bought items. "You've been cleaning, I see."

Beth looked around the kitchen. "Yeah. It helps distract me. Well, actually it doesn't really, but it's better than eating my way into the biggest size available. Never paid much attention to how small this place was—doesn't take long to clean."

"You should come early Christmas morning and watch the kids open their stuff," Trudy offered.

"Yeah, just what Tim and the kids need . . . me, bawling on the couch on the happiest day of the year."

"I'm serious, Beth. You shouldn't be alone."

"No, I probably shouldn't. But I will be. Thanks for worrying, and thanks for the milk and eggs. Surprised the market's even open. I need to stay here. He may call, he may send a note—heck, miracles happen, right? He may even walk through that door. So I need to be here.

Whatever he's going through, Kenny needs to know I'm here when or if he decides to come home."

* * *

Beth hit the REPEAT button, and Bing Crosby sang— for the fifth time—his rendition of "Silent Night." Both Michael and Kenny made facial contortions each year when she played the CD. It had been a gift from Kenny when he was younger. She'd give anything to listen to Kenny's whining right now.

Since her home had been cleaned, polished, swept, and laundered, she didn't know what she'd do tomorrow. She could wrap Kenny's Christmas gifts—just in case. She pulled her robe around her as she walked to the front room window. It was late and her neighbors were asleep— at peace in their nice, comfortable lives. She took a deep breath, closed her eyes, and wondered where hers had gone wrong.

She thought of her parents and their desire for her to be at the top of her graduating class. She had been surrounded by the importance of education. The necessity of proper education was poured at every meal, just like milk. Her mother had earned her degree—insisting on being just as educated as her husband—in case anything ever happened to him. Nothing did. They were both still alive, although her parents had entered therapy when she'd eloped with Michael. At the time, Michael was a prison guard at the state penitentiary in their hometown of Lyle.

*They thought I would eventually grow out of it. Typical teenage rebellion. After all, Martha grew out of it, and Steve's a judge now. Here I am twenty years later, divorced and alone. Mom and Dad finally got to say, "We told you so." Did I marry him out of spite?* She'd asked herself that question many times throughout the years. Somehow the man she fell in love with at sixteen and married at eighteen wasn't the man yelling at her today. When had that started? She couldn't remember. When had the swearing started? She couldn't remember that, either. When had the anger started? That she *could* remember, but it *all* had to have had a beginning. *How does one get to this point and not know how it all began?*

She jumped when the phone rang. "Hello?" she said quickly. "Oh. Hello, Jennifer."

"Hope I'm not callin' too late," Jennifer Chandler said quietly.

"No. Not at all," Beth replied. "What can I do for you?"

"I was just wanting to—"

Beth waited, but no reply followed. "To . . . what, Jennifer?"

"Well, it's not my business really. I'm not sure Ken would like it if—"

"Jennifer," Beth's voice took courage. "I know Kenny's your friend, and you probably don't want to break a promise, but if there's something you know that can help us find him, please, please tell me."

"Well, I— Sorry, Mrs. Moon. I can't talk now, my dad just got home."

The line went dead. Beth sighed. She turned for her bedroom, leaving the winter scene and Bing Crosby behind. But just in case, she left alight the bright lamp perched in the front window.

\* \* \*

"There you are, Barkley," Jessie whispered. Something had brushed against her leg while she'd been retrieving a spoon from the kitchen drawer. "Since that big overgrown monster is asleep for the night, you've decided to roam freely now, hmm?" She picked the cat up and nuzzled her face in his fur before setting him back down on the floor. She used hot tap water to make a cup of chamomile tea and warmed it as quietly as possible in the microwave.

Tea and candle in hand, she climbed the staircase and settled into the recliner in the reading loft. This was her other favorite room, although there was no backup power on this floor. Since the third floor was the last, the ceilings here matched the vault of those at the back of the cabin and were dotted with skylights.

The howling wind accented the faint flicker of the candle as Jessie closed her eyes and forced her thoughts to Ken. Where had he come from? He wasn't from Stone Ridge, or Gramps and Ryan would have known him. Summitville was too far away for him to have made such a distance in the storm. Then again, they had no idea how long he'd been on the run. Still, it was more likely he was from either Castle Rock or Lyle County.

"Hey there, kitty. You're awfully brave to be venturing up here," she said, detecting a noise behind her and leaning over to pick up the cat.

"Actually, it's me," Ryan replied.

Startled, Jessie pulled her arms back. "Oh. How come you're not sleeping? Was I too noisy?"

"No. Like I said before, it's been a while since we've had a late-night talk." Ryan stepped past her to the couch.

"Oh, brother. Have you really stayed up hoping I couldn't sleep?"

"You haven't been sleeping for a few weeks now, from what I hear."

"Apparently I've got to quit confiding in Gramps." As she said it she caught a whiff of his cologne, and the slightest chill formed at the base of her spine and increased throughout her body.

Ryan leaned over and handed her the crocheted afghan that was always folded by the couch.

"Thanks." Jessie readily accepted the afghan, feigning that the cold was the only thing that affected her. "Look, Ryan, I already told you—"

"Thought we could head out at first light and hunt for a tree," he interrupted.

"Oh, but I thought it would be too difficult in the storm," she said, her smile concealed in the flickering shadows.

"There are a couple small spruces behind the barn that have been partially sheltered. I think we can cut one of them down without too much trouble. We're going to need the kid's help though."

"Wonderful. Thanks, Ryan."

"Not a problem."

"That's not all you want to say, though, is it?"

"It's not about your issues, or the boy."

"He has a name. It's Ken."

"I know."

"Then you could try to use it." Jessie's breaths had become short and audible. She was becoming uncomfortable. It had been in this loft that she'd first told of her childhood to Ryan, how she had been hurt by most of the key people in her life—physically, psychologically, and in other ways that little girls should never hurt.

She was five when she and her two-year-old sister Katie had been abandoned by their mother at a theater far from home. Despite her mother's efforts to sever any trails that might lead authorities back to their father, social services finally located him. She and Katie had been sent back. Their drunken father had abused them, as well as his new wife and her four sons. As the boys grew older, they'd retaliated against the abuse, though it wasn't their father they took it out on. Jessie had suffered even more then.

Jessie's stepmother worked long days as a cook or waitress. Her father's days were spent wallowing in self-pity at the local bar after locking Jessie and Katie in the basement each day. The stern threat that they never tell anyone was always impressed upon them. Most days he'd forget to turn the light on when he left, and on stormy days it got very dark and scary in that dungeon.

Ryan seemed to read her body language and waited for Jessie to feel comfortable again. She calmed as her mind focused on the positive steps that had brought her to this loft and had begun her healing.

Here in this loft Jessie had relayed the traumatic loss of Katie's life. It had been an accident, but Jessie's father had blamed her, since she was the one who fed Katie the hotdogs. Not only had she been haunted by the recurring nightmare of Katie's dying face, she had lived through the constant and heartless accusations of her father. While Jessie was finally able to verbalize the torment and guilt of losing her sister, the inner scars from that battle still existed. She had been forced to dig deep into her mind to the real source of her problems. Blaming her father had been easy, and blaming God had seemed essential—after all, He had let her travel that horrible road, alone. Those *were* safe places for her anger, but it took Ryan to point out the true source of her anger.

*Tonight isn't about my issues. Take a deep breath and relax,* she thought. *Give Ryan a chance to—*

"You have something that belonged to my wife."

Ryan's softly spoken words forced Jessie out of her trance. *What?*

"I saw it on the nightstand when I went into Ken's room, beside the matches."

Any perceptible breaths were silenced. The mention of matches brought Jessie's comment about Ryan's past to the forefront of her mind and turned her stomach. She hadn't fully apologized for that yet; she'd been waiting for the right time.

"Ryan, I don't know what you're talking about."

"You have Brecca's Book of Mormon."

She groaned inwardly. In an instant she realized Ryan hadn't been the slightest bit concerned about Ken having matches. It was a convenient cover for the confused turmoil he must have been feeling. *Now his behavior makes sense. What on earth am I going to say to him?* she thought frantically.

"Jessie, can you explain *why* you have Brecca's Book of Mormon?"

"Yes." Her hands trembled as she picked up her tea. She placed her long slender fingers completely around the mug. "But first I'd like to apologize for my earlier remark concerning the matches. I was out of line."

"Yes, you were. Apology accepted."

"I'm wondering, given the circumstances with the boy being here and all, if this should wait?" She bit her lip hopefully.

"His name is Ken—as I've been reminded. He's exhausted. He'll sleep a long, long time."

"I . . . I asked Ruth if I ought to give it to you. She said that it wasn't necessary and that I should keep it—just to read. And then she died, and well . . . I didn't know . . ." She began making vague gestures with her hands, few of which could be easily seen.

"It wasn't Ruth's to give," Ryan returned softly.

"Yes, I know that. I was waiting for the right time. But I know how you feel about the Mormons."

"You do? And how *is* that, exactly?"

"I saw how you treated Bishop Grant when he came to give Ruth the blessing, and then how you wouldn't have the funeral at the church, and how it gnawed at you to have Ruth's house inundated with Mormons after the funeral. It's obvious you don't approve of them." Standing reluctantly, Jessie's words were softer. "I'll go and get the book."

"I haven't asked for it back yet."

She looked at him shrewdly through the shadows as she eased back into the recliner. "You *don't* want it back?"

"When did you start reading it?"

"Ryan, with all due respect to our friendship, I'm not sure that's any of your business. You have a right to the book, but not to the choices I make about reading it."

"Oh. You're reading my late wife's Book of Mormon, and it's none of my business. That means you believe what you're reading, you're talking with the missionaries, and you're beginning to accept their views."

"I'm thirty-plus years old Ryan. I've pretty much earned the right to read what I want, talk to whom I want, and choose a religion," she retorted, her arms providing the proper emphasis.

"You're right, your religious preferences are solely yours. My feelings about that put aside for the moment, I'm concerned about your sudden turn to God."

"Meaning?" Jessie's voice softened. She knew that if anyone *was* capable of putting his own feelings aside to help someone else, it was him.

"It wasn't too long ago that you were bitter toward God."

"Go on."

"Then you have an experience, which, incidentally, I'm still in the dark about, and suddenly you're meeting with the missionaries and reading Brecca's Book of Mormon."

"I've only met with them a few times. But what is it you're going for here?"

"I'm suggesting that you've replaced one expedient with another. Being angry with God is what kept you going through the years . . . Now *leaning* on God is what seems to be keeping you going."

"Hmm. *Expedient* denotes an unethical means to an end. I'm not sure how *leaning* on God could be considered unethical, but somehow you managed to drift from your issue—to mine. We're not supposed to be discussing my issues, remember? The ball hasn't dropped at Times Square yet." Her voice conveyed a tone of satisfaction.

"Technically, this issue is both of ours."

"Do you want the book back or not?" Jessie snapped, her anger rising.

"No. I would've liked knowing that you had it, that's all."

"Ryan, think about this. Look how upset you were tonight—you, who are unusually calm. If I had told you months ago that I had it, and was reading it, how would it have been any different?"

"You *didn't* tell me months ago. That's the point, Jessie. If you viewed our relationship as strictly professional, would you have told me about the book?"

Jessie remained still, staring into the darkness. She searched for his face, wondering what expression it held. Yes, if her connection to him were purely professional, she would have happily discussed her newfound knowledge. But he wasn't her therapist anymore. He was in love with her, and worse—as difficult as it was to admit—she was in love with him. But she couldn't answer this question out loud.

"Let me try a different approach," Ryan continued. "Your reading of the Book of Mormon and your reservations about telling me. Are those the reasons why you keep avoiding me lately?"

"Yes."

"So you've taken what little you know regarding my past, the few incidents you've witnessed, and without getting my views, decided that I'm incapable of discussing your feelings about the Mormons? Jessie, what can I do to assure you that no matter what either of us has been through or are going through I'll be here for you?"

"If you *are* open to the subject, as you've indicated, then why didn't you tell me Ruth belonged to the Mormon Church that Sunday I wanted to go and pray on her behalf? You said there was only the Catholic and Methodist churches. That was a deliberate lie, and you promised you'd always be honest with me." Barkley had found his way into Jessie's lap, and Jessie was relieved to have something to fidget with since her teacup had long since been emptied.

"I knew if I told you of Ruth's church you'd have chosen to attend, and . . . I didn't want to deal with that chapter of my life. I made a mistake. It was wrong and I apologize. Jessie, I don't dislike *all* Mormons. And while your reading of the Book of Mormon does make me nervous, I won't stand in your way. I chose to leave the Church . . . but that doesn't mean there isn't some truth to the gospel—there's a difference. If you're wanting to go there, I won't stop you, and it won't change my being in love with you. I would just want to be sure you're accepting the teachings of the gospel on their own merits and not just replacing one crutch with another."

"I'm not sure about truth, but I have found peace." Jessie heard his sigh. "You don't believe me?"

"I think you're convinced you've found peace, which is better than your alternatives—fear and pain. But you're still experiencing nightmares. I can't help you help yourself if you're intent on keeping things from me."

She sniffed, feeling through the darkness to the coffee table for the tissues that were always there. "Have I mentioned lately that I really *don't* like you?"

"Yeah, usually when I'm right. The truth is, you like me much more than you're ready to admit—or we wouldn't be having this conversation."

"I'm tired. Am I giving you back Rebecca's Book of Mormon or not?"

"No. Return it when you're through with it. I am curious how you came by it though," he said.

"I found it at Ruth's. It was in the room I stayed in. Will you tell me sometime why, exactly you left the gospel?"

"Left the Church, you mean."

"Right. There's a difference, you said. But I don't know what that means."

"The gospel is truth—the teachings of Jesus, if you will. The Church is merely the institution made up of imperfect people that attempts to carry out the teachings of the gospel in an organized fashion."

"Hmm . . . So you've left the Church, but *not* the gospel?"

"It's a bit more complicated than that, but I'll make you a deal. When you're ready to tell me about your experiences—namely how you knew where to look for your mother's letter last summer, and about the nightmares—I'll answer your questions."

"What happened to opening up to me, building my trust, letting me in, and allowing me space to do the same?" Jessie teased.

"As I remember, you were quite specific about me *not* using those techniques anymore."

# CHAPTER 6

Lyle Community Park was bustling for a wintry Sunday. Inner tubes were everywhere. And where there was an inner tube there was a child laughing or crying. In some cases, adults too. Jennifer Chandler sipped at the hot chocolate she'd bought for only ten cents. *That little kid's going to be an entrepreneur when he grows up,* she thought to herself. There had been a steady stream of people lined up in front of the little boy since she'd arrived an hour before.

Several teenage girls her age walked past and gawked openly at her appearance. She was used to the odd looks and comments, and had learned from experience it was better to ignore such incidents. Most around town knew her and were friendly. But holidays always brought out-of-towners and lengthy stares. She enjoyed the Gothic look of dark spiky hair, dark makeup, dark clothes, and silver jewelry. Her style wasn't a matter of low self-esteem; it was a matter of keeping people at a distance. At present most was covered up by winter apparel.

"Hey babe, been waiting for you all my life."

Jennifer didn't waste time looking over her shoulder. "Clint Palmer. Could recognize that adolescent voice anywhere."

"Huh?" the high-pitched voice returned.

"Forget it. What are you doing here? Drugs don't sell well on Sundays?" Jennifer said roughly.

"Ouch, she got you there, dude," said a tall, slender boy who fell in beside Jennifer on the wet bench.

"First Laurel and now Hardy," Jennifer replied dryly.

"Who?" Clint asked. Jennifer rolled her eyes and let out a sigh.

"He can't really be *that* stupid," Jennifer said to the kid they all called "Rapper."

"Yeah, he really can."

Jennifer's eyes spotted the sedan in the distance, then turned her face away from Rapper. "What'd he do, pay someone to plow that area just for him?"

"Look, Jen, wish I could say we were here just to annoy you, but it's business."

"Nope. Not talking. Catch you later, boys." Jennifer immediately stood and walked toward the line of people waiting to donate to the future Donald Trump. After collecting her second cup of cocoa, she meandered through the maze of inner tubes and ducked down an alley a few blocks from her home. The snow was knee deep, but she didn't want to walk the path the town had plowed. She knew who would be waiting for her at the end. She rounded the corner and smacked into the barrel of a .38.

* * *

"I wonder what the good bishop would say if he knew you were out here on the Sabbath cutting down a tree?" Ryan asked with perverse satisfaction.

"*I'm* not cutting it down, you are," Jessie dutifully corrected. The snow which had continued to fall heavily through the night now offered them a momentary reprieve, leaving only the lightest of flakes suspended ethereally about them. The sun was at work in an effort to burn its way through the dark and thickened sky, but the effort, Jessie thought, though valiant, was in vain.

"You warm enough?" Ryan snickered.

"What is that supposed to mean?"

"You look like a five-foot-eight version of one of those Weebles toys."

"Love that sense of humor of yours."

The spruce tree Ryan had in mind was nestled snugly behind the stable surrounded by its older sibling. It was perfect, Jessie decided. She couldn't wait to decorate—although she didn't have any idea what she was going to use. She hadn't planned on being trapped here, and of course had brought nothing with her. She would make do, even if she had to sacrifice all of the remaining red-and-green miniature marshmallows to a Christmas chain.

Ryan leaned the handsaw against the stable wall and blew into his hands. "I'm going to need Ken's help. You want to get him?"

"Absolutely." Jessie walked around to the front of the stable and waved at Gramps. He stood on the balcony of Ryan's study peering through the glass.

Entering the stable, Jessie found Ken filling the water bucket for a paint horse named Zeus. Jessie was amused by Ryan's attraction to Greek and Norse mythology. She'd need to become better educated on that subject, she decided, if she were ever going to get more involved in his life. Ryan was sure to have suitable literature in the library.

Jessie's research was often Internet-based, due to the Web's vast content and speedy access, but she preferred the feel of a book in hand.

Jessie pulled her hood down and removed her gloves. "Hey, Ken. He's a beauty, huh?"

"Yes, ma'am." Ken turned the water spout off and turned to face Jessie.

"No need for *ma'am*, Ken. *Jessie* works just fine. You were brought up well, however. Haven't known many teenagers to be so polite."

"Yes, ma'am."

"Are you ready to tell me who might be concerned about your being missing?"

Ken closed Zeus's stall door and returned the brush to the grooming box. "No, ma'am."

Jessie followed. "I left home when I was sixteen."

"Uh-huh."

"I was a little more prepared than you, though. I had money, a job, and I didn't leave in the middle of a blizzard. So you know what that tells me?"

Ken had no comment and proceeded to fidget with the grooming equipment.

"It tells me that this adventure wasn't premeditated," Jessie continued, following his expressions closely. "That it was a spur-of-the-moment kind of thing. Possibly brought on by a burst of sudden anger. And anger is merely a code. A cover-up, if you will, for other things. Maybe you were fearful, or frustrated, threatened, jealous, humiliated, depressed, or a mixture of any of those."

Ken rearranged the items in the tack trunk—none of which were out of order. "You a shrink or something?"

Jessie smiled. "Psychologist. So is Ryan."

"Great."

"Yep, you picked an excellent spot to drop in the snow."

"I don't need fixin', ma'am. I'll be outta here first chance I get."

"Hey, you know how much we make an hour? Trust me, when you're thirty, you'll be sending us thank-you notes for saving you a ton of money."

Ken quickly turned his back toward Jessie. She had again procured a smile.

Ryan threw open the stable door. "Hey, which part of 'I need help out here' got lost in the translation?"

"Coming," Jessie yelled, then turned her attention to Ken. "We're bringing in a tree and Dr. Ryan over there needs our help. If we don't hurry, he's liable to drag it in himself, and then I'll never hear the end of it. Would you come help, please?"

"Yes, ma'am."

\* \* \*

Gramps held the door while Ryan and Kenny threaded the tree through. Gramps noticed the intensity with which Ken worked. "You're quite strong there, kid. Done a bit of physical labor, have ya?"

"Yes, sir," Kenny huffed in response.

"Good thing. Comes in handy from time to time. Nothin' wrong with good, hard work."

"No, sir."

"Kid know any other words?" Ryan whispered to Jessie as he and the tree shuffled past her.

"No, sir," Jessie echoed.

It took almost thirty minutes for Jessie to hone to perfection the placement of the tree. On one occasion she had Ryan and Gramps threatening to put it in the middle of the kitchen.

Jessie's eyes sparkled, the child within spread uninhibited across her face. "It has to be just right," she kept saying.

"Tree's gonna be pretty bare underneath. 'Fraid Santa ain't gonna be able to find us, let alone land his sleigh," Gramps said with a snicker in his voice.

"Gramps, knowing Jessie, she started buying gifts weeks ago. There probably won't be a naked spot on the tree skirt."

"You have a tree skirt?" Jessie asked, even more excited than she'd previously been—if that were possible.

"Somewhere. Yeah. It'll take a few minutes to find the right box, but we should be able to come up with a few things. If we're going to have a tree, might as well do it right. Otherwise, you'll be forced to resort to all your decorative tea bags."

Jessie grinned. "You know me well."

"Where's the lad?" Gramps asked.

"He was right here," Jessie answered.

"He's in here somewhere or we'd have heard a door," Ryan surmised.

"Can't see that he could have slipped upstairs without us noticing," Jessie said. "But, I'll go take a look after I've checked his room." Jessie left the men in the family room assessing the frozen tree.

"By the way, son," Gramps said as Jessie went upstairs, "wanted to wait till I had you alone to tell ya. I heard somethin' about the boy on the news. Wasn't anything last night, but this mornin' there was. Seems a fifteen-year-old son of a cop over in Lyle has disappeared. They haven't said he run away, just that he was missin'. Showed a picture, and it was him all right. Name's Kenny Moon."

* * *

Jessie checked Ken's room, then headed for the stairs. Halfway up she thought maybe he had slipped into the Jacuzzi, but dismissed the idea since he'd never been in the solarium and they had all been standing right in front of its entrance when they noticed him gone. Then she remembered the game room. It was a room she rarely entered, but Ryan seemed to spend a bit of time there—a male thing, she decided. It housed a pool table, Ping-Pong table, a couple commercial pinball machines, an old arcade game, and an entertainment center. Sure enough, there in the corner staring at the arcade game Galaxia was Ken.

"Hey, there," said Jessie sweetly.

"I can't find a backup power outlet in here," Ken said casually.

"No? Guess Ryan didn't think playing games was an emergency kind of thing." She walked toward him, but kept her distance by leaning on a nearby windowsill, directing her eyes outside rather than on him.

"The old man knows where I came from."

"Is that right?"

"He was listening to the news this morning. I heard it too. Hasn't he told you yet?"

"Nope. Maybe he was hoping you'd tell me."

"You're just trying to make me feel like I can trust you."

"Is that what I'm doing?"

"Yes, ma'am."

"Well then, let me put you at ease. If you call me *ma'am* one more time, I'm going to show you what made me a brown belt."

"Yes ma'—" Jessie didn't let him finish.

"Now I realize you're being polite, although if we're being honest here, that's simply a cover too. You don't want to be polite at all. In fact, you'd probably like to tell us all to drop dead, but you won't because you know darn well that you haven't any other choice—for the time being—but to be here."

Ken rolled his eyes to a fixed point on the ceiling and exhaled deeply, letting Jessie know that he didn't want to hear any of this.

"Ken, I'm not telling you to spill your guts, but at least quit the games and be yourself. You can continue putting up the front, but you're not fooling me, Ryan, *or* the old man. None of us are that naive. But, if there *is* something we can help you with, we'd all be glad to do it."

"You're going to make me go home, right?"

"We can't allow you to just take off when the storm's over. We are obligated by law and more importantly, our consciences, to get you home—unless home places you in some danger we're currently unaware of?"

"Does this mean I can't have any privacy? I came up here to be alone, and here you are. You all going to be in my face every minute?"

*There it is, finally, an emotion breaking through,* thought Jessie. "Give us a reason not to be in your face, and we won't."

"I'm going to run first chance I get!"

"Great! First honest thing I've heard yet! Keep that up, and you might just get that privacy you're looking for." Jessie turned and left the room.

"Women *are* weird," Ken said as the door closed.

\* \* \*

After she'd opened the door, Beth wished she'd have pretended not to be home. This was company she didn't need. Her ex-husband's wife and kids.

"Roads are so bad, we barely made it!" Janice Moon said, her three daughters trailing her into Beth's front room.

Beth watched as all three girls and mother transferred the snow from their boots to her newly polished floor. "Where's Michael?"

"He's shoveling out a spot for the car."

"Here, Mom," said the oldest girl, Diana, as she handed over three coats. Diana resembled their mother the most with her long legs, slender build, and long brown hair.

"Can we have some hot chocolate?" asked Andrea, the second oldest.

"Certainly not!" barked Janice. "You know what that sugar will do to you. These are your important years; can't put that weight on now! But maybe Beth has some lemons for water?"

*They're shaped like sticks,* thought Beth. *Gaining a pound is the least of their worries.* "Lemons? I don't think I have actual lemons—not something I typically have in the middle of December—but I may have some lemon juice," Beth offered, plastering a fake smile on her twitching face.

"It'll do, I guess." Janice threw the coats on the recliner and then instructed the three girls to sit on the couch. Each did, sitting perfectly still.

Beth escaped into the kitchen. She and Michael had agreed after the divorce that they needed to maintain an amicable relationship for Kenny's sake. Unfortunately, Michael interpreted this as extending the amicability to his current wife and her daughters. Michael had blindly thought that Janice and Beth would like each other and that the kids would all get along, but it was not the case. Michael had met Janice only a month after their divorce and was married within the next month. Beth couldn't stand Janice, and Ken wanted nothing to do with the girls. Diana was thirteen now, going on thirty. Andrea was eleven with a firm grasp on the middle-child syndrome, and Allyson, age nine, knew exactly how to get her way.

"So, Beth, how are you really?" Janice asked, entering the kitchen. "You've got to be just miserable, I'm sure. Mike said they've called out the dogs, not that they'd be able to sniff out anything in this weather anyway. But what that must feel like, I can only imagine. Your second child lost, exactly the same time of year that Patrick—"

"Yeah, okay," Beth interrupted. She placed the lemon juice on the counter and pressed both eyes with her fingers. The slam of the door saved Janice from the repercussions of Beth's deteriorating patience. *What does Mike see in this social clod?* Beth wondered angrily.

"Mike, honey? Is that you? I'm here in the kitchen with Beth. Make sure the girls aren't eating any of those candy canes on the table." She turned back toward Beth, whispering, "He's such a bad influence on them, you know. I think he really misses your cooking. Can't seem to get that out of his system."

A blank stare froze on Beth's face as she moved past Janice.

"I'll just go ahead and do these lemon waters," Janice called over her shoulder.

Beth walked past the statues on the couch and caught Michael's coat before it landed in the rocker. "No need taking it off—you're all leaving."

"Now, Beth, whatever she's said, I'm sure—"

Beth grabbed Michael by the arm and marched him toward the front closet. "What in the name of heaven were you thinking, bringing her here? Do you really hate me that much?" She kept her voice low but allowed the irritation to blossom unrestrained.

"Now, Beth, I can't leave her home all the time."

"Why not? Did you lose the keys to her cage?"

"Shh—the girls—"

"I'm serious, Michael. If she calls you *honey* or brings up Patrick again, I'm liable to vomit."

"Allyson! No!" By the scream Janice let out, Beth thought Allyson just got hit by a car in the living room. Beth shook her head as she watched the young girl being reprimanded for sneaking a candy cane behind her mother's back.

"Here, drink this." Janice placed three glasses of water spiked with lemon juice in front of the girls and glared at Beth. "We put popcorn on our tree. Not only is it quite time-consuming—allowing time to think of Jesus and all—but it's also not as unhealthy as all that sugar."

Beth's face held a perplexed expression as she tried to find the link between Jesus and popcorn, or Jesus and the woman before her.

"Beth?" called Andrea.

Beth turned her attention toward the middle child. "Yes?"

"Where's Kenny?"

"He's out with some friends, sweetheart," Janice replied quickly.

Beth looked up at Michael, who was half in and half out of his coat. "You haven't told them?" Beth asked.

Michael and Janice glanced at each other, then back at Beth. Janice's mouth started to open, most likely in protest, Beth guessed. "No. Just stop there." Beth put her hand up in front of Janice. "Girls? I'd like you to go upstairs to the room on the left. You'll find a deck of cards on the table by the bed. You know how to play Go Fish?"

All three girls nodded in the affirmative.

"Good. Well, I'd like you to play a few rounds on the rug by my bed and, Diana, would you close the door behind you, please?"

"Sure," Diana replied. The girls didn't even look in their mother's direction to see if it was okay. They never got to play with cards, except in *their* home. The upstairs door slammed before Janice had a chance to argue.

"Now, Beth . . . " Michael began.

"No, Michael. Now, I don't know why you're keeping Kenny's running away from the girls, but I won't lie to them, especially under my own roof. It's wrong and I won't stand for it. If you didn't want them to know, then you shouldn't have brought them."

"Good gracious, Beth, we can't leave them home alone!"

"You live ten minutes away. Diana's perfectly capable of watching the other two. They're not babies. You need to let them grow up." Beth knew she was headed into territory she hadn't any right to be in, but she couldn't help herself.

"Oh, like you have all the right parenting skills!" Janice barked.

"That's enough, both of you!" shouted Michael.

"Mike, I think now is a fine time to tell her." Janice flipped her long brown hair out of her eyes.

"No, Janice, we'd better just get the girls and go."

"Tell me what?" Beth stared back at Janice. "Is it about Kenny?"

"No. Girls!" Michael yelled up the stairs.

"We're pregnant," Janice roared over Michael.

The pitter-patter of feet could be heard on the landing. Michael looked up and growled, "Get back inside!" The confused girls promptly retreated.

Beth sighed as she moved to the kitchen table and sat down. While used to Janice's lack of consideration, this comment had crossed the line, even for her.

"This isn't how we planned on telling you," Michael began. "We were going to wait until Kenny was back." He narrowed his eyes and looked at Janice, who had folded her arms across her chest, momentarily dwelling in victory.

"I see. Well, I guess congratulations are in order," Beth replied softly.

"Beth . . ." Michael began.

"Really, I'm happy for both of you. Do the girls know, or is this another secret?"

"We wanted to tell Kenny first," Michael responded.

"It's a boy," Janice said, her contempt apparent.

"Of course it is," Beth said dryly.

"Girls, let's get a move on," Michael called up the stairs. This time he dumped the girls' coats into Janice's arms and shoved her toward the bottom of the stairs.

The girls came running down the steps. Janice grabbed at arms and headed toward the front door.

"Wait for me in the car," Michael said.

"It's freezing out there!" Janice countered.

Michael's eyebrows rose as his hands motioned toward the door. Janice made some undistinguishable sound and marched out the door with the girls.

Michael sat at the table in the chair across from Beth.

"Does Kenny know about the baby?" Beth asked, looking down at the gingerbread-man design on a placemat.

"I don't see how."

"You think those girls didn't hear what we were just talking about?"

"They were upstairs."

"Michael, haven't you learned anything after raising two boys and three girls? I guarantee they were listening. They heard the whole thing through the heater vent. It's probable that Kenny knows about the baby, and that could explain why he's left."

# CHAPTER 7

"Hope I ain't keepin' you from anything important," the eyes behind the .38 said.

Jennifer's first instincts were to scream, but the sound wouldn't come. She had felt fear before, but this was entirely different. She instantly felt warmth on her legs and knew she'd just done the unthinkable. She took a slow breath and muttered, "What do you want?" She was wishing now that she *had* talked to Clint and Rapper. Maybe this would have been avoided.

"My friend Joe and me were sent to give you some advice." The man lowered the gun enough for Jennifer to see the black ski mask in full.

"Well, you've got a captive audience."

"It's simple. Wanna keep your mama alive, you'll tell us where your friend is."

*Simple,* thought Jennifer. "Truthfully fellows, my 'mama' has been dead to me for almost ten years now. Taking her off those life support machines would be a blessing. Do what you gotta do. I haven't a clue as to where Ken is . . . I assume that's the 'friend' you're talking about. But knowing him, he's long gone. Now, unless you have orders to take me out, I'm outta here."

Jennifer pushed past the two men and trudged toward home. Her breaths were shallow. She may have sounded calm to them, but she was terrified within. *Have they been given orders to shoot?* she questioned. *I can't believe I said that about Mom. Did they buy it? Would they really kill her?* She silenced the urge to turn around, and kept walking.

\* \* \*

"Hey, Ken, would you grab the last box up there and bring it down?" Ryan asked, balancing three large boxes while feeling his way down the spiral staircase.

Ken did as requested.

Ryan set the boxes on the floor beside the Christmas tree, and Jessie watched in disgust as he blew the layered dust off the lids. Her first inclination was to cry out in horror as the small particles danced in the air, knowing perfectly well they were going to land somewhere else. It was Jessie's nature to be obsessive-compulsive when it came to cleanliness and order. This part of her had turned in constant turmoil since moving to the country, where dirt seemed part of the decor. After shivering, she leaned over and snooped into the boxes.

Ryan pulled out a round, quilted tree skirt. "Here it is." It was bright and festive with all the colors of Christmas and tied with red yarn.

"Oh, Ryan. It's marvelous. Did Ruth do this?"

"Nope. Done up by his grandmother," Gramps replied, hoarsely.

"It's in great condition," Jessie added.

"Well, there's four different kinds in here. This one went under our 'heirloom' tree. Then somewhere in here is a white one which was used under the 'peace' tree, and a red-and-green striped one that went under the 'goodie' tree. I could never figure out what that odd-looking one was all about, but it went under our 'hodgepodge' tree."

Jessie tried to conceal her shock at hearing the growing excitement in Ryan's voice. "If you'd like, I can do my best at making things look like what you're used to," she offered.

Ryan's eyes held hers briefly. "No, Jessie. You do this tree your way."

"Well, all right then. Ken, it looks like we have a long evening ahead of us."

Ken dropped back toward the hall. "I'm going upstairs."

"Oh, you're not leaving all this to us, are you?"

Ken continued to climb the stairs in silence.

"Fine. But I hope the guilt doesn't get to you when you find presents under this tree addressed to you!"

"Think I'm ready for my nap," Gramps expressed heartily.

"Oh, come on! You can't leave too."

"Now Jessie, I'm an old man, remember?" There was a twinkle in his eyes as he wrapped both thumbs around his suspenders, then gave them a snap. He rocked back and forth on his feet. "Gotta rest so I don't keel over and die before the holiday."

"Oh that's just fabulous, just fabulous." Jessie sighed as she turned back toward Ryan.

"I suppose you've got an excuse too?"

Ryan grinned. "Nope. Thought I'd grab a snack and follow orders."

Jessie tried hard not to stare too long into those deep blue eyes, but frankly she was caught a bit off guard.

"Really? I hoped someone around here would get a little Christmas spirit!" Her eyes followed him as he left for the kitchen. She allowed her thoughts to drift back briefly to their first and only kiss. It was during the summer, after they'd found the buried letter from her now-deceased mother. It had been a vulnerable moment, and she had given into the gentle kiss. But an intimate relationship would never last, she'd told herself over and over.

Ryan was simply a tool on her path to emotional recovery. These days it wasn't so much the fact that she'd been manipulated and emotionally hurt by several men in her past, but that she'd convinced herself that, inevitably, Ryan would be the one to get hurt. While she loved her new home and environment, sooner or later she would have to move back to the city and get on with life. Her savings were becoming depleted. The time was drawing near in which she'd have to decide on a new career path. She would have to return to her city apartment that she'd been subletting since the summer. She was well aware that a change in her life was good when it served a healthy purpose, but ultimately she had to deal with what made her leave . . . and that left little room for Ryan.

Jessie was pulled out of her thoughts by the tinkling of bells. She turned to find Ryan hanging a small sprig of mistletoe on a hook above the entryway to the kitchen. "Might come in handy," he teased, walking toward her.

"Yeah, well just remember, stupidity killed the cat." She turned toward the boxes in an effort to hide her smile.

"I believe that was curiosity."

"That's what everyone *believes,* but in truth, the cat knows better."

"The sun's breaking through the clouds," Ryan said, digging through a box.

"Yes, I saw. How can it be snowing so hard with the sun shining?" Jessie replied, dragging strands of white lights gently across the floor.

"I've come to the conclusion that the weather is a lot like a woman," Ryan said.

"How's that?"

"Everything can be calm and serene, and then seconds later the wind kicks up and the next thing you know, you're in the middle of Hurricane Helga."

"That's very romantic, Ryan. You should use that next time you're out with someone."

"I don't go out. You keep turning me down."

"Well, maybe if you came up with something a little more endearing than 'women are hurricanes,' I'd consider it."

"No you wouldn't," Ryan chuckled. "But speaking of romance, Gramps told me Elliott paid you a visit at your place before the storm hit."

Jessie stilled at the thought of her obsessive ex-boyfriend and boss. "We were having such a nice conversation, Ryan, why'd you have to go and ruin it?"

"Fine. I'll go back to asking you out."

Jessie plugged the lights into the backup power outlet to test them. "Right, then. Elliott. It was a good thing Gramps happened by or Elliott may have been another Christmas guest. After fifteen minutes of hearing Elliott ramble on, Gramps came in the kitchen and began working on a crossword puzzle. He gave Elliott that piercing look of his every time something foolish fell from Elliott's lips—which was just about every ten seconds. He was going for one last try, showing me the official divorce decree."

Ryan took a turn at unwinding a clump of white lights. "And?"

"And I think I finally convinced him that it doesn't matter. I don't want him in my life. It's a good thing he made it out of town before that storm hit. The last thing anyone's holiday needs is him." Jessie felt a twinge of sadness at the words. Elliott had been good to her for a time. Making her partner at his firm gave her career an incredible boost. And he was the first man she'd allowed into her heart. She believed him when he first said his divorce was final, so the relationship had become romantic. Then, by accident, Jessie found out he wasn't divorced, and she ended everything.

She was grateful, however, that he had forced her to get help with her past, landing her at Ryan's.

Jessie turned in time to see Ken's shirttail leaving the balcony. How long had he been there? she wondered. Minutes later Ryan and Jessie found themselves under the entryway of the kitchen, each holding a strand of lights to plug in. Ryan smiled and glanced up at the mistletoe.

"Isn't going to happen. Besides, I'm not actually *under* it," Jessie said.

* * *

"Whatcha readin' there, kiddo?" Gramps asked as he leaned over Ken's shoulder. Ken had been deep into the story and hadn't even heard Gramps enter.

"A book."

"Makes sense, this bein' a library and all. Mind sharin' which one?"

He didn't answer.

"Well, it must be a good one, or you'da heard me come in. Don't got any books about girls that I can recall, so could be just about anything, I guess."

Ken didn't move an inch, except to glance down and make sure the book was completely covered by his hands.

"And, as you can see, there's lots of choices, so if you get bored with that one, help yourself to another." The library's walls were lined from top to bottom with books. A rolling ladder of brass and maple was attached to the old-style bookcases that spanned the majority of the room. "Well, since you're not in the mood for conversation, I'm just gonna grab my readin' glasses and hightail it on outta here. That should make you right happy."

Silence.

Gramps shut the door and turned into Jessie. "Hey, doll. Flustered with that boy of mine already?"

"Just need an extension cord. Well, actually I suppose I am a bit flustered. But what would my life be without a certain level of flustering, eh? Have a good nap."

"By the way," Gramps said, "kid's readin' an interesting book."

"Oh yeah? What?"

*"The Giver."*

"What? Out of the millions of books in there, he chose that one?"

"Yep."

"Any chance he has the sequel with him, too?"

Gramps scratched the back of his head. "Don't believe so, no."

"Wonderful."

\* \* \*

*"The Giver?"* quizzed Ryan.

"Yep," Jessie answered.

"Could just be curiosity. It's won some awards, and it's been banned by some school districts—that's enough to make most kids curious."

"Yeah, well, I hope it's just that."

Ryan and Jessie each stood back to appraise their handi-work.

"Now for ornaments," Jessie began, searching through boxes again.

"You find them, I'll hang them," Ryan said, trying to match her enthusiasm.

"Great!" Jessie pulled out several boxes of candy canes off the top of what appeared to be small boxes of orna-ments. "Okay, I'm almost afraid to ask how long these have been in here."

"Sugar has a guaranteed shelf life of ten thousand years. I read it in a book. They'll taste just fine."

"Okay then, start with these."

"Actually, these go before the tinsel, but *after* the orna-ments."

"Uh-huh. 'Do the tree however you want, Jessie.' That lasted a long time." She grinned and placed the candy canes and tinsel off to the side and began gently unwrap-ping the ornaments.

Ryan took a handful of snow-white crocheted snowflakes of various sizes and shapes from Jessie, then began to make his way around the tree. "So, what *is* the reason behind Ken's reading choice, Dr. Winston?"

"Hard to say, really. If he's never read it before, then I would draw your immediate conclusion—curiosity. If he *has* read it before, then there are other reasons to draw from."

"Such as?"

"Well, the main character, Jonas, didn't have much time to plan for his journey, for one. Like Jonas, maybe Ken had been thinking about it for a while, but then something happened that made him rush, and so he grabbed the necessary items for his journey."

"Those being the bike, food, a little clothing, and his cell phone."

"Yes. The bike is obvious, a quick getaway. The food was to sustain life, and clothing to keep warm."

"And the cell phone?"

"Link to his past."

"Jonas didn't have a link to his past."

"Yeah, I know. Threw that in myself."

"Ah. And so Jonas took the baby to represent a future. What did Ken take?"

"That would be the gun."

Ryan stumbled out from behind the tree, nearly knocking it over. "Gun?"

# CHAPTER 8

Sunday was coming to a close at Beth's home. As to be expected, Beth's mood was sullen. She poured the rest of the pricey store-bought wine she had been saving for New Year's Eve, flipped off the lights, and turned on Bing again. She lay across the once brightly colored flower design of her couch and closed her eyes. She hummed softly to Bing's rendition of "I'll Be Home for Christmas," tears cascading down her cheeks.

Within minutes she found herself sitting on Kenny's bed. He had assured her he was safe, but she yearned for his return. "Wait a minute," she said out loud. "He said he'd call when it was *safe*. What did he mean by safe? Is he in some kind of danger?" She closed her eyes and forced her thoughts elsewhere. She was soon lost in the memories of his childhood, focusing, curiously, on his laughter when he'd told jokes that were amusing only to him. He had been such a happy kid. He was the one who always looked for and found the bright side of things. Everything changed when Patrick died. The laughter ceased, and seriousness set in. He was hardly talking to her now. The only thing she was good for was to find things that he'd lost. "Mom, where's this?" and "Mom, where's that?" or,

"Mom, have you seen my such-and-such?" was almost all he said to her. That's all he seemed to need from her now.

The divorce had taken place before his thirteenth birthday—almost three years after Patrick's death. Beth thought about the first time he'd been to counseling. He never said a word. When it came to Patrick, Ken had been quiet and moody and refused to discuss his feelings. She knew he kept going just to ease her mind—until this year. He said he'd had enough and refused to continue.

Looking around the room she wondered if he'd like the organizing she'd done. *He'll probably be irritated because he won't be able to find anything. Maybe I should have left it alone.* Searching the chaos might have offered her clues about what was happening. But it was too late. Everything was in order now. The only thing she hadn't touched was the small sandbox in the corner—a battleground full of miniature pewter figures. She knew enough about sand therapy to recognize that the scene before her held a significant meaning. On one side of the sandbox every battle figure stood together in a large group. On the other side, half buried, was a lone figure, his weapon knocked away. What had done that? *Perhaps Kenny feels alone, no one on his side. Helpless against his enemies? Or maybe I'm overanalyzing and he was simply acting out his favorite show.*

But why take the gun? she wondered. Kenny couldn't ever hurt anyone. Was it for protection? Had he, heaven forbid, planned on using it on himself? *Have things come that far? Have I missed the signs?* There were usually signs connected with suicidal thoughts. She'd already learned that. Kenny had been aloof lately, and messy and skipping school, but wasn't that just a typical phase for a teenager? Were those signs?

*Patrick didn't have any signs.* She stopped that thought process. She bent down and looked under Kenny's bed at the small box he'd left for her. It would stay with the spider she didn't have the heart to kill. She wanted her son to give her his gift.

She suddenly felt incredibly alone. She missed her sons. She missed Michael. Friends and neighbors came and went, she thought, but family should have always been there.

* * *

Before Jessie continued her conversation with Ryan, she stood back and tilted her head to see if the snowflake she'd just hung on the tree was crooked. "Yeah. The gun would represent Ken's future. The question is, though, is it going to be the *end* of his future?"

"JESSIE!" Ryan's face was shocked.

"Hmm?"

"GUN?"

"Shhh, keep it down."

"Keep it down!? How come I'm the only one upset here?"

"You *are* upset. Wow, Ryan. You think I'd allow a loaded gun in here? Please, I'm much more sensible than that," she whispered.

"So, there's *not* a gun?"

"Oh, no, there's a gun, just not a *loaded* gun. I took the bullets out the second I found it. He's most likely unaware of that, though. I'm sure he's checked to make sure his stuff is still intact, but he won't think to check for the bullets—at least not until he's ready to actually use it. Hopefully by then he'll have changed his mind."

"Even with the gun empty, we have someone here who is potentially dangerous."

"He's not dangerous, Ryan. He's confused, alone, hurt, frightened, and possibly looking for a way out. If he'd meant to harm us, he would have attempted it before now."

"When did you find it?"

"I went snooping when he was asleep."

"Wait a minute. You jumped all over me for being curious about his backpack, and *you* went snooping?" Ryan had long since quit decorating the tree, choosing instead to poke at the now-ebbing fire.

"Remember when Ken joined us for dinner and you alluded so thoughtfully to the possibility that he may have a knife or a gun in his pack?"

"That's what I'm talking about."

"Yes, but do you remember what his response was?"

"Not really."

"So does this photographic memory thing only work when you want it to? I thought once the information was stored it was always there for instant recall."

Ryan glared at her sarcasm as he recalled that evening's conversation. "He said he didn't have a knife," he replied a split second later.

"Good boy! He didn't say, 'I don't have a weapon,' or 'I don't have a knife or a gun.'"

"How did I miss that?"

"I'm sure the match thing was a distraction. There was also an envelope full of money. I'm guessing a few hundred dollars." She looked down. "Oh Ryan, this is adorable! Did you make this when you were a kid?" Jessie had pulled out a tongue depressor, which had been painted white and decorated with red and green beads all around the edges. From the top to the bottom was written, "Mary Crismas."

"Yeah. I think I was four."

"So there *was* a time you didn't have a perfect knowledge of all things."

"Why did that sound like a passage from the Book of Mormon?" Ryan chided.

"Did it? And would you look at these! Did your mother make these for you?" Jessie dangled a sky-blue pair of handmade booties before him.

"No." Ryan turned from Jessie and continued poking the kindling in the fireplace. "Brecca made those for Joshua. I'm not sure what they're doing in there."

"Hey there, that tree's lookin' mighty nice," Gramps called, stomping down the steps with Nelly at his heels.

Jessie was grateful for the distraction; Ryan was most likely thinking of Joshua. The first time she'd learned of his son was when she'd found Ryan kneeling at a grave last summer. That was when he told her of his past. He hadn't been the model husband to Brecca. She had come from a long line of horse entrepreneurs, and her share of her grandfather's legacy had been in the millions. The money, coupled with Ryan's egotistical view of himself as the greatest psychologist in his field, created a monster. He had it all, but it was never enough. He became unhappy, turning to alcohol for comfort.

Not wanting his drinking binge to be interrupted, he'd turned off his cell phone the stormy night Brecca had gone into labor. Jessie learned Gramps had been the one to find her rolled car. It had been too late for her and for the baby. That had been eight years ago. Ryan had finally let go of tormenting himself for his role in Joshua's and Brecca's deaths, but Jessie wasn't sure he'd ever be able to completely rid himself of the pain and sadness. She knew that Ryan, while not antagonistic toward God, certainly resented His not taking him, instead of his wife and son. That's the way it should have been, Ryan had told her— the innocent spared and the guilty punished.

"Come on, girl, time for you to go out," Ryan said, nudging Nelly toward the front entrance. Ryan opened the door, and Nelly got a taste of the winter's crisp bite. She turned quickly around and headed back to the family room. "Oh no you don't. Now come on, Nelly. Nelly! You get back here!"

Jessie reached Nelly before the dog leaped up the stairs. "Ryan, you've got to learn how to talk to women. We don't respond well to loud, irritable speech."

"I wasn't being irritable. You have a better idea?"

Jessie smiled and began using baby talk, all the while scratching Nelly gently behind the ears. "Come on, sweetie, you gotta go out now. I know it's cold, but it won't take you long." Nelly was at her side now, following her to the door. "Just go on out there and do your thing." With a pat on her back, Jessie opened the door, and out Nelly went. Jessie shut the door and walked past Ryan.

"Please don't ever do that again," he said. "The hair on my arms may never lay flat."

"Say what you want, but you've got to admit it worked," Jessie said loftily as she headed into the kitchen.

"So that's how women want to be talked to? My voice has never reached that pitch, not even during puberty."

"Well, maybe once," Gramps cut in.

"You stay out of this," Ryan retaliated. "You're the one who brought her downstairs and then walked away."

"Ain't my dog."

There was an immediate bark at the door. Gramps smiled as Jessie let Nelly back in. She went straightway upstairs to resume a nice cozy nap at Ken's feet.

"So, Gramps, what shall we have for dinner?" Jessie asked.

"There's some leftover stew on the top shelf of the fridge. Thought I'd heat that up with the leftover corn bread."

"Sounds fabulous," Jessie responded. "I'll set the table. Ryan, would you put another log on the fire? I'm determined to finish that tree tonight."

"Hey, Ken!" Gramps yelled from the kitchen.

"Yes, sir?" Ken called from the top of the stairs.

"You gonna join us in some stew and corn bread?"

"Yes, sir."

"Ever wonder if that kid knows more than the standard ten words he's used in the past couple of days?" This whisper wasn't directed to anyone in particular.

"I think he's reached about twenty, Gramps," Ryan answered mechanically, filling a saucepan with the stew.

The table was set as Ken entered the kitchen. He sat across from Jessie. She was, after all, the most pleasant choice to look at.

Dinner conversation consisted of weather, horses, and the Christmas dinner menu.

"You mean you haven't planned the entire meal yet?" Ryan grunted toward Jessie while buttering his bread. "I'm amazed."

"How come you're so rude to her all the time?" Ken suddenly ventured.

Ryan and Jessie glanced at each other before Ryan spoke. "Have I been rude?"

"Seems so to me."

"It does, eh? Well, is it my choice of words that seem rude, or the sound of my voice?"

"Do all you guys do that?"

"Do what?"

"Answer questions with other questions?"

*Smart kid,* Jessie thought.

"Yes. I suppose it is an occupational hazard. Does it bother you?" Ryan asked.

"See? There you go again. You couldn't just stop at 'Yes. I suppose it is an occupational hazard.' You had to add, 'Does it bother you?'" Kenny used his corn bread to wipe the inside of his bowl. The stew was good. Not as good as his mother's, but darn close.

"So, it does bother you," Ryan said, nodding to himself.

"Ken, are your parents often rude to each other?" Jessie cut in.

"Doesn't matter."

"Ryan and I will try to be more patient with each other. He's gone through a great deal in life, though, in the last year even. And sometimes when people are on edge with their own emotions, it's hard to remember to be kind to those around them."

The stew-filled ladle in Ryan's hand stopped in midair. There was absolutely nothing he could say to that, even though somewhere inside he wasn't thrilled she had shared that with their fifteen-year-old, uninvited guest.

"What's he gone through?" Ken's curiosity had been piqued.

"Well, it isn't my place to tell you—no more than it would be for me to tell him why you left, that is, if you'd told me." Jessie finished the last bite of her corn bread and laid her napkin on the table. "You have your reasons, and Ryan has his."

"So, what've you been through?" Kenny didn't look directly at Ryan, but only an idiot wouldn't know who the question was directed to, Ryan thought.

Both Gramps's and Jessie's eyes rose to meet Ryan's, their spoons finding a place of respite in their bowls.

Ryan understood on a psychological plane what Jessie was doing, but he would have preferred she'd chosen *her* life to be this evening's illustration. He breathed deeply, resting both elbows on the table. "My mother died giving birth to me. My father split when I was five because he couldn't stand looking at me. Gramps, here, and my Aunt Ruth had to raise me. When I was a little older than you, I set fire to a friend's house and burned it to the ground. I spent the night in jail, then Gramps made me spend months rebuilding their house, and I had to pay for it myself. Eight years ago my wife and unborn child died because I was too busy being a drunk on the night she went into labor. Had I been where I should have, I could have driven her safely through the night's storm to the hospital.

"After that I buried myself so deep into my career that I burned out. I retired and threw myself into my late wife's million-dollar business of breeding and selling horses—which by the way *is* a positive thing. Last summer Aunt Ruth died. And last, but not least, around that same time I heard my dead wife's voice and smelled her lavender scent everywhere I went."

"You burned someone's house down?" Ken asked in shock.

"Why, after all that, is that the first thing of interest?" Ryan shook his head and returned to his stew.

A light went on in Ken's head. "That must be the match thing. And how old are you anyway?"

"I'm thirty-eight."

"And you're retired? Wow."

"Ken, Ryan learned the hard way that life doesn't owe us anything," Jessie began. "I believe society fails to teach that it's not life that owes us, but rather *we* that owe something to life, as well as to those around us who share it."

Ken didn't comment, but the blank stare was enough to say he hadn't a clue as to what she meant.

"Let me ask you something. Do you like Nelly?"

"I guess so."

"Why? What does she do for you? She really isn't good for a darn thing. She's constantly in the way, it's difficult to get her to do anything you want, she sometimes has accidents in the house because she's too lazy to go outside, and she goes through more dog food than I'd care to think about. So, what could you possibly like about her?"

"She stays with me and lets me pet her, I guess."

"Yes, she keeps you company. That's a good reason. We all put up with that big overgrown dumb animal—no offense, Ryan." Jessie smiled.

Ryan returned the smile. "None taken."

"Because she keeps us company and lets us love her, and once in a while she'll nuzzle us or bark at the right moment. There aren't any other expectations. That's simply what she lives for. Life for us is to find out what *we* live for. Is there someone we can be company to or let love us just because we exist?

"We depend on others, just as Nelly depends on us. We do, however, have the added responsibility of depending on ourselves for food, and shelter, and work. We have to make those things happen. Life is a journey, a gift. It's up to each of us, no matter what our circumstances, to make out of life what we can. If we expect others to allow us to lie on our feet and be petted all day, sooner or later that gets old, and we have no purpose. And we all have a purpose, Ken."

"Not me." The words were soft and bitter.

"Yes, Ken, you do. At fifteen you have an incredible purpose."

"You don't even know me."

"You're right. I don't know the ins and outs of you. But I know that you're going through one of the most difficult times of life. This is when you start evaluating yourself and figuring out your own identity. You've realized that you're not going to be Superman, like you thought when you were four. You're probably not going to be that astronaut or the top-gun fighter pilot that you role-played when you were eight. You're trying to find a place to fit in with your peers. You're realizing that you're eventually going to be out there, on your own—a scary prospect by itself. You're discovering what your place is in the universal scheme of things. You're choosing your values and defining your personal philosophy. You're at a pivotal point, Ken, and what you do now can, and most likely will, determine the ultimate direction your life will take."

"You know this just 'cause I'm fifteen?"

"Yes. And the fact that you've left home. It could mean there's stuff going on there that goes against your belief structure—whether or not you're even aware that you have a belief structure. You're quiet, which means you're reflective. Running away alone also indicates you *feel* alone."

"Maybe I was on my way to meet somebody."

"Then you would have called someone other than your mother."

"You listened?" Ken challenged in disgust.

"Yes. You hadn't earned your privacy yet."

"You need help with these dishes, or can I go to my room now?" Ken mumbled between clenched teeth.

"It's up to you," Jessie replied kindly.

Ken banged his dishes in the sink. "You don't want me here." The words were short and crisp.

"Ken," Ryan began, "anything I've said in the negative shouldn't have been directed at you. I was—"

"Not talkin' about you. She's the one who said it." He nodded toward Jessie.

"Me? I've never said you weren't wanted."

"Yes, you did! When you two were doin' the tree, I heard you. You said, 'The last thing this holiday needs is him'!"

"You've got to hone your eavesdropping skills there, Ken. That wasn't about you. It was about a love-sick maniac who won't leave Jessie alone," said Ryan.

Jessie flinched. "Gee, thanks for that kind and thoughtful narrative, Ryan."

"No problem."

"Oh." Ken promptly left the kitchen and practically flew down the hall to his room.

"Wow, he *can* move faster than a snail's pace," Gramps said, folding his crossword puzzle and setting his glasses inside his shirt pocket.

"Think he overheard everything?" Ryan stared at Jessie, not wanting to bring the gun issue up in front of Gramps.

"Doubt it. If he had, he'd have known about Elliott." Jessie stood and began clearing the table. "At any rate, I just blew our first real talk with him."

"Not at all. I was impressed. I've never seen you in action before. Ready to accept my offer as partner of Valhalla Retreat?" Ryan leaned back in his chair and rubbed his chin.

"If I actually considered it, you'd have to change the name."

"What? Why?"

"Ryan, naming a youth summer camp after Norse mythology is . . . well, it's morbid."

"Oh, come on. No it's not."

"Your goal, I assume, is to *help* them, right? I did some studying lately, and I realize that Valhalla was a 'great hall' where fallen battle heroes went, but I'm not sure that's the right angle. Besides, Norse mythology is different from other mythology. They believed that even though the gods were immortal, they would be destroyed in the final battle between good and evil. Don't you think that's . . . a bit ghoulish?"

"It's mythology, Jessie."

"Exactly my point. Why not give it a name from reality?"

"You agree to work with me, and I'll reconsider the name."

"Good. I'll let you know by New Year's."

"This New Year's, right? Not next year or the year after."

"Yes, Ryan, *this* New Year's."

# CHAPTER 9

Jessie awoke perspiring. Had her screams been real? Since neither Ryan nor Gramps were seated next to her, maybe the cries of terror were only part of her nightmare. She wouldn't sleep now and she needed a change of scenery. A walk in five feet of snow should alter her subconscious, she thought, and it wasn't long before she stepped out into the night.

The night was moonless black, and the gusting wind caused tree branches to rustle and snow to whirl around her. "Okay, imagination, no overtime please," Jessie whispered, thankful that it was the month of December and not October. She switched her thoughts to something more productive.

After a few minutes of trudging through the snow, Jessie spied a light in the stable. It was well after one in the morning by now. Either Ryan left the light on or someone else couldn't sleep either.

Jessie peeked cautiously through the window, then realized that if it *was* a stranger, she was certainly in no shape to flee. Thankfully it was just Ryan, walking about with a cloth in one hand and a bottle in the other. The wind howled as it thrust Jessie inside.

"Well, hello there," Ryan called in surprise.

"What are you working on at this wretched hour?" Jessie asked. She removed her gloves and pulled the scarf off her face.

"Gramps's Christmas gift."

"Really? What is it?" Jessie's voice was filled with excitement.

"Not telling."

"Oh, come on! I won't squeal." Jessie walked toward the corner where Ryan was perched on a stool.

Ryan stood and blocked her view. Since his hands were full, he placed his elbows on her arms and pushed her back gently. "Nope."

"You're no fun. No fun at all."

"So you keep reminding me." He lowered his eyes to meet hers as a smile set on his face. He didn't want to break the touch.

"Did you make something for me?" Her green eyes twinkled. She was surprised she felt no need to push him away.

"Maybe."

"Well, I got you something."

"There's only one thing I want." Ryan smirked as his eyes set on the stable doors.

Jessie glanced over to see another small sprig of mistletoe hanging. "Oh, you've got to be kidding! How many of those things have you hung around here?"

"Lost count."

Now she did push him away. "Well, your present's already wrapped, so there."

Ryan set the bottle down and shooed Jessie away while he covered Gramps's surprise with a saddle blanket. "So, another nightmare wake you up?"

"There's that great gift of subtlety again."

Ryan moved toward Zeus and sat on a stool in front of his stall. "Come on, tell me about it. You might as well—we're both wide awake."

Jessie ignored the therapy attempt. "Don't sell Joanie. At least not to Zeus's buyers. If you're intent on selling her, you could sell her to me instead." Jessie pulled another stool toward Ryan and sat down. "I know with all the money I've put into fixing up my house this year there isn't a great deal left, but I think there's enough for a down payment. Please, Ryan?"

"Hmm. Something to bargain with now." Ryan leaned back on the stool and winked.

"What do you mean?"

"You want Joanie, and I want a kiss."

"Oh, Ryan, don't be ridiculous!"

"I'm not," he chuckled.

"You mean you'd sell her to me if I gave you a kiss?" Jessie said, mentally assessing the idea.

"Absolutely."

"Oh brother. You really need to get out more often. Fine, stand up; let's get it over with." Jessie stood and shook her whole body, as if she were preparing herself to eat something that was still alive.

Ryan remained seated. "Hmm. Not exactly the way I had imagined."

"Do you want a kiss or not?"

Ryan stood and stretched. "Not if it's going to cause you extreme discomfort. I'm sure Joanie will love her new home in Mexico."

"Oh, Ryan, please. I can do this . . . I mean I *want* to do this, really." Jessie pressed her hand gently on his arm. She closed her twitching eyes and leaned in.

Ryan shook his head back and forth as he watched her cheeks tighten and her hands tense. "Jessie, it's okay. If you want Joanie, you can buy her—same price as the buyers. I was just being male."

Ryan turned and rummaged through a tack box. Jessie knew it was an attempt to cover his obvious humiliation. "I told you that I would hurt you," she said. "I told you when this relationship started months ago that this would happen."

"You've misinterpreted what just took place. *I'm* not the one hurting. You are."

"I can't believe you're going to get psychological about a kiss," she returned.

"It's not about a kiss."

"Ryan . . ."

"Hey, you're the one who came in here. You came in here either because you wanted to see me or because your subconscious wanted to be analyzed."

Jessie said nothing.

Ryan laid a blanket out on the floor and sat down crossed-legged, patting the spot next to him. "It bothers you when I'm right, doesn't it?"

Jessie grudgingly sat across from him. "It's like chalk screeching across a board. Makes me just want to stomp you into little tiny bits."

Ryan smiled. "Jessie, I told you I'd wait, and I'll wait. In time you'll realize I'm not the manipulative jerk that you expect me to be, and you'll wish you'd have jumped in sooner."

"You'll be snatched up long before that. Why did you say *I* was the one hurting."

"Oh, Jessie, come on now, that's high school psychology."

"Don't insult me, Ryan."

"You're hurting because you wanted to kiss me, and didn't."

"But you've just said it wasn't about the kiss."

"Right."

"I'm continually amazed that you made an above-average living at this."

Ryan smiled and remained silent. He knew it wouldn't take long for her to figure it out.

A few neighs passed through the quiet.

"It's about the *wanting*," Jessie offered.

"And?"

"And—I still can't trust. Amazing, isn't it? I've dedicated years to teaching abused children that even though they were mistreated by those who should have protected them, they *could* trust again—they just needed to learn how. I *know* how, and I still can't do it."

"You've been able to forgive your father and your stepbrothers."

"Yes, I suppose I have."

"And you've forgiven God."

"Yes. But I still can't trust, Ryan."

"I know."

"Is it my mother?"

"You tell me."

Jessie sighed and looked off into space. Wasn't she over that? she questioned herself. Initially her mother was the source of her buried anger. But didn't that end when she'd found the letter? "There are still many unanswered questions. For instance, why did she choose to leave Katie and me at the movie theater? Why didn't she just drop us off on the steps of the child welfare department? Was she still alive when I was being abused and when Katie died? When exactly *did* she die? But the questions don't seem to consume me like they used to. Somehow I know that they'll all be answered or it will cease to bother me completely. So, having said all that, there's only one other possibility."

Ryan's eyebrows rose. Was she actually going to acknowledge it?

"Me. I don't trust me."

"Yes." Ryan let out the breath he'd been holding in.

"You know what will happen, don't you? If our attraction continues?" snapped Jessie, annoyed at how easy the answer seemed to be in his mind.

Ryan's eyes narrowed while his head leaned to one side. He had no idea where this topic had come from. "What?"

"Sooner or later, our individualism will reassert itself."

"Meaning?"

"I'll want to go to a movie, and you'll want to stay in. You'll want to go out to eat, and I'll want to eat here. You'll want to go riding, but I'll want to read a book. You won't like my friends, so I won't like yours. I'll want to go to church, and you'll want me to stay home. So, sooner or later we'll be individuals again, and not one in purpose."

"Want to explain to me how we jumped from 'trust,' or the lack of it, to 'you won't like my friends'?"

Jessie stood up and began to pace, her hands punctuating and emphasizing her speech. "Confusing, aren't I? There's so much, Ryan. I don't have a clue where to start. I'm feeling overwhelmed. I know you care about me and would wait, but—"

"I haven't meant to pressure you, Jessie."

"Yes, I know. But it's still there, Ryan."

"You've been avoiding me quite well, until this snow-storm."

"That's just it. I don't *want* to have to avoid you. I have enough things to *avoid*."

Ryan attempted a different route. "Tell me about the nightmare."

"Ken loaded the gun with Christmas marshmallows and shot the arcade game, and all the little Galaxia ships came alive and attacked us," she said melodramatically.

"Okay, well, that won't take much analyzing."

"Nope. How about we talk about Ken?" She too hoped for a change in subject.

"No. Let's get back to you not wanting to be challenged. What's changed?"

"What do you mean?" Jessie returned to the stool.

"You said that reading the Book of Mormon has brought you peace. Yet, you're not wanting to trust your instincts or be personally challenged. I hate to be the one to tell you this, but as I recall, the gospel of Jesus Christ is full of things that are considerably challenging."

"So, you're right. Are you happy now?" Jessie was off the stool again.

"I'm not sure what it is I'm right about, Jessie."

"The finding something else to lean on. The crutch thing."

"Ah."

Jessie's ritual pacing continued. "Why can't things just be simple?"

"They are," Ryan said. "How does that saying go, 'Peace is fitting into God's plan, stress is fitting God into our plan.'"

"Oh, what—now *you've* found religion?"

Ryan restrained his laughter. "I'd like to be privy to what led you to find that letter from your mother. It might facilitate figuring out what's going on in that pretty little head of yours."

"Not to mention the fact that you're dying of curiosity," Jessie retorted, smirking.

"That too, sure."

Jessie stared, the welling tears barely perceptible in her eyes. She was finally becoming sleepy. And there wasn't another blanket close by to wrap up in for security. "It's awfully late."

"Yes, it is."

"Gramps will have breakfast at the crack of dawn."

"Yes, he will. Are you finished changing lanes?"

"Ryan, I've said more than I'd intended. I'm not going to be a wreck for the holidays. I want to enjoy Christmas."

"After Christmas, you'll tell me how you found the letter?"

"Yes."

"Done."

Jessie sighed in relief. "It's really beautiful out here this time of year. Although, next year I'll have to be a bit more prepared. It's a good thing I'm with you and Gramps. I'm actually tiring of crackers. By the way, how come *you're* not sleeping? You could work on that project anytime." She pointed toward the corner.

"The dinner conversation set my mind into overdrive."

"Yes, I've been going over that too."

"What do you think Ken's dealing with?" Ryan leaned back on his elbows.

"Hmm. Best guess would be—I have no idea."

"No clue? That's not like you."

"Kids have different things to survive than adults, Ryan. Adults with past issues are working *through* their childhood. Kids are *living* it. Sometimes it's obvious, like abuse or drugs, and sometimes it's not so obvious. It's not being accepted by their peers or feeling inadequate, not getting into the right college, not meeting family expectations, not feeling loved, being dumped by the love of their life—the list goes on and on. It's not just 'tell me about your mother.' Adults usually manage to overcome their phobias because they have a greater base of experience, and those who can't end up seeking help. Kids don't know how to express what's going on, let alone how to get help. They just know they're frustrated and unhappy. Then they meet up with someone who can make them 'feel' better with either drugs, physical intimacy, or the idea of the ultimate escape—ending it all. And most parents don't see the signs until it's too late."

"From his remarks regarding us, there's tension in the home."

"Yes," Jessie replied unhappily. She picked up a stray piece of hay and began twirling it between two fingers.

"You ready to tell me about the nightmare now?" Ryan asked with quiet steadiness.

Jessie met his gaze. "What—you didn't like the Galaxia explanation?"

"I'll admit it was a premier attempt for being put on the spot."

"I wouldn't really call it a nightmare," Jessie said softly.

"People don't typically scream in dreams."

"Yeah, well, you got a point there. I'm cleaning all the time."

"Did we switch topics again?"

"No, you idiot! In the nightmare! Honestly, Ryan!"

"Sorry. What do you mean you're cleaning all the time?"

"People are surrounding me, vying for attention, and all I want to do—actually *want* isn't the right word—all I *can* do is clean, to the detriment of all else."

"So what does that tell you?"

"I'm avoiding things that I don't feel I'm good at or scared of."

"Like intimacy."

"I'm cleaning because I'm not happy with my social life?" Jessie asked, incredulously.

"Just a thought." Ryan pulled himself back up to a seated position.

"I think I'm fanatical about cleaning and order because that's the one sure thing I *can* control, and I'm good at it. I've accomplished something that's tangible. I can't do that with people."

"Sure you can."

"No, Ryan, I can't. People change, dusting doesn't. Dust always appears on the same things, day in and day out. It's dependable."

"I sense you're judging all of mankind based on the handful of men you've managed to get stuck with in life."

"Probably. So, you think if I create positive relationships my compulsion with cleaning will stop?" she asked.

"I said it was a thought, Jessie. Cleaning, in and of itself, is not bad. It's something I see you enjoy doing, odd as that may be. It's to the extent that you take your cleaning that may be in question. You *don't* have to mop the floors or wash all your trash cans on a daily basis. You don't have to wipe your baseboards and your—"

"Yeah, yeah, okay. I got it. But I've done it for so long, I don't know how to stop."

"Yes, you do."

"You want me to call someone every time I get the urge to overclean and have them distract me?"

"Not a bad place to start. Why not call me?"

"You know how many times a day I'd have to be distracted! We're finished here. I've told you about the nightmare, you've analyzed it, now I'm ready for sleep."

"Gramps saw Ken on the news. His last name is Moon," Ryan said, putting on his overcoat.

"Ken mentioned that Gramps knew where he came from."

"I've met his father. He's an ex-prison guard from Lyle Penitentiary turned cop. We had a horse stolen that turned up in Lyle. Moon was assigned the case. He talked more with Brecca than me. Seemed like an okay guy." The wind swirled softly around them as they left the barn.

"Having a cop for a dad can be rough for some kids," Jessie called over her shoulder. "You're sure it's the same family?"

"Lyle's a small town, Jessie, and the kid's build—he's Moon's son, all right." The sound of the crunching snow echoed as Ryan and Jessie retraced their steps through the drifts. "You think he's suicidal?"

"I believe it's crossed his mind. But I also believe he's still grounded in his love for his mother. He hasn't reached peace with the decision to end it all."

"So we watch for a change in personality?"

"Yes, for now. If he becomes happier immediately and less resistant to us and our desire to help, *then* we take more drastic measures."

# CHAPTER 10

The morning light inched across Gramps's crossword puzzle as Ryan entered the kitchen. Gramps peered over his glasses. "Mornin', son."

Ryan poured himself a glass of juice. "Why is it so quiet around here? Where is everybody?"

"Hmm. Well, the kid hasn't moved since last night. He's still asleep in his room. At least I think that's him snorin' away in there. Nelly's on his feet. Didn't think that bed could hold that much weight. And Jessie, well, I don't know, son, but there's a note over there with your name on it." Gramps pointed to a poinsettia-decorated envelope underneath a candy-cane magnet on the refrigerator.

Ryan sat across from Gramps as he quickly began to read the note. "Oh, for crying out loud! Gramps, why didn't you stop her?"

"What you jumpin' on me for?"

Ryan stood quickly, shaking his head. "She's walked back to your place."

"What? What did you do now, son?"

"What do you mean, what did *I* do? I didn't do anything. She says here she had to get a few things." Ryan walked to the utility room and returned with his winter gear. "You're going to have to keep a close eye on Ken. It's a mess out there, but with Jessie and me gone, I wouldn't put it past him to try to sneak off. It hasn't snowed for a couple days, but even with the sun, that snow is way too deep to get anywhere. Unless of course you're Jessie Winston. What in the world was she thinking?"

"She's got a mind of her own, son. You told her you love her yet?" Gramps placed his eyes back on his puzzle.

"If it's bothering you all that much, why don't *you* tell her—if she's still alive after today, that is. What does she need from your place anyway?"

"Now, now, son. It's Christmas and she's a woman. That should be enough explanation. And don't you go gettin' all mad when you see her. She *was* thoughtful enough to leave you a note. Few months ago, I don't believe she'd a done that."

"Yeah, okay, fine." Ryan rubbed his face, then slipped on his gloves. "I'll try the phone when I get to your place. If you don't see or hear from us by dark, don't plan on us for Christmas dinner."

Gramps watched Ryan mumble something unintelligible to himself as he made for the door. Any concerns for the welfare of his grandson were put on hold as he smiled at the changes he'd seen in Ryan over the past few months. As an adult, Ryan had always been calm, especially with Rebecca. "Even-tempered" was what she called him. They were both easygoing and unemotional—only Ryan's drinking had brought contention.

Jessie was bringing out a different side of him, and it had been interesting to watch. While Rebecca had been good for Ryan, Gramps had to admit he liked spunk in a woman—believed it forced a man to become better. Since having met

Jessie, his grandson's life had changed dramatically. He had finally been able to let go of his emotional hold on Rebecca. His desire to help people had returned, and a dream long forgotten had been remembered. Jessie would help him put Rebecca's money to good use when they opened their retreat. He had to admit he didn't like Ryan's name for the camp, either. He was sure it would change if Jessie had the final say. The thought brought a chuckle to his lips.

\* \* \*

"The sun's shining and you still can't get through the streets," a disgruntled Michael yelled. He shook his head as he moved away from the police station's front window. "This coffee's awful! Whose turn was it?" he shouted between clenched teeth.

"I'm sorry, Lieutenant," replied a timid Officer Smoot, biting her lip.

Michael slammed his coffee mug down on her desk, splashing the dark liquid onto the piles of paper. "That's the same miserable tune you whistled yesterday. Wanna keep your pitiful job? Learn to make a cup of decent coffee!"

"Yes, sir."

Michael stormed past the wet-behind-the-ears officer and slammed the door to the men's bathroom.

"Hey, don't worry about that, Smoot," said Officer Sanders. "Can't blame him for being in a mood. It's gotta be rough having his son missing, with the weather and all. He already lost one kid."

Officer Smoot scooted out from behind her desk and strolled over to Sanders. "What happened?" She perched herself on a stool next to his desk.

Officer Sanders looked over his shoulder before he whispered, "Well, rumor is the kid killed himself."

"Oh, how awful! How old was he?"

Sanders threw his forefinger to his lips and squinted his eyes. "Shh!" His voice went back to a whisper. "That's the other odd thing—he was the same age as this kid, fifteen."

"No!" Officer Smoot's eyes grew wide as she leaned in closer.

"The missing kid's the one who found him."

"How long ago?"

"Let's see . . ."

"It's been five years," Michael interrupted, standing at the bathroom door. "And rumors are full of discrepancies."

Officer Smoot skirted away quickly, muttering something about finding some new coffee beans. Officer Sanders stared at Michael with a terrified grin.

\* \* \*

"Jessie?" a cold and tired Ryan called as he kicked off his boots by the front door of Gramps's place.

Jessie pushed through the kitchen door holding a pair of scissors. "Ryan! Please tell me you didn't forge your way through that mess out there just to hunt me down?"

"Thought you might want some help."

"You're dripping!"

"Well now, doesn't that just beat all?"

"The least you could do is drip on the tile and not the carpet."

"Are you finished scolding me?" Ryan asked, staring down at her while she helped pull off his parka.

Those eyes and his proximity were taking their toll. She cleared her throat. "Watch it. I'm holding a pair of scissors."

She let go of the parka and backed away. "Ryan, what *are* you doing here? We've gone over this. I'm not a little girl. I can trudge through snow for a few miles without keeling over."

"Let's play a yes-or-no game, okay?"

"Oh, here we go." Jessie sat on the couch and sighed.

"Humor me."

"Fine."

Ryan had successfully accomplished the task of removing his snowpants and gloves and was shaking the water from his hair. "It's obvious I care about you, right?"

"Yes."

"And not *just* as a friend?"

"Yes."

"And so, if I hadn't come after you—if I had let you not only walk one way, but *both* ways, carrying *who knows what* on the way back—you would've been okay with that?"

Jessie's eyebrows rose. She let out a deep breath while looking at the ceiling. She longed to release deceiving words from her lips but couldn't. She hated the part of her that forced integrity. "Would you like some coffee?"

The hint of a smile formed on Ryan's cold lips. "I'll take that as your way of saying, 'You're right, Ryan. Thanks for coming to help.' Is there *any* chance there's any *caffeinated* coffee in this house?"

"Nope. Coffee is bad for the heart," Jessie said triumphantly as she headed toward the kitchen.

"They're teaching that now as part of the Word of Wisdom, eh?"

"Hmm? Who?" Jessie raised her voice as the door closed behind her.

Ryan joined her in the kitchen. "The Mormons."

"Nope. Read that on the Internet. Haven't studied much about the Word of Wisdom yet. Apparently it's in the Doctrine and Covenants, which I haven't gotten into. So, you want cinnamon tea or hot chocolate?" Jessie was holding a tea bag in one hand and a container of mint-flavored chocolate mix in the other.

"You know, teas and hot chocolate aren't necessarily good for you either," Ryan stated, smirking.

"Huh?"

"From what I've seen, your tea could boil an egg."

"And that's bad?"

"The Word of Wisdom isn't necessarily about caffeine, Jessie."

"It's not?"

"No."

Jessie set her belongings down on the table. "Well, are you going to elaborate?"

Ryan chewed the inside of his cheek. How did he manage to become the teacher of Mormon religion? It was an inevitability of things to come, he decided. However, he could always attempt to change the topic of conversation. "Jessie, why are you here?"

"When Bishop Grant asked me that, I told him that earth was the only known planet with both oxygen and water. When that didn't get a response, I said it was because I probably had some kind of purpose. But, like I told him, if God knows *everything,* then He knows what I'm going to do and what I'm not, and so even if I did have a 'purpose,' does it really matter? If God knows the intents of our hearts, then why do we even have to *be* here? The bishop then said something about 'a test.' Whatever that meant." Jessie had been waving the tea bag around with such intensity that the bag tore free of the string and landed in front of Ryan.

Ryan chuckled and leaned back in his chair, raising the two front legs off the floor. "Actually, I was asking why you came back here to Gramps's."

"Oh. Sorry." She retrieved the tea bag from its new resting spot, then headed toward the cupboard. "We were talking about the Word of Wisdom and then you asked why I was here, and well, it just sounded like . . . anyway I came back because I wasn't bright enough to bring all our Christmas gifts with us. I didn't believe we'd be cooped up in your cabin all this time. I'm a city girl trying to turn country too soon, I guess."

Ryan smiled inwardly. He had enjoyed their time together these past few days and selfishly hoped the sun would fade again behind an even blacker sky. "Have you got them ready to go?"

"You're not upset?" She placed her mug into the microwave.

"Of course not."

"I kind of enjoyed your bout with anger."

"Yeah, well, I didn't."

"I have two more small things to wrap, and then I'm all done. That pile over there needs to go." Jessie pointed to the corner by the hallway.

"You're kidding, right? *All* of those need to go? There's no way the two of us are going to be able to handle that!" Ryan's chair landed back onto all fours.

Jessie's face looked smug as the microwave sounded. She stood to get her tea. "He's back," she sang.

"This isn't anger, Jessie. This is—slight frustration."

"Right. Whatever you need to tell yourself in order feel good there, Ryan. We'll manage with the presents. Since you're here, I won't have to make two trips. I found some good-size pieces of wood in the shed, and some rope. We can build a couple of makeshift sleds." Jessie brought her steaming tea to the table and sat across from him. "Now, can you tell me what my hot tea has to do with the Word of Wisdom? If not, it can wait till I see the missionaries after Christmas."

Ryan drew in a deep breath. "Part of the Word of Wisdom says something like 'hot drinks are not good for the belly.' Research has proven that really hot drinks cause damage to the lining of the mouth, esophagus, and stomach."

"Well then, if it's the temperature, couldn't we just drink them warmed, or cold, like ice tea?"

"Sure, you can rationalize anything, Jessie," Ryan teased. "Teas can also have tannins and caffeine, you know. The Word of Wisdom isn't about what kind of tea we buy. It's about principles of health. It talks of foods, herbs, proper amounts of sleep, alcohol, and tobacco—but people typically expend their energies in the 'hot drinks' end of it."

"Chocolate has caffeine too."

"Yeah, that seems to be the typical comeback. Here again, you're assuming that's the reason we don't drink tea and coffee, yet that has never been officially stated as *the* reason. When the revelation was given to the early members of the Church, the majority were only drinking tea and coffee, so maybe that's why the revelation is left at that."

"You drink an awful lot of coffee." Jessie smiled.

"Yeah, well lately it's been warm *and* decaffeinated."

*"Now* who's rationalizing?"

* * *

Gramps was startled by Nelly as she pounced into the snow beside him. "Well, good mornin', girl. 'Bout time you got outta that room." Gramps turned slightly and caught Ken out of the corner of his eye, shovel in hand, walking up behind him.

"You want some help?" Ken asked, a hint of caution in his voice.

"Never been known to turn down a helpin' hand." Gramps perched his elbow on his snow shovel. "Don't know exactly where to start, but thought I might try to find the mailbox. Isn't anything in it, but I miss seein' it."

"Where's it at?"

Gramps pointed in front of them. "'Bout thirty yards that direction."

"Why don't I start the path and you come in behind and clear what I miss?" Ken said.

"All righty. Let's give it a shot."

Ken and Gramps watched Nelly as she chased the snow that took flight from the end of their shovels. It was only fifteen degrees above zero, but it felt warmer, as the wind was still and the heat of the sun was intent upon showing its superiority.

"So what did you think of *The Giver?*" attempted Gramps.

Though Ken didn't stop shoveling altogether, there was a dramatic decrease in energy. "It was okay."

"Just okay?"

"Yeah."

"Read it before at school?" He was glad the kid was slowing down. His heart was beating far too rapidly.

"Yeah, couldn't read it when I was in middle school, but the high school had it."

"Why not middle school?"

Ken wondered why the old man had picked this topic, but it was better than talking about his family. Talking and shoveling simultaneously made it difficult to breathe. He stopped and turned toward Gramps.

"Suppose it's all the stuff about death."

Gramps noticed how red Ken's nose was. "Want a sip of chicken broth?"

"Sure."

Gramps shuffled back to the porch and picked up a thermos. He poured Ken a lidful and handed it to him. Gramps sipped out of the mug.

"Schools always gotta have something to fight," Ken said.

"Seems that way," Gramps replied, wiping his mouth on his parka sleeve.

"Don't think that one's any worse than other stuff we've read."

"Maybe it makes suicide or murder seem okay."

"I don't think so. Nobody thought for themselves in the book, so how could they know one way or the other? That's what the Giver was trying to do—give them back their chance to choose. Adults are always looking for ways to shelter us."

Nelly sat at Gramps's feet, apparently waiting for her turn with the broth. "Hey, you ain't gettin' any of this. Go on now, scoot on outta here." A deflated Nelly wandered away, looking occasionally over her shoulder.

"You worried I wanna kill myself?" Ken ventured.

While Gramps hadn't flinched, the question had caught him off guard. "Do you?"

"Not today." Ken turned and began shoveling again.

"None of my business what's goin' on in that head of yours, but suicide's a waste of a good life. Do me a favor and stay alive while you're under our roof. Been enough dyin' round here. Besides, anyone gonna die, the next in line oughta be me."

# CHAPTER 11

The faint knock at Beth's back door forced her out of the rocking chair. Who would be at the back door? she wondered. "Kenny!" she burst out as she opened the door.

"It's me, Mrs. Moon."

"Jennifer? Oh, I'm sorry. You looked like Kenny in that coat. For heaven's sake child, you're not dressed warm enough to be out in this! Why did you trudge through that snow and come in the back?"

"I'll explain in a minute," Jennifer replied, her body shaking with cold.

Beth pulled Jennifer in and watched as she began working on the buttons of Kenny's old coat. Beth had thought it strange last week when Kenny had asked for it back. He hadn't worn it since he'd gotten his new one.

"Come sit by the fire, Jennifer, and I'll get something to warm you up. You want soup or hot chocolate?"

"Hot chocolate, please," Jennifer answered through quivering lips.

The phone rang as Beth handed Jennifer a mug of hot chocolate with marshmallows. "Excuse me, Jennifer, I need to get that. It could be Kenny."

"Right."

Beth quickly picked up the receiver and said two or three hellos. When there wasn't a response, she hung up. "Nobody there," she said to Jennifer.

"Oh, there was someone there all right."

"What do you mean? Are you or Kenny in some kind of trouble?" Beth returned to the recliner.

"Well, I'm always in *some* kind of trouble. But it's not about me this time. It's about Ken."

"Kenny?"

"Mrs. Moon, *Kenny* is fifteen, not two. I'm sure he would rather you called him Ken. Anyway," she continued as she stirred the lingering marshmallow mixture, "I figured you don't know much about who he's been hangin' with."

"Other than you? No, I guess I don't."

"Thought so. He hasn't been keeping the best company for a while. He's been going around with a pretty rough group. There was Greg, and then Clint, and a guy known as Rapper," she finished as she rolled her eyes.

"You're right. Those are names I haven't heard. Wait . . . Greg—Greg Roberts? The boy whose body they found?"

"Yeah. They're all pretty messed up and into some heavy stuff."

"Stuff like . . ." Beth felt her heart racing. *What has he gotten himself into?*

"They're runners for Randolf Thornton."

*That* name Beth knew. She tried hard to suppress her shock. "How do you know that Kenny's involved with Thornton?"

"'Cause I've seen him hangin' with Greg a lot. And Greg was Thornton's number one."

"Number one?"

"Top runner." Jen let out a frustrated breath. "You *are* out of it." She placed her mug on the table as she saw headlights streaming through the front room.

Beth squinted at the lights for a second. "Jen, are you mixed up in this too?"

"Not like you're thinking, no. I'm just known because I hang with Ken."

"*Hang* as in . . . ?"

"As in we're together a lot."

Beth finally understood her son *liked* this girl. At least he didn't buy her an expensive piece of jewelry—just gave her his old coat.

"But that's not why I'm here, Mrs. Moon. If you were to go look out your front window you'd probably see a black sedan. It was parked at the end of your street when I got here. The guys that pulled a gun on me earlier are most likely the ones in it."

"What?" Beth was out of her seat in no time. She went to the window. There it was, the black sedan, engine running. "It's next door."

"They've moved closer," Jen said cooly.

"They held a gun to you? Do you know where Kenny is? Is that why they're after you?" Beth asked, trying to remain calm and rational.

"Yeah—that's why they're after me. But I don't know where Ken is. He wasn't supposed to leave until after New Year's. He must have felt threatened when the bodies were found."

"He was supposed to leave later? So he was planning on running away *before* these guys came back? Was his reason the same, to get away from these guys?"

"Can't go there, Mrs. Moon. That's between you guys. I'm here just to let you know to watch your back."

"But why haven't they asked *me?* Why go after you?"

"You're a cop's ex-wife. I'm a nobody. Makes sense. I'm easier to scare. Well, I'd better get going. I'm going to head out the back."

"No, Jen, you won't be going anywhere. I'm going to call Michael and—"

"Mrs. Moon, I'm not going to a police station to give a statement. I try to avoid that place. Plus, that would only make it worse for me with these guys. They need to think I'm scared." Jen walked to the fireplace and picked up her coat. "I didn't see their faces anyway, so I can't rat anyone out. I've been in trouble before, so it wouldn't be easy to convince the police about what happened. They'd think I was just looking for attention. If these guys wanted me dead, I'd be dead. It's as simple as that."

Jen put on her gloves and headed for the back door.

"Jen, please. I can get Michael over here in minutes." Beth was walking behind her. "He can see that you stay safe."

"Thanks, but no."

"Jen, I can't let you go out there."

Jennifer smiled. While she wouldn't admit it, it felt good to have someone worried about her. "Mrs. Moon, I've already been threatened. They'll probably continue to harass me, but they won't hurt me. I just wanted you to know you're being watched."

Jennifer bent her head as she stepped into the cold air. The howling wind joined with the sound of a bullet shattering the door's glass window.

\* \* \*

"Mighty fine job there, young man," Gramps said with enthusiasm. The mailbox had been completely uncovered, and a clean pathway now led to the house.

"Thanks," said Ken.

"Well, I don't know about you, but I've worked up an appetite."

"Can I go check on the horses? Jessie's taught me some. I think I'd do okay."

Gramps squinted and looked off toward the barn. Ryan wouldn't be thrilled to hear he'd left him alone. But this kid needed to have someone trust him. "Fine by me. But remember, you weren't in the mood to leave this world today, so I'm gonna hold you to it."

"Yes, sir." Ken maneuvered his way to the barn and yelled over his shoulder, "Tomorrow we ought to shovel a path from the house to the barn."

"Sounds good, that is, if I'm still able to move by then!" Gramps yelled in return.

Ken removed his parka, leaving on the snowpants that Ryan had loaned him. It wasn't a perfect fit by any means, but it kept him warm. He immediately set out to clean each stall. He still found himself rubbing his nose from time to time, but Jessie had been right, he was getting used to the odor. He liked being in here, he decided. He wished he'd run away in the summertime; maybe Jessie would have let him ride one of the slower horses.

Neighing brought him to a Paint; he remembered she was called Tawny. Her coal-black head was accented with a white-blazed face. Her white frame was splotched with black oval spots. "What's the matter, huh, girl? Will you let me pet you?" Ken reached his hand up to her nose and, using long strokes, pet her gently. He then ran his hands down her sides. That's when he felt the prick. He looked at his hand first, and not seeing anything, looked at Tawny's right side. There it was; something prickly was sticking into her skin. "Hmm, well, no wonder you're uncomfortable. That can't feel all that great. I'll be right back."

Ken looked through all the tack trunks until he found the first-aid kit. Inside he located a pair of tweezers and some antibiotic cleaner. He rubbed her nose again and made sure his voice was soothing. "Okay, now, girl. I don't think this will hurt all that much. But just in case, let's be nice and not kick me, okay?" He used the tweezers to pull out the thorn. Tawny turned her neck around as if to watch, then neighed loudly. "It's all done now. Just gonna clean the area." Ken remained for a few minutes imagining what it would feel like to ride her.

His thoughts turned to his mom. He wondered how long it took her to realize he had run away. He hadn't gotten very far in the snow. She would know that, too. He would have to get a head start on the search party. If the clear weather kept up, he could leave in the middle of the night tomorrow. And if everyone stayed up late because it was Christmas Eve, then he'd just have to leave on Christmas.

But he would miss being at home for Christmas. His mother had said he would love his present. *But then they always say that, and then you unwrap a sweater that's totally out. I want a new computer and a dog. Computer's too expensive and the dog—well, it's a dog.*

Then Ken's mind strayed to why he wouldn't be home in the first place, and he gritted his teeth, firming his resolve. *Thornton's not gonna kill me, because he ain't gonna find me. I'll get out of here soon and work my way to someplace he'd never think to look. He'll forget all about me.*

Ken finished up feeding and watering the horses and said his good-bye to Tawny, then headed back to the cabin. He peeled off the layers of warmth and hung them up to dry. He could smell something good cooking and was glad he'd worked up a real appetite. Sure enough, there was a large pot of something on the stove.

"Hey there. Got here just in time. Heatin' up some chili if you're hungry," Gramps said. "Horses doin' all right?"

"Yes, sir. The little one seems kind of anxious."

"It's Buddy's first winter. She's used to being in the valley, but she'll be fine. Good eye, son."

"Not really. Anyone could see she's upset by the way she jumps around." Ken grabbed a bowl and ferried it to the stove where Gramps was stirring with a ladle. "Smells really good."

"Yep. It's my best chili yet. There's some crackers there, if you need to make it weaker."

"Nah. I'll eat it plain." Ken made his way around the island and settled onto a barstool across from Gramps.

*'Bout time he's relaxing,* thought Gramps as he filled a bowl for himself. He preferred to eat at the table, but figured since the kid had obviously sat there to be sociable, he'd better join him.

"Tawny had a thorn in her side. I used some tweezers to get it out and then cleaned it with the antibiotic stuff I found."

"Good job. A thorn? Wonder how she got that? Must have been in there for quite a while. Bet you're her new best friend."

"Ryan got any books on horses?" asked Ken.

Gramps's cheeks flushed pink from the heat of the chili. "Most certainly does. They're in the library on the north wall. Start lookin' and it won't take ya long to find 'em."

The front door flew open, and Ken and Gramps turned from their bowls to find the source of the interruption.

Ryan's head peeked stealthily around the foyer's wall. "Hey, is that chili you two are downing?"

"Yep, but I planned on you dyin' out there, so I only made enough for me and the kid here."

"You couldn't cook for two if your life depended on it."

Gramps winked at Ken. "Where's Jessie? You leave her behind again?"

Ryan took off his gloves and hat and shook his head, smiling. "Yeah, decided she was slowing me down, so I built her an igloo and told her I'd be back in the spring."

"Actually, he did threaten to do that!" Jessie called, still unseen. "Oh man, that smells great! Will that ever hit the spot."

"You know you really should have used the side door. Now you're gonna have to lug all that wet stuff clear down the hall," Gramps said. "Go on and hurry now while I dish up your dinner."

* * *

Ryan watched as Jessie dug into her third helping of chili. "Good thing we're not rationing food."

"You ate more than I did," Jessie retaliated.

"No, I didn't."

"You most certainly did."

"I only had two bowls," Ryan countered.

"Yeah, but you had four scoops in each bowl. I, on the other hand, only had two in each bowl. So that's my six to your eight."

Ken was wiping the kitchen counter when Gramps came up behind him. "Don't worry, kid. They're not fighting, they're competing. It's what they do. I've learned to let it go in one ear and right out the other."

"Who usually wins?" Ken asked.

"You're kiddin', right? If you ain't learned it yet, let me teach you now—women always win. It's better that way."

"Fine, you win," Ryan gave in.

Gramps's eyebrows rose as he turned toward the sink. "See?"

"I could use some help with the horses," Ryan said to Jessie as she used the last of her bread to clean the inside of her bowl.

"Um, you bet. I'll just help Gramps finish the cleanup and I'll meet you out there."

"Kid's already done it," Gramps interjected.

Both Ryan and Jessie looked at each other briefly, then at Ken. "You mucked and fed and watered?" Jessie asked, impressed.

"Yes, ma'—" Ken stopped instantly, remembering the beating she had promised if he called her *ma'am* again. "It's all done. You might want to check, though, in case I missed something."

"You've been busy today. Between the horses and the shoveling, you must be exhausted," Jessie said, scrubbing a plate.

"I'm okay."

"Told the lad I'd teach him to play Tile Rummy tonight, if there's no objection."

Jessie stole a quick look at Ryan. None of them had played since Ruth's death. It had been their favorite pastime. Ryan typically won. However, Jessie was getting quite good. But she hadn't dared mention the game.

"Okay with me," Ryan mustered. "Jessie?"

"Yeah, I think that would be great."

Ken could feel something in the air, but hadn't a clue as to what it was. He spoke directly to Gramps, with his hands tucked in his front jean pockets. "If you guys don't want to play, I can go look for those horse books you were telling me about."

"Naw. We haven't played in a while. 'Bout time we got back into it."

* * *

Beth regained enough composure to pull Jennifer inside as she watched the man holding a gun escape around the corner of the house. Beth slammed the door, locked it, and ran to the telephone to dial Michael's cell phone.

"Michael? We've just been shot at! Jennifer and me! I don't know . . . Michael, just get here!" She slammed down the receiver. She was visibly shaking as she retreated to her front window again and peered cautiously through the blinds. There was no sign of the black sedan.

It was only minutes before Beth and Jen heard the sirens. Beth watched as Michael's large frame plowed its way through the snow, followed by several uniformed officers. She opened the door wide to let them in.

"You all right?" Michael asked quickly.

"Yes. We're fine. Startled, but fine," Beth responded with a hint of nervousness. "The glass in the back-door window is broken."

"We'll check it out, sir," an officer said as he headed down the hall.

"We'll need a statement, ma'am," another officer interjected.

"Of course." Beth ushered Michael and an officer into the front room. Jen narrowed her eyes at Beth, who knew instinctively the girl didn't want their earlier conversation to make it into the statement.

"And you are?" the officer asked Jen.

"Jen Chandler."

The officer stopped momentarily after he'd written down the name. "Ben Keaton's daughter?"

"Yeah." Jen rolled her eyes, and her foot started tapping the floor.

"You a friend of the Moons?"

"Yes," Beth interrupted. "She came by to see if our son had returned. We were saying good-bye at the door when we were shot at."

"Why were you going out the back way?" asked Michael.

An officer looked at his lieutenant as he motioned Michael toward the back door. "Sir, could I see you for a minute?"

After both men disappeared, Jen sighed. "And so it begins."

"What begins?" inquired Beth.

"They're discussing me."

"Jen, Michael *is* a cop. He's bound to know about whatever trouble you've been in, right?"

"So?"

"So, he's never told me about it. He knows you spend time with Kenny—Ken—and so if he thought you a bad influence, I'd have heard about it. He must not be too worried about you. Therefore, whatever that officer is saying over there isn't going to get very far with him."

"Okay, let's get back to my question," Michael said as he and the officer returned. The officer sat down and didn't look at either woman.

Beth gave Jen a quick glance. "The front door was, well . . . we," Beth attempted.

"I didn't want to be seen by anybody," Jen rescued. She smiled at Beth, showing her appreciation. Ken had mentioned his mother didn't tolerate lying and wasn't very good at it herself.

"I was here telling Mrs. Moon about some of the guys I've seen Ken hangin' with. I was concerned because the black car that had been following Ken was parked at the end of this street."

"A black sedan?" Michael asked.

"You know about this?" Beth gasped.

"I know Thornton's buddies drive black cars. Several shootings have been tied to him—even if they've never been proved. But rumor has it he got out of town the minute we found his accountant dead. Is there more I should know?"

Beth motioned for Jen to fill Michael in. Jen sighed and relayed the entire story.

"Wearing that coat and sneaking around back, they must have thought you were Kenny," Michael said.

"Yeah," Jen replied. "They wouldn't waste a bullet on me."

"I'm going to leave Smoot and Reynolds here for the night, Beth. I'll take Jen home and talk with Ben. I'll fill him in and let him know we'll have a uniform at the care center to watch over his wife, just in case."

Jen picked up Ken's coat and walked toward the front door.

"Jen, wait," Beth called as she walked over to her. "Thank you. I know you must have risked a lot to come here."

# CHAPTER 12

For over an hour Jessie wrestled with sleep. The guilt of having cheated at Tile Rummy was eating away her remaining peace of mind. After the fourth game, she had tied with Ryan, then she had won the tiebreaker. Ryan had held the family record for years but managed to accept defeat graciously. In reality he *still* held the record.

She wasn't sure how it happened; it went against everything she stood for. And the only way to get rid of the guilt was to tell Ryan. *What was I thinking? I never cheat, at anything!* She thought about how arrogant he'd been about his winning record. *He had to be humbled, right?* She sighed at her own justification. *Look, Heavenly Father, I'm sorry.* The words were offered in silent prayer, but the next few came with more difficulty. *I was being selfish. He's just so annoying sometimes. It was important to me to win, but . . . I know it was wrong.* Jessie rolled over, thinking how, on an intellectual side of things, that prayer had been ridiculous. God already knew how she felt. Did she really have to verbalize everything? Her old ways were much easier, she decided. But what her "old ways" were lacking was the peace the gospel had given her. And, if for no other reason, that one was strong enough to keep her trying even if she wasn't completely accustomed to her new ways yet.

She reached over to the nightstand and pulled out Rebecca's Book of Mormon from the top drawer. She'd read a few passages earlier that had moved her. She searched through the section called "Mormon" and reread verses eighteen through twenty-one from the ninth chapter.

> *And who shall say that Jesus Christ did not do many miracles? And there were many mighty miracles wrought by the hands of the apostles. And if there were miracles wrought then, why has God ceased to be a God of miracles and yet be an unchangeable Being? And behold, I say unto you he changeth not; if so he would cease to be God; and he ceaseth not to be God, and is a God of miracles. And the reason why he ceaseth to do miracles among the children of men is because that they dwindle in unbelief, and depart from the right way, and know not the God in whom they should trust. Behold, I say unto you that whoso believeth in Christ, doubting nothing, whatsoever he shall ask the Father in the name of Christ it shall be granted him; and this promise is unto all, even unto the ends of the earth.*

She thought of the miracle she had received, when she was trying to understand how her mother could have left her and Katie at the theater. She would never have found her mother's buried letter if God hadn't interceded. It was the Spirit who'd told her to look under the lilac bushes of her old home. There she found the old ammo can of her father's which had contained the letter. In a fit of anger he'd hidden the letter to spite her, and had spent years tormenting her about the hidden letter.

That letter brought her the understanding she needed. Jessie wondered why *she* received a miracle and not her mother. Couldn't God have cured her mother's cancer so that she could have taken care of her daughters? What *exactly* was the difference? Considering the verses she'd just read, her mother's belief was certainly stronger than hers, and her pleas had to have been considerably more passionate.

Pen in hand, Jessie wanted to underline the verses, but this wasn't her book. After the holidays, she would get her own, she decided. *Where does one buy such a thing?* she questioned herself. Surely the missionaries would be more than thrilled to get her to the right place. She reflected on the numberless invitations extended for sacrament meeting—each of which she had graciously declined. She hadn't yet felt the need to attend church.

A soft knock at the door brought her to her feet. She threw on her flannel robe and cracked open the door.

"Hey," Ryan said.

"Hey yourself. It's only midnight. Off to the stables till morning are we?" she asked. She had let her hair down and it now swung freely, lit from behind by the bedside lamp. Ryan fought the urge to express how beautiful she looked.

"Ryan? You okay?" Jessie's face turned to a worried expression.

"Yeah," Ryan answered, clearing his throat. "Saw your light. Thought if you weren't ready for sleep you could come out and help in the barn. I'm sure the kid's done fine, but the horses may need some grass and hay. More than likely he gave them the grains again."

"Yeah, you're probably right. I haven't taught him to alternate. Give me a couple minutes and I'll be down."

Ryan was ready to go when Jessie entered the front room. She quickly layered on her winter attire, and she and Ryan slipped into the deepening cold of night. The sky was clear and the stars seemed only a rooftop away, their light bathing a perfect carpet of reflecting white. Neither spoke, taking in the stillness around them.

Jessie recalled a winter of her youth when she had skipped school to spend the whole day in the park. She'd filled as much of the park as she could with snow angels, then climbed a spruce tree that overlooked her collective masterpiece, and reflected on the magic of the day. It was a pleasant memory—until she at last recalled the bite of the belt upon her return home.

Inside the stable, both Jessie and Ryan removed their parkas and set about their work. Within the hour, the horses were dozily munching their midnight snack. Ryan pulled down a blanket from a cabinet and spread it out on the floor. "Ken's interested in reading about horses."

"Yeah, I caught that." Jessie moved in to help smooth the blanket's corners. "He's good with them."

"Want some hot chocolate?" Ryan gestured toward the blanket as he unscrewed the cap of his thermos.

"What? You don't have coffee in there?" Jessie smiled as she sat across from him.

"When my choices are limited to herbal tea, chocolate, or decaffeinated coffee, chocolate wins out."

"Yes, well, speaking of winning . . ." Jessie's hands trembled slightly as she took the cup Ryan had poured for her. Ryan quietly sipped from the thermos.

"I, um, well, I don't know quite how to say this." Jessie placed the now jiggling cup on the blanket beside her and set about waving her arms.

Ryan leaned onto his side and grinned. "What's up?"

"I, uh, well you see . . . It's like this—I cheated at Tile Rummy tonight." Her heart was pounding.

"I know." Ryan's eyes danced as he smiled.

"What? How? How did you know?"

"Because I lost."

"What? Oh, come on. You are so arrogant. That's exactly why I cheated! I can't stand that arrogance. You know, one of these days I really *will* beat you fair and square, then what will you have to say—hmm?" Her protestation had brought her face within inches of his. His smile forced her retreat.

"It'll never happen. But I do believe it's time to be buying a new game. That way the outside of the Jokers will be the same tint as the rest of the pieces—no more yellowing."

"You did know!" Jessie's checks flushed.

"Yes, ma'am," Ryan said proudly.

"Hey, wait a minute. If I could spot them, then so could you! Is that why you've been winning all these years? And here I'm feeling awful."

"Do you remember any game in which I used the jokers?"

She hated to admit that she hadn't. "That doesn't mean you haven't in the past—before I came along," she said, kneeling up and waving her index finger in his face.

"I've never cheated, Jessie."

"You're going to tell me that in all these years, you've never *once* used those jokers?"

"There have been a few times, when I haven't paid attention as to where they were, that I've picked them up on accident. But that's been rare."

"It's just not humanly possible. Not even you can be *that* disciplined. It goes against your character. What about in your drinking days, hmm?"

"Ouch."

"Yeah, okay. That was uncalled for. I just can't believe that you've *never* cheated." She poured another capful of hot liquid and waited for both her mood and the chocolate to cool.

"There's no fun in cheating."

"But wait—aren't you cheating if you choose *not* to use the jokers?"

"Come again?"

"Well, you could have drawn the jokers naturally, like the rest of us always do—except for me tonight—but by not so doing, you've cheated because you altered the natural course of your game," Jessie said with finality.

"That almost makes sense. Must be the influx of chocolate to my brain."

"Ah-ha, then you admit you're a cheater!"

"I'm not a cheater, Jessie. I believe that I've played an honest game, given the circumstances. I'll continue to come out on top, even with new game pieces. You're just going to have to come to terms with being number two." Ryan's eyebrows rose with his smile.

"Oh, you're so smug."

"Ken's behavior has improved." Ryan changed direction casually.

"Yes, it has."

"Apparently Ken asked Gramps if Gramps thought he was suicidal."

"It came out of nowhere?"

"They had been discussing *The Giver*."

"How did Gramps respond?"

"Turned the question back to him."

"And?"

"He responded with 'not today.'"

"Hmm. How did Gramps end it?"

"Told him that suicide was a waste of a good life, and if he did have intentions of going through with it, it had better not be under our roof. He told Ken that if any dying was going to occur, he had seniority."

Jessie chuckled. "Gramps ever consider a career in psychology?"

"I've proven to have more than enough psychoses for him."

"True," Jessie agreed. "Ken's more energetic and a bit more talkative, but I don't think he's suicidal yet. He's still in turmoil, though, and tomorrow's Christmas Eve. That only gives us a couple days before Tucker gets here."

"To do what?"

"Figure out what's going on with him, duh."

"Jessie, when did you become deluded with the idea that we could solve all this kid's issues in a few days?"

"We have to solve them. It's as simple as that." The passion of the subject at hand drove Jessie to her feet. "Besides, if not us, then who? Don't you think it odd that he landed here?"

"He's from Lyle, Jessie. It's fathomable that he'd head this direction."

"Nothing's this direction, Ryan."

"My point exactly. He wasn't *headed* anywhere."

"You're saying he intended to go as far as he could, then shoot himself? Don't take this the wrong way, but you're simply not ready to work with kids." She picked a track and started to pace. "You need some more schooling, or plain old common sense. If he was simply going to shoot himself, he'd have done it somewhere warmer. He wouldn't have gone out on his bike in a blizzard with a backpack full of survival items."

"You haven't lost sight of the underlying reason you want to help Ken, have you?"

Jessie finished the last drop of chocolate. "There's a fifteen-year-old runaway whose life has progressed to a state in which he wants out. I'd say that's a decent motive for my wanting to help." Jessie's pacing made Ryan feel as if he were a spectator at a tennis match.

"Your motives aren't in question. You've given the day after Christmas as a deadline."

"I don't want him running off at first light before Tucker gets here—so what? Why is it we can be having a nice, peaceful conversation one minute, and then you throw me into anxiety?"

"Are you feeling anxious, Jessie?"

"Oh, stop it. I hate that, and you know it."

"Jessie, come and sit down."

"I can't sit, and you're back to using my name too much." She was becoming annoyed.

"I'd like you to try this one time to sit and relax."

"I am relaxed," she replied through clenched teeth.

Ryan reached his hand up to her. "Come here, Jessie."

She ignored the gesture. "You've told me to pace when I'm anxious, remember?"

"Do you have a focus object?"

Jessie rolled her eyes and turned away sharply. "Concentration meditation doesn't work for me. Neither an object nor a mantra, so you can check that off your list."

"So if you're obliged to say it doesn't work, then that means at some point you *had* an object?"

"Ryan!"

"May I ask what it was? It may offer some explanation as to why you can't sit."

"I can't sit because I don't *want* to sit."

"Your focus object?"

"A horse!" she replied, flippantly.

Ryan closed his eyes and breathed heavily. "Ah."

"Ah?"

"Let me guess. Your horse isn't lying in a beautiful pasture, basking in the sun, is he?"

"*She's* a Bloodstock Thoroughbred headed for the Puissance wall."

Ryan rubbed his face. "And you didn't see the problem with that?"

"This is ridiculous, Ryan. I'm exhausted. I'm going back to the cabin."

"You won't sleep. Have you considered the fireplace? Its blaze may offer you something to lose yourself in, allowing your mind to be free—"

"I know what it does, Ryan," she interrupted. "I'm going now, and I *am* going to sleep. I came out to apologize and end up getting analyzed. Tomorrow's Christmas Eve. You keep this up, Blake, and Santa's going to leave you a huge pile of coal and quite possibly some reindeer droppings." If the stable door could have slammed, it would have been heard for miles.

# CHAPTER 13

The screech of pain echoed through the loft. "Well, dang it, Barkley, you can't just lay there in the dark and expect people to step over you!" Jessie's tea sloshed onto her hand, and most likely to the white carpet below. She felt for the end table, stowing the cup safely on its polished surface before dropping to all fours in search of the offending liquid. Armed with only a napkin, she patted the one damp patch she could find, then snuggled into the comfort of the recliner.

From the constant licking coming from her right side, she surmised that Barkley had settled himself on the top of the couch to begin his ritual bath. As she pulled the afghan tightly around her robe-clad body, she realized that the majority of her many child clients also felt more secure wrapped up in a blanket or two. Odd, as the blankets were never able to defend them, or her for that matter, and yet they still continued to offer a sense of protection. Jessie knew she had nothing more to fear; she controlled her environment now as well as the people she associated with, but the little girl inside still yearned at times for the security that somehow came from being wrapped in a blanket.

As Jessie's eyes adjusted to the dark, she was relieved to find that Barkley was indeed the only one occupying the couch in front of her. It wouldn't have surprised her at all to have found Ryan lounging there. It seemed his nature to be one step ahead of her. He'd been right about tonight. She'd only been able to sleep for a few hours. She reclined back as far as the chair allowed and closed her eyes. Maybe she could get another hour or so of shut-eye before Gramps woke and started breakfast. She tuned her mind to the sounds of the night, which tonight consisted only of the endless bathing of her adopted feline.

* * *

"Wanna come play?" the girl with the pink hair bow asked. Her face was a mature twenty, but her clothes and her voice mirrored that of a typical preschooler.

"I've got to clean!" Jessie shrieked, frantically wiping the stark white linoleum.

"Bor-ring," the girl sang; now she spun on a horse-filled merry-go-round.

"Lilacs! Get your lilacs," yelled the man at the baseball game. "All for one and none for all," he continued.

"Throw me the ball, throw me the ball!" the twenty-year-old child called to Jessie. The girl was bent over home plate sporting a red-and-green pot holder as a glove.

"I don't know how!" Jessie's voice carried through the crowd.

"Boo! Boo! Throw the bum out! New pitcher, new pitcher!" cried the spectators.

"Breathe, Katie. Breathe!" Jessie screamed at the limp, blue-faced child in her arms.

"Hey, you okay? Jessie, you okay?"

The question echoed, the confusion compounding itself until at last Jessie broke free from the swirling grip of terror that haunted her sleep. "What? Oh, Ken," she sputtered, forcing a cough and clearing her throat of the dry tension that muted her voice. "I'm sorry, did I wake you?" Shifting the chair into its upright position, she patted at her tangled hair with perspiring hands.

"I was up in the bathroom when I heard you. You okay?"

"I'm fine. Just having a bad dream."

"Hate those."

"You get them too?" Jessie focused on the vague form of Ken standing a few feet away from her. She glanced around, wondering where Ryan and Gramps were. Surely if Ken had heard her, they had too.

"Well, not so much now, but I had 'em all the time after my brother—" Ken froze, then taking a step back, tried to stick his hands into the nonexistent pockets of the pajamas Gramps had lent him.

"After your brother . . . what?" Jessie asked, hopeful of a possible revelation.

"Uh, it's nothin'. Since you're okay and all, I'm gonna go back to my room."

"The clouds have lifted, from what I can tell. Sunrises are incredible to watch from up here. It's close to time, if you'd—"

"Seen lots of them before," Kenny muttered as he headed down the stairs.

Ryan held his grip on the railing as Kenny moved past him. "You okay?" he called up to Jessie as he ascended the staircase.

"Yep, just dandy. Thought I'd watch the sunrise." Jessie and her blanket were snuggled against the windowpane. "Care to join me?" *What?* her mind whispered.

"Sure." Ryan concealed his surprise.

It was a sight worth seeing. The sky was a sea of glass washed from the deepest blue to an intensifying orange. The surrounding peaks, plastered in white, reflected every nuance of the changing heavens. Ryan was toying with an appropriate comment when the sun broke free of its reins, momentarily blinding their view and bathing the snow-covered valley in the magic of first light. Words were no longer necessary.

It was Jessie's voice which finally cut through the silence. "Did I wake you too?"

"Yes."

Jessie lowered her head and turned away from Ryan. Closing her eyes, she inhaled slowly and deeply. *He's going to bring it up again now. I shouldn't have asked if I woke him. Of course I woke him! I don't want to get into . . .*

"It's Christmas Eve," Ryan said softly, still enjoying the transition of power that would usher in the day. "You have any traditions I should know about?"

*He's not pressing?* "My stepmother used to bake. The house was filled with delicious smells the whole day. I did enjoy her fudge. I've got the recipe memorized."

"Brecca always put on *It's a Wonderful Life.*"

"I haven't seen that one in years."

"So then, are we baking today?" He turned to look directly at her.

"I hadn't given it much thought, really. Besides, I don't think you have everything I need."

"What goes into fudge?"

"Sugar, cocoa, salt, butter, milk, vanilla, and nuts. And I'll need a double boiler."

"Surprisingly, I have a double boiler, and all the ingredients, except for the nuts. But you won't need them."

"Why not?" She was finally able to face him.

"I'm allergic to nuts."

"You're kidding."

"Nope."

"Fudge isn't fudge without nuts! And speaking of allergies, you never told me whether you were allergic to lavender or not."

"Yes, I did."

"No, actually, you sidestepped it every time. It's been weeks since the last time I asked." Jessie's stare was distracted by Barkley circling between her legs.

"I don't believe I sidestepped it, but no, I'm not allergic to lavender. Good thing, too. It was Brecca's favorite scent. It was in everything around here—soap, candles, perfume . . . I think she even used it as a spice in her cooking."

"Her scent came with the whispers then, is that it?"

Ryan simply nodded.

"What did she whisper to you last summer when you heard her voice?"

"You believe me, then?"

"I've always believed that our spirits can speak in a way to those we love. Besides, it's either that or admit you've lost your marbles."

"Yeah, well, remember that this is just between you and me. I'm sure the rest of the world would more readily adopt the marble theory."

"So, what did she whisper to you?"

Ryan's lips moved into a wide grin. "That ball drop yet in New York?"

A frown pasted across Jessie's face as she settled onto the couch. "Ken's being here has something to do with his brother."

"He said that?" Ryan considered joining her on the couch, but knew she'd be uncomfortable. He opted for the recliner across from her.

"No, not really. He woke me from my . . . dream. I made reference to it, and he said he used to have bad ones a lot after his brother . . ."

"His brother, what?"

"Yep, that's where it ended for me too."

"Died?"

"That's my first guess. Maybe if we can get him to help us with the fudge, he'll drop some more clues."

"Not if I'm around," Ryan said.

"Then you'll just have to keep busy doing something else. You finished that project for Gramps yet?"

"Almost. Another couple hours and I'll have it done."

"Well, then you'll have something to do while we work in the kitchen."

"That's if you can coerce him into helping you."

"My fudge will get him there."

* * *

"Beth, you here?" Michael called as he closed the front door.

"Have you found out anything?" Beth jumped from the chair she had settled on in the kitchen.

"Yeah. Got word a half hour ago." He started removing his coat.

"Well, what already?"

"Hold on a minute." He turned to Smoot and Reynolds. "Any problems?"

"No sir, everything was quiet," Smoot answered.

"Michael!" Beth yelled.

"Okay, okay. I got a call that he's in Stone Ridge."

"Stone Ridge! That's not far, Michael. I'll grab my coat."

"Now hold on there, Beth. The way this storm hit, there's no way we can get to him."

"What about a helicopter?"

"Closest one is in Denver. I might be able to get the chief to pull a few strings. But because of the weather, he doesn't believe Kenny to be in any immediate danger. It's not worth the taxpayers' money to go to any extraordinary measures to pick him up."

"You've got to be kidding! Not in immediate danger? Does he work for Thornton too?" Beth went to the front window, her fingers pushing back the brimming tears.

"He's safe and in good hands. I know the guy he's with. Met him a few years ago—the guy's a psychologist. He's not gonna let Kenny slip away. It might even do the kid some good. I filled him in on what's going on. Kenny's okay, Beth. It's just a matter of time."

"Thornton's got connections. *He'll* get a helicopter out there, just you watch. If he gets there before we do, I'll never forgive you, Michael." Beth's temper was at its peak.

"Mr. Blake said that the road to his place will be plowed the day after tomorrow. I'm plannin' on leavin' as soon as I get word from Blake."

"I want to call him." She headed to the phone.

"Now, Beth—"

Beth turned sharply his direction. Her cheeks were a vibrant red. "Don't you 'now Beth' me. I want to talk to my son!"

"Blake and I figured it's best we don't."

"Best! Best, why?"

"'Cause he doesn't know that we know where he is. And telling him about Thornton may make him run again."

"I thought you said they were keeping an eye on him!"

"Beth, let's sit down."

"You sit. I'm going to get my son."

"He's *our* son."

"No, he's not. He *used* to be *our* son, but you gave up the *our* when you left." Beth knew that sounded ridiculous, but she was in no mood to be rational. She sat down anyway.

# CHAPTER 14

Jessie organized the ingredients in front of her. She picked a bag of chocolate morsels and shook her head. She wanted block chocolate or cocoa. She'd never used morsels before. *Shouldn't be a big deal,* she decided with resolution. Ryan was in the stable, and Gramps's snoring in the next room could be heard for miles. Ken was sitting on a barstool, reading Jessie's neatly written recipe.

"How come there aren't any nuts? My mom always uses nuts," Ken asked.

"Yeah, well, I use nuts too. But apparently the good Dr. Blake is allergic to them. So there aren't any to be found."

"Bummer."

"Yes, it is. Okay, lets get this chocolate melted."

"You want me to throw it in the microwave?" Ken asked.

"No! I mean, yeah, I suppose that would work, but it takes all the fun out of it. And I'm already depressed enough at not having any nuts. We need to *stir.*"

"Whatever," Ken said, walking to the stove.

Jessie showed him how to melt the chocolate in the double boiler. "Heard you've been reading *The Giver.*"

"Yeah. And no, I'm not plannin' on killing myself."

"Okay, well, thanks for clarifying. Although I didn't think you *were* planning on it."

"Yes, you did," Ken pushed.

Jessie took a deep breath as she watched him wipe his nose, cough into his hand, then continue stirring. *Well, at least it's the season for sharing,* she thought to herself. "No, I really didn't."

"Then how come you took the bullets from my gun?"

Suppressing even the slightest sign of surprise, Jessie responded, "It was the safest thing to do. I knew nothing about you. I had Gramps, Ryan, and myself to consider."

"So you thought I was going to shoot *you?*"

"It's only logical that I considered the possibility, and at the time I had no way of knowing one way or the other. You were a complete unknown to us. I'll give your bullets back when you leave . . . or rather, I'll give them to your parents." Jessie walked over to where he was stirring and added the sugar, salt, butter, and vanilla. "Okay, keep stirring for a few more minutes. So, what did you think of the book?"

"Not sure what the big deal is all about."

"You mean with the schools?"

"Yeah."

"I think it has something to do with all the controversial themes. Okay, this is ready to pour into the pan." Jessie watched as he poured the chocolate concoction into the pan, licked the spoon, then stuck it back into the pan to even out the mixture. *And he seems like such a bright boy,* she thought as she cringed inwardly. Instead of saying anything, though, she just took the pan and placed it in the fridge to chill, still wishing it had nuts.

"But, like I told Gramps, it was part of their society. It was as natural to them as driving at sixteen is for us," Ken said. "There's worse stuff on the news than what happens to characters like Jonas."

"I see your point."

An awkward moment of silence fell. "Think I'll go to my room," Ken said as he headed out of the kitchen.

"Ken? Can I do anything to help you?"

He stayed in the doorway. "What do you mean?"

Jessie chose her words purposefully. "Is there anything I can do to help ease the situation that has apparently forced you to take a Jonas-like journey?"

Ken stuck his hands in his pockets and lowered his head. "I'm not taking a journey like Jonas. Mine was planned."

"His was planned too. He just had to leave sooner than scheduled. And from the looks of how you packed and the fact that you rode your bike this far in a blizzard, I'm thinking the same about you. Jonas left in an effort to eventually make things better. If there's something I can do, I'd like to help."

"That's not why Jonas left."

"No?"

"He left because he didn't want to be like everyone else anymore."

"Hmm."

"I'm going to my room now."

"Thanks for your help with the fudge. Even without the nuts, it should be good."

He nodded.

* * *

Ryan stomped the snow from his boots before heading to the utility room. He could hear Gramps's snoring, and since Nelly wasn't around to greet him, he figured Ken was in his room. He heard Jessie in the kitchen humming "Silent Night." The last time he'd heard her sing was at Ruth's funeral. He immediately realized how much he'd missed hearing it. He listened quietly in the doorway as she gradually wound into full voice, unaware of her audience. It was gentle yet precise and for him, hypnotizing. "Hey," he said as she finished, "can I hear another one?"

Jessie's face turned the slightest shade of pink as she attacked the already-clean countertops with renewed vigor. "How long have you been standing there?"

"Not long enough. I only got one verse."

"And that's all you're going to get too."

"Is the fudge done?"

"It's setting."

"So I have to wait?" Ryan stared at the refrigerator.

"What a smart guy. You just don't get the credit you deserve." She smiled to lighten the sarcasm, then changed her tone. "If you're hungry, there's some chocolate left."

"I'm assuming Ken's in his room with Nelly sleeping on his feet?"

"Yep. We had a nice chat," Jessie stated as she rinsed the dishcloth and set it down neatly by the sink.

"You did?"

"It was short, but interesting." Jessie took the next few minutes to relay their conversation.

"So he's trying to be someone he's not. Anyone in particular?"

"Not sure exactly. I have a hunch, though."

"Okay." He knew Jessie would let him in on it when she was ready. "The phones are working. I called Ken's dad through the police station."

"How'd that go?"

"Not bad. It was obvious they've been beside themselves, and there was definite relief in his voice when he heard that Ken was here and that he's all right. I told him that we found him half frozen in a drift in front of the house. I think he hopes we'll send him back all fixed up. He knows I'm a psychologist."

"Did you discuss any of that?" she asked.

"Any of what? We don't really know anything."

"Are they coming to get him?"

"Not until after the roads get cleared. But there is something else," he added.

"What?"

"I think we have the explanation as to why he ran away." It was Ryan's turn to relay information, and he passed on what he'd heard about Thornton.

"Hmm. Wow. Didn't take him for a drug runner," Jessie said in disbelief.

"We don't really know him, Jessie."

"True. If he thinks Thornton killed that boy and is after *him,* then he certainly had good reason to run. Not to mention what it's done to his psyche. But my instincts tell me there's more." She walked into the family room and settled into the couch. "I thought Thornton was in prison."

Ryan followed and sank into the recliner. "The case was dropped because his Miranda rights were read incorrectly."

"You're kidding. I never heard that."

"You've been out of the loop too long, eh?"

"Suppose so. We better be a bit cautious. We ought to tell Gramps, but definitely not Ken. Although, he's a smart kid and that could explain why he took the gun."

Jessie pulled herself off the couch. "Well, I've got a few things to do in my room and then I'm headed outside."

"Huh?"

"I'm going to play in the snow."

"Play in the snow?"

"Yep," Jessie replied.

"I thought we were going to be *cautious?*"

"I'm going to play in the snow *cautiously*," Jessie answered, leaving a confused Ryan staring at her receding form.

* * *

Beth sat at the table in her usual place and sipped at her coffee, offering some to Michael. "So how do you know these Blake people?" she asked after she also offered coffee to the officers in the sitting room.

"They had a horse stolen years back. Remember that lady old Stanley stole one from? He figured it was owed him since the one he bought died."

"Oh, yeah. Big place, lots of land, right?"

"Yeah. Lots of good places to hide. It's hard to believe they found him," Michael said.

"Thank the heavens for hearing our prayers."

"Amen to that. Anyway, Blake's wife died in a car wreck a while back. Terrible thing. She was pregnant and the baby died too."

"Seems I remember that story," Beth said. "That was her? Oh, how awful."

Michael drank the hot coffee in two gulps. "Now this is coffee. I sure do miss your cooking."

*Yeah, I've heard.* "There's something I've not told you," Beth said slowly.

"That Kenny's got the gun?"

"Yes, but how—?"

"Checked already."

"Why didn't you get after me?" Beth asked.

"You were feelin' bad enough as it was."

This was the Michael Beth remembered. Rough on the outside, soft on the inside. She felt a little out of breath. Was she still in love with him? she wondered. *How can I still love him after all he's done?* "Did you tell the Blakes?"

"Yeah, but they'd already found it and unloaded it."

Beth let out a huge sigh, then bit her bottom lip sharply.

"What?" Michael asked.

She reached for Michael's mug and stood to refill it. "Truth is, I was afraid he took it to kill himself. But with all that's happened I'm betting he took it for protection."

Michael's cell phone began ringing. He looked down to see who was calling, sighed, and then answered. "Yeah? . . . That's because I'm not at the station, remember? Takin' the day off . . . Because you were sleepin' and I didn't . . ." Michael leaned back in his chair and stared at Beth. "I needed to get a couple more things for tomorrow . . . Now? I'm givin' Beth the news about Kenny . . . Because I didn't *want* to leave a note." Michael turned his gaze from Beth to the ceiling. "Of course she's here. Look, I've got a couple of stops to make, then I'll be back."

Michael stood and pushed his chair into the table. "I better get goin'. We're gonna keep Smoot and Reynolds here, just in case."

"Michael? Is that what happened his birthday weekend? Was it then he made that delivery? Or was that when he found out about the baby?"

"I don't have all the details yet." He put on his coat and started for the front door.

"Sooner or later, you're going to have to deal with Patrick's death," Beth said softly. Despite her tone, Smoot and Reynolds stopped what they doing in the next room, looked at each other, then at their lieutenant. It only took a fraction of a second for them to find a different room to be in.

"Where did that come from?" Michael asked, fidgeting with his cell phone.

"I'm pretty sure Kenny ran away this time because of Thornton's men, but his previous runs couldn't have been."

"What does this have to do with Patrick?" Michael held the knob of the door, ready to make a brisk exit if necessary.

"He won't talk about Patrick's death any more than you will. Both of you have kept it bottled up inside, and it's changed who you are."

"Kenny blames me."

"I know that. But neither one of us knows *why*."

"Can we talk about this later?"

"I don't know. If I lose another son because I just sat here doing nothing . . ."

"We're not going to lose Kenny. Let's get the boy home, then we'll talk about going to counseling together for Kenny's sake. Okay?"

Beth was shocked. Was he just trying to pacify her? she wondered. "Okay. But I'm going to make you stick to it this time, Michael—for Kenny's sake as well as yours."

# CHAPTER 15

"Where you headed, sir?" Ken asked Ryan, who was pulling on his slightly soggy boots.

"Seems Jessie's in the mood to play in the snow. I thought she was joking at first, but she's been out there a good fifteen minutes now."

"Snow's deep."

"Yep. She's probably buried in a drift somewhere and can't get out."

"Want some help?"

Ryan was slightly surprised at his offer. "Sure, why not."

It took only a minute for them to find Jessie. The backyard was beginning to look like a choir of snow angels.

"Come join in the fun!" a cold-sounding voice called.

Just then Nelly came around the corner of the house, leaping through the drifts, and tore between the two men who were staring at the frolicking white blob they assumed to be Jessie. Nelly headed straight for Jessie, who had by now caught sight of her impending doom. She stopped, momentarily frozen in time before disappearing under the slobbering beast. Jessie could barely discern the raucous laughter of Ryan and Ken over Nelly's jubilant panting and licking. She pushed the huge dog off her chest. *There's another reason I prefer cats.* She arose slowly, trying to wipe the worst of Nelly's now-freezing slobber from her face. The approaching laughter met her glare and she barreled toward them. Ryan, now but a few feet away, stopped in midstep just before getting tackled. Despite the handfuls of snow being forced into his mouth, he couldn't stop laughing. He finally collapsed, smiling as he caught site of Gramps in the tropical comfort of the enclosed forest at the rear of the cabin. Gramps watched as the three built fort walls, then prepared for war—letting loose a barrage of flying snow that would make any parent proud.

After their afternoon cavorting, Ryan, Ken, and Gramps headed for the Jacuzzi. Jessie had declined, stating she had more wrapping to do. Ryan was the first to enter the warm water. *What could she possibly have left to wrap?* he thought in annoyance as he leaned back.

Today had been the first time in months that he and Jessie had actually had "fun" together. It felt good. He had let her win the snowball fight and helped her build her fortress wall. It was possible she was being overly kind because Ken was there, but he hoped that she was simply distracted to the point that she was letting her heart lead instead of her head. He liked the playful side of her and naturally wanted more.

"This feels great," Ken said as he relaxed into the water.

"Nothing like a good hot tub after a day in the snow," Gramps added, following suit.

"All you did was watch," Ryan scoffed.

"Yeah, well, these old bones wouldn't have lasted fifteen minutes out there buildin' forts and tossin' snow grenades."

"So, you two gonna get married?" Ken's question came out of nowhere.

"Who? Me and Jessie?" inquired a stunned Ryan.

"Yeah."

"Uh, well, if I had my way . . ."

"She doesn't want to?"

"She's not ready," replied Ryan.

"How come?"

"Like you, she has some things to work through."

"Huh." Kenny seemed thoughtful. "Well, maybe you shouldn't put it all on her."

That ended that conversation, but the room wasn't tense with discomfort as Ryan had anticipated. Rather the atmosphere was relaxed, the air sweet with the scent of the solarium's flourishing life, and the water was warm and comforting.

Kenny looked around at the indoor forest, the river with its redwood walkways and the lush tropical plants, and wished he'd asked sooner to use the Jacuzzi. He wondered if this kind of luxury made life any easier. He thought of his small home and what his parents went through just to afford that.

But then the memories of happier times floated through his mind—of his childhood and brother. Patrick had always been kind to him. He had never teased Kenny like his friends' older brothers teased them. Patrick had helped him with schoolwork and taught him to tie his shoes when his mother had given up. Sometimes during Patrick's late-night readings, he would signal that the coast was clear and let Kenny join him under the flashlight-lit covers.

With cruel suddenness, the horrible day of Patrick's death intruded into his thoughts. Kenny had run home during his lunch hour because he'd forgotten a book report. Out of breath, he'd thrown open the door to their room. The room was meticulous—except for the blood. Kenny had run to his brother and lifted his head. He'd heard himself shouting his brother's name over and over, his mind gone limp. Then he'd just sat there, cradling his brother's head in his arms until someone came home.

Kenny forced his mind elsewhere. He looked up through the glass windows above him. Though the evening was still relatively young, the stars had bloomed and were now glowing brightly. "Shrinks must make really good money," he said to no one in particular. Both Ryan and Gramps laughed.

"They do okay. Depends on how many hours you choose to devote yourself to it, and how many clients—things like that," answered Ryan.

"You must've worked a lot, then."

"Most of what we have around here isn't because of my efforts, but rather to my late wife's. She inherited a dynasty of horse breeders."

Gramps set about extracting himself from the hot tub. "I think it's time I started somethin' in the kitchen."

"I'm really hot," Ken said, following in Gramps's wake.

Ryan figured Ken didn't want to be alone with him. The boy was most likely afraid that he'd try to find out what was bothering him. Besides, it was Jessie the kid was relating to.

Late into the evening everyone adjourned to the great room to watch *It's a Wonderful Life.* Ryan sat down by Jessie, which, to his surprise, garnered no disapproval.

Jessie, playing therapist, kept a close eye on Ken during the movie. While it appeared Ken ran away because of

Thornton, she still had an uneasy feeling that there was something deeper going on. *Will his conscious mind be influenced by George Bailey and his journey to the bridge? Will this movie upset him?* As it turned out, if he had been bothered by it, he gave no indication. Maybe, like most teenage boys, he wasn't watching it at all, Jessie thought. He was probably spending the entire time thinking about cars or girls.

\* \* \*

"You're in here somewhere, aren't you?" Jessie's subdued voice filtered through the darkness as she reached the top step of the loft near the game room. It was almost midnight and she'd been trying to sleep for an hour.

"Yes," came the reply.

"Figures," she retorted.

"I had a great time today. It's been a long time since I've played in the snow."

Jessie made no response as she walked to the window. She was wrapped in a blanket and holding her tea. She opened the blinds to let the moonlight stream in. Now she could see Ryan, his feet stretched out in the recliner. Nelly was nowhere to be found. *Probably glued to Ken,* she thought as she stepped past Ryan and nestled into the couch.

"I would think you'd be exhausted tonight. Nightmare wake you?" Ryan gently asked.

"No. You want to put the presents out?"

"If you'd like," Ryan replied.

After a few minutes of silence, Jessie let out a soft sigh. "Look, I know I'm going to regret this, but I have a question."

"I'm all ears."

"What's the *real* reason I want Ken fixed by tomorrow?"

"I can't tell you that."

"You mean you *won't*." Jessie inched the blanket closer to her face. "Fixing him has nothing to do with me."

"Then why did you bring it up?"

"Because you think you know everything!" Jessie hissed, louder than she had intended.

"Okay then, *you* tell me why you wanted Ken fixed by tomorrow."

"I already did. But you didn't believe me."

Ryan leaned forward, placed his elbows on his knees, and locked his fingers together. His facial expression was serious. "All right, try again. Maybe this time you'll be more convincing."

"Like I said before, he's a messed-up kid and there's something that's not right at home. I mean, other than the Thornton issue. Generally kids don't just decide, 'Hey, I want to be a drug runner.' There's usually something that pushes them that direction."

"It's not about motives, Jessie, it's about timing," Ryan cut in.

"Come again?"

"It's about fixing him by a certain time, not fixing him in general."

"I'm not following."

"Yes, I can see that."

"Well?"

"I'm not going to give it to you, Jessie."

"Then be quiet and let me think," Jessie said somewhat sharply.

Ryan watched as Jessie moved into her usual thinking position; pacing, wrapped in a blanket, and jiggling a teacup. "I'm going to grab some more coffee. You want me to reheat your tea?" he offered.

"Whatever," she said in distracted frustration.

Jessie found herself at the window again. The valley below was exquisite. The moon's reflecting light was so intense that it made her seriously contemplate the purpose of the "lesser light to rule the night" from Genesis. It was, for a moment, distracting. *This wasn't the Christmas I planned. But what did I expect? I haven't really talked to him since we found my mother's letter.*

When Jessie had first made the choice to stay in Stone Ridge, she was distant to say the least. But as time went on, she'd opened up and brought Ryan a little closer to her world. But when he'd gotten too close, she'd instinctively shut him out. She had used her newfound religious beliefs as the reasoning for ignoring him, but that was a lie. She wasn't protecting him from anything, she was alienating him.

*I knew this storm was serious. I knew by going to Gramps's I would inevitably end up in Ryan's arena. I need to let go of my pride and just talk to him.*

Ryan reentered the loft and cautiously extended his hand holding her cup toward Jessie. "Here." He was prepared for anything. She'd either accept the tea graciously or punch him in the nose, sending the hot liquid cascading down his body.

She chose the gracious approach. "Thank you." She walked to the couch and slowly sipped at her tea.

"I'm not sure—" he began.

"Ryan, wait. I'm the one who asked you the question, so I know that I'm the one searching for an answer. I'm scared because I don't want to depend on anyone other than myself. It makes me feel weak and vulnerable, and that inevitably I'll be hurt." Jessie paused, surprised at her commentary.

Ryan slowly edged his way to the recliner. This he hadn't expected. He decided to remain quiet since he had no clue as to the direction she would go.

"That's just the way life is," she continued. "Trust and hurt are synonymous. Maybe not to you, but they are to me. This relationship has been cemented in my mind for years. A few months of you and your wisdom can't change that for me. I didn't want to be here when Elliott put me in the position he did. But I came because I didn't see much choice at the time, and I *have* become a better person because of it. I like Stone Ridge, I like the country, and I love being around the horses. I've grown to love Gramps and, well, I've grown accustomed to you too." Tears were building in Jessie's eyes, but her will held them in check.

Jessie cleared her throat before she continued, "The reason I wanted Ken's issues resolved by tomorrow was because I was planning on leaving then, and I wanted closure. I was planning on going back to the city. I don't want to be a therapist anymore. I have nothing to offer. There's so much I don't understand. I can't stay here with you when I don't know who I am. Running is what I do, so I know you're not surprised. You need to get on with your life now too. It's up to me to create that opportunity for you."

She forged ahead before Ryan could respond. "You were right. I came here to hide from reality. I'm not sure if I'll ever stop hiding. I thought . . . I thought that having received an answer to my prayers, things would be different. But they're not. God finally answers me, and I'm more confused now than I was to begin with. I should never have found that letter from my mother." Her tears finally won out.

"Will you tell me about that?" Ryan's words were soft, soothing.

Jessie readily conceded. "That night I knocked on your door, I felt like I'd been given a miracle. That was when I realized you were right and my anger *was* with my mother. She wasn't there to protect me when I needed her. I decided to pray, even though I still also harbored resentment toward God for not being there. I begged to know why the two most important people in my life weren't there for me. That's when the word *lilacs* came to me. I didn't understand it at first, so I prayed harder. Then I got it. I immediately realized that my father would have hidden the letter that she intended for me. He could never have brought himself to destroy it."

"That's when we went digging."

"Yes. To my place of refuge—the lilac bushes. He buried it right under my nose. I didn't know she had cancer. I know she didn't want Katie and me to watch her die, and it wasn't *her* desire that we end up with our father. *I* altered that course when the people at the theater read the note my mother had pinned to my coat. I corrected them when they stated our last name as Smith. So I shouldn't be angry with her or God, right? But I still am. It's not easier. I can't seem to let go. I keep trying, but . . ." She wiped her nose with the tissue from her pocket. "I thought that after such an experience, the hurt would be gone."

She sighed. "I don't want to lean on God. I don't want to lean on you. And if I stay, I'll have to keep dredging all this up and I don't think I have the energy. Why do I have to anyway? I can be alone and paint, and who does that hurt? And *don't* say it hurts *me,* because it doesn't. That's how I want it to be. You have to let me go." She retrieved her tissue and blew her nose hard. "I'm sorry to have spoiled your holiday."

Ryan fought the urge to move closer. He waited to be sure she was finished. "Will you come with me?" He stood and placed his hands in the front pockets of his sweatshirt.

She pulled the blanket tight. "Where to?"

"Come." Ryan extended his hand.

"Ryan—"

"Please?"

Jessie breathed deeply. "Can I bring the blanket?"

"Absolutely."

# CHAPTER 16

It was Christmas Eve and Beth had grown tired of her police guard. She wanted to be alone. If Thornton wanted to get at her, so be it, she decided. She called Michael and insisted Smoot and Reynolds be allowed to leave. After much coaxing he agreed, with the understanding that she use the cell phone he had left her with to call the second anything out of the ordinary happened. She now felt more relaxed than she had in days as she placed the simple gifts she'd bought for Trudy and Kenny beneath the tree. There were even presents for Michael, Janice, and the girls—purchased in a moment of weakness. It was, after all, a season of love, she told herself.

She took a large heavy box from the kitchen pantry and pulled it upstairs to Kenny's room. She turned on the light and shut the door. She took the wrapping paper she'd put aside for this, and began cutting and taping, topping the package off with a large red bow. Now she placed the neatly wrapped package in the center of the room. *Michael is sure to throw a fit about the new computer.* Then she stopped herself, remembering that the relationship had changed. *It isn't his business anyway. I'm the one that worked overtime.*

Beth sat at Kenny's old computer and, for some unknown reason, turned it on. The computer screen appeared before her with Kenny's desktop full of icons. She recognized most of them as games, but surprisingly a few were actually educational. The desktop also included a word-processing icon and an encyclopedia. *Where did all these come from? I didn't buy them.* She went into the word processor and began rummaging through his file folders. Most were school papers, but her eyes fell to the one marked "personal." She figured opening this file would be violating her son's privacy, but the mouse seemed to have a mind of its own as she clicked on it anyway. Any guilt she might have been feeling disappeared as the password box popped up. "Password?" Beth muttered. She didn't know such a thing existed for a word processor. She didn't know enough about computers to get around the process, so she banged on the keys for almost an hour, considering every possible password she could think that might represent something important to Kenny. Realizing this file might provide information about his disappearance, she was determined more than ever to get into it.

* * *

"You're cold," Ryan stated as he watched Jessie pull the blanket tighter around her body.

"Well, this isn't the warmest room in the house." Jessie smiled.

"True. Let me find you another blanket." Candle in hand, he began walking back toward the loft.

Jessie reached for his arm. "I'll be fine, Ryan. What *are* we doing in here? Ken's already told me that this room doesn't have an emergency outlet anywhere, so I'm inclined to believe we're not here to play games."

"Come over here." Ryan guided Jessie to the other side of the room. It was a vast, almost empty space. Its only contents were back-to-back folding chairs on the wall to her left, along with a painting of a rose that Ryan had repainted twice. Through the filtered light, Jessie stared at the soft, lavender-colored roses. Ryan wasn't as talented a painter, but his techniques could be improved easily with her help, she decided. She remembered the first time she'd learned of this painting. It had once held only two roses representing Ryan and Rebecca. After Rebecca died, he'd removed one rose and painted the background black, reforming the isolated rose to a wilted and lonely state. It was just the previous summer that he was able to lift the spirits of the remaining rose by adding four more to the bouquet. The roses were symbolic of his reasons to appreciate life. He'd told her who four of the roses stood for, but the fifth rose he'd left unidentified. But she was intuitive enough to figure it out on her own.

"Okaaaay . . ." Jessie held a blank expression, looking at Ryan, then at the painting and back at Ryan again.

"You remember who the roses represent?"

"Yes. One for Rebecca, one for your son Joshua, one for Ruth, and one for Gramps," Jessie replied proudly.

"And the last one?" Ryan leaned his shoulder on the wall and looked directly at her.

Jessie began fidgeting with the blanket. "Well, I suppose I could make an educated guess."

"Go ahead."

Jessie furrowed her brow and then suddenly broke into a grin. "Nelly?"

Ryan shook his head and sighed.

"Okay, okay. Me?" Her voice was low and her breathing became rapid.

"Very good."

"So what happens when I leave? Will you take a rose out, like you did when you lost Rebecca?" She instantly wished she could take it back.

"First of all, you're not going to leave. And secondly, I didn't remove Brecca's rose. I removed mine, remember?"

"I'm sorry, it's just that . . . what do you mean I'm not going to leave?" The humility she'd felt was beginning to wilt in the presence of her rising temper.

"You're not going to leave because you want to stay."

"Ryan! Haven't you heard one word I've said?"

Ryan stepped in closer and took Jessie's hands in his. "Heard every word but tuned in more closely to your body language. It said something completely different."

Jessie yanked her hands from his. "See, there you go again, thinking you know everything." She dropped the blanket to the floor, the robe over her pajamas falling open. The heat from her anger now sufficed to keep her warm.

Ryan suppressed his laughter. There before him stood an attractive, intelligent, and competent thirty-two-year-old psychologist—housed in what appeared to be reindeer-covered sweats. "It's time that—"

"No, Ryan. Stop. It's Christmas now, and I want to unwrap presents, eat fudge without nuts, and pack."

"You want to know why I stopped going to Church?"

"Oh, sure, throw that out there," Jessie chastised. "You think that after you tell me that, I'm going to just spill it all and miraculously morph into whatever it is that you need me to be? You're soooo off the mark, Blake. I don't even have my stupid tea!" Her unspoken need to move now pushed her around the room like an Indy-500 race car.

Ryan slid to the floor and leaned against the wall beneath the painting. He folded his arms across his chest and waited.

"Go ahead and spill it. Just don't expect me to follow suit," Jessie blurted.

Ryan's eyes followed her laps about the room. "I never felt good enough to be a Mormon."

Out of the corner of her eye, Jessie could see Ryan's chin lower to his chest. *Good move, Blake. Whatever you do, Jessica Nicole Winston, do not, I repeat, do not, fall for this strategy . . .*

"My mother and father were Latter-day Saints. I don't think you knew that," Ryan said. "My dad joined the Church when he and my mom began dating. She was a strong member and had her sights on a temple marriage. But after a year of being together every day, their teenage hormones took over. It wasn't long before her dreams were shattered—I was the result. But they were in love, so they married civilly, convinced that after a year they'd get to the temple."

Jessie's demeanor instantly softened. "Which never happened because she died giving birth to you."

"Yeah." Ryan watched as Jessie's pacing slowed and her tensed body relaxed. He continued, "When I found my mother's old paints, I also ran across a notebook she used as a journal. I skipped a day of school to read it in its entirety. While my dad loved my mother, his testimony was solely based on his desire to please her."

"So when she died, any desire he had to continue on in the Church died with her," Jessie supplied. "But wasn't Ruth a good support?" she asked, now completely engaged in the conversation.

"I'm sure she was. But more than likely my dad was simply going through the motions. He had never been *converted*. And if you're not converted, all the efforts of the well-intentioned will get you nowhere. With no real sense of who he was or what the gospel offered, and a kid who reminded him daily of what he'd lost, he cracked. He hung in there for five years, though. I have to give him credit for that.

"I went through Primary just fine, which is the Church's organization for children. The kids wondered why I didn't have a mom or dad . . . but the things they said were never too big a deal to me. But as I grew older, kids were meaner, and for some reason I was the victim. I didn't handle it as well.

"When I was fifteen—this was after I'd read my mother's journals—a kid named Randy and I had a fight at church because he'd been ripping on my dad. As I look back on that, I'm sure that all the remarks from the years previous must have just built up inside, and with Randy's stupidity, they erupted. When our teacher asked what happened, every boy in the room said that I had provoked the fight—Randy hadn't done anything wrong. I *was* strong and had worked him over pretty well. The teacher, who happened to be Randy's father, sent me out of class and talked with Gramps and Ruth. He told them that I was welcome back as soon as I apologized. Not only to Randy but to the entire class."

"Ouch."

Ryan mustered a smile. "You can imagine how well that went over with me."

"Yeah." A good portion of her angry tension was now dissipating, leaving Jessie short on energy. She slid down the wall closer to where Ryan was, careful to remain at a "safe" distance. "So you stopped going?"

"Yes and no. I went to sacrament meeting and then came home. I didn't go to the other meetings, and I never went to activities."

"I thought you stopped going *altogether* before Rebecca came along."

"Yes, I did. Remember the burning incident when I was seventeen?"

"Yeah. I kinda figured that played into it somehow."

"The plan was just for me and this kid Robert to help our friend Paul get back at a guy named Mark. Mark was going out with a girl that Paul insisted should have been *his* girlfriend. I got along well with Robert and Paul. They never hassled me—let me be who I was. So I didn't mind causing a little mischief on their behalf. That night, though, Robert brought another guy along."

"Ah, let me guess. Randy?"

"Yep." Ryan turned slightly toward Jessie. "I considered leaving, obviously the wiser choice, but I didn't want to appear spineless to my buddies. Randy was the reason the small fire we started got out of hand."

"I thought you said the wind picked up and it spread out of control."

"Yes, it did. But it wouldn't have if Randy hadn't soaked the surrounding area with gasoline to 'give it a kick.'"

"Oh, Ryan—like you didn't see him holding a gas can?"

Ryan raised his eyebrows and looked directly at Jessie. "No, *Gramps,* I didn't know about the gas can—it was dark at the time."

"Sorry. And so after the fire spread to the house, everyone ran—except you."

"Yeah."

"Why did you never tell anyone who the other boys were?"

"I took responsibility for what I did. It wasn't my place to rat out those who didn't."

"Wow. Remarkable constitution at seventeen."

Ryan stretched his legs and offered a weak grin. "I was raised by Gramps, remember? Although if my constitution were so remarkable, I wouldn't have been there in the first place."

"So you were ticked at the boys, had to rebuild Mark's house, and then said, 'No more church for this guy'?"

"There's just one more thing. Robert confessed about a year later—his guilt got the better of him. But Paul and Randy never came clean. Paul's dad was our stake president, and Randy's dad—"

"Was your old Sunday School teacher," finished Jessie.

"Yeah, but at that time he was in the bishopric as a counselor."

"Ah," replied Jessie. Although, if truth be known, she hadn't a clue as to what a counselor was. She knew being a bishop was a big deal, so a counselor must be too, she decided.

"Those two guys got away with a lot of things because nobody ever wanted to tell on them," Ryan continued. "They both went on missions and were continually praised for their greatness. In truth, I learned they didn't serve well at all. Both their fathers knew what kinds of things they'd done, but let it go. By the way, Randy's last name is Grant."

# CHAPTER 17

Jessie's eyes widened as her breathing came to a halt. *Of course! Bishop Grant's son.* This explained why Ryan had been belligerent to the bishop that day at the hospital when he'd come to give Ruth a blessing.

Jessie and Ryan listened to the wind pushing against the cabin. After a few minutes, Jessie quietly spoke. "That would explain your dislike for Bishop Grant."

"Yes. Fortunately, though, you've put things into perspective for me over the months, and now I'm able to let go of that."

"You've forgiven Randy and the bishop?"

"Yes."

"Wait a minute. What could I have possibly done to help you to let go of all those years of anger? And even so, how can you just 'let go'?"

"You've managed—through your grief—to turn to the only true source of comfort, even though you were angry with Him."

"You mean God?"

"Yes. I find it commendable that you've let go of your pride long enough to recognize that you want peace and to find something better than the bitterness of anger and grudges. It doesn't serve any purpose other than to hold you back from living the kind of life you were born to live. You've been an amazing example to me. When I said I never felt good enough to be a Mormon, it was because I failed so many times in the gospel. I should have stood up for the truth that day in class, I should never have agreed to help set fire to someone's property, I should never have flaunted Brecca's money, and I shouldn't have started drinking to forget my problems. If I hadn't, I might not have lost Brecca and my son. I'm still not sure why God took her and left me. Seems an unbelievable waste. But He did, and I'm left to suffer the consequences of my choices."

Jessie was silent, so he continued. "The whispers from Brecca were for me to 'let go.' At first I thought it meant to let go of *her* and get on with my life. And while I believe that was part of it, the bigger picture was that by hearing her voice, she was inviting me to let go by forgiving and healing. I can't bring her back. There's no way to make a physical restitution for what I've done. But I can forgive those I've conveniently blamed, and I can use the knowledge that God has granted me and the wealth which Brecca left and put it to good use in helping others."

After a moment's silence Ryan added, "Feelings of inadequacy and incompetence distract us from doing good. Heavenly Father has put us here to succeed gloriously, not to fail miserably."

Jessie cut in with a familiar quote. "'Our deepest fear is not that we are inadequate. Our deepest fear is that we are powerful beyond measure'—"

"'It is our light, not our darkness, that most frightens us,'" Ryan finished the quote from Nelson Mandela. They stared at each other for a moment. "And if you can realize that, then I ought to be ashamed of myself. I've had the truth for a long time, but I've allowed it to get buried beneath my pride."

"So you're better now because your wife spoke to you from the dead and because I've turned myself over to God?"

"I'm not *all* better, Jessie. The realizations have come, but like you've said before, it's been years that I've carried these resentments. While I have 'let go,' the patterns of learned behavior and thought are still there. And now I have to struggle to overcome those patterns.

"And as far as you and I go, well, if you choose to leave, even though I know you don't really want to, I'll let you go. I won't run after you and publicly proclaim my love or how desperately I need you. The choice to stay has got to be yours. I can't rescue you from this choice. *You* have to make it."

"But, Ryan, somehow you've missed the point. You're under the illusion that I'm better. I'm not—not at all. The miracle of finding that letter has done nothing for me. Look at me, I'm a wreck!"

"You're a wreck because you're choosing to be. You're scared to 'let go' of your old self and your old patterns. That miracle is what broke the shackles that bound you. You just haven't decided to leave the captivity of the cell. It's all you've known, and there's comfort in that."

Jessie's eyes watered again, and she was feeling as if tranquility was just beyond her grasp. "I'm a therapist for crying out loud. I know exactly what to tell people when they're where I am—why can't it work for me?"

"You know why. The same reason it takes your clients time to change—you've been taught from childhood that you'd amount to nothing, that you were no good and had nothing to offer. Your miracle can't change that or take away its hurt. It just opens the door for you to recognize what you need to face. I know you've said you've found a place to forgive your father, and even your mother. But I believe you did it only cerebrally, because of what you learned from the letter. It just seemed the correct course of action. I'm just not sure you really felt that release for them in your heart."

Ryan watched as the woman before him became child-like in her expression as the tears flowed freely. "You gave what you weren't prepared to give because it was the right thing to do. The anger is still there, and rightly so. You were hurt, Jessie, physically, emotionally, and spiritually in ways parents should never hurt a child. You got it all—and it's time to acknowledge that anger in a healing way."

Jessie wiped at her eyes, and in a quiet voice said, "So what's the textbook answer here?"

"There's not a *textbook* answer. You know that, but the world has taught us how to convince people that there is. You're searching in the wrong arena. The answer lies in the book of Isaiah when he declares, 'And with his stripes we are healed.' Real healing is offered us through the Savior, who said, 'I have heard thy prayer, I have seen thy tears: behold, I will heal thee.'" The instant the words issued from Ryan's mouth, he felt a warmth spread through him that he hadn't felt for a long, long time. He could no longer deny what he'd always known as truth.

Jessie pulled her knees to her chest, her auburn hair falling around her sobbing form. Ryan grasped the collapsed blanket and wrapped it tightly around her shoulders and pulled her to him.

"I can't heal you, Jessie, even though I desperately want to. But I won't abandon you in the process. What's left to be done involves a personal connection with your Savior. He is the only one that truly understands how you feel. He was there. And He was also there for Katie and your mother, and your father, and understands their part in it. But most importantly, He has already borne sins and the hurt for all of you."

Jessie gently pulled herself away to look at Ryan. She was surprised at his sudden religious fervor. "Don't take this the wrong way, but I don't understand. You haven't done all this, have you? But here you are, suddenly ready to save the world?"

"Not the world, Jessie, just you and me, and in reality we've already been saved. Enlightenment *can* be sudden. I've simply had a shift in identity. Not forgiving Randy, the bishop, myself, and blaming God allowed me to live with my egotistical self. Remembering and accepting that I am indebted to Him for everything and that life's journey is to become like Him has helped me shift to my eternal self. Most of us walk around only getting glimpses of enlightenment. It's a rare few who can regard it as a permanent state.

"You also have to realize that my own actions, when I truly knew better, caused my issues and problems. And I knew at every step the way out. I just haven't owned up to it until now. You, on the other hand, were a child when this was all thrown upon you. You had no wise counsel available to help you. You were left to the pain, misunderstanding, and injustice born of a cruel environment. Nothing that happened to you was *your* fault, and the misunderstanding of it and the lack of your ability as a child to cope with it created the patterns of hurt and self-doubt that haunt you now.

"I struggled because I denied and acted against the happiness available to me. You're struggling because you've had a glimpse of happiness and of your true potential, but your old self, which evolved to protect you from your childhood pain, is preventing you from embracing change and your new spiritual awareness."

"But you lost Brecca and your son. You had loss too. Where's your pain?"

"Let me back up. You asked if I've allowed myself to feel the hurt from all my wounds. The answer is yes. I've visited my Gethsemane, if you will. I've cried for my loss, and I've agonized over my choices, but some of my losses were of my own doing and I understand now why I made the stupid choices that I did. I'm in the process of forgiving myself for things that I basically understand. Not so for you. Your situation is more complex, although the solution isn't. So it's been easier for me. I still feel sadness about Brecca, about the baby, but I know what's next for me. You mentioned something about Bishop Grant asking if you knew why you were here, and about a 'test'?"

"Yeah?"

"Has he talked to you yet about what he meant?"

"No, but before you get into it, I have another question."

"Go ahead."

"How come you know so much if you quit at seventeen?"

Ryan drew in a deep breath and pinched the top of his nose with his fingers. "I learned a great deal from Ruth's lectures and had many discussions with Brecca. The gospel isn't something you easily forget, anyway. Truth is truth. It's no less powerful simply because you choose to ignore it. Now I need to do something about it."

"Okay, this life is a test. It's only a test . . . right?"

"Partly, yes. It's a test of many things—of our faith, patience, strengths, how we adapt, our priorities, desires, and our beliefs." He paused. "C.S. Lewis said, 'You find out the strength of a wind by trying to walk against it, not by lying down.' That's what this test is about—testing ourselves against what life can throw at us. We're struggling to reach our potential, but to do that we have to overcome and change." He paused to look at her.

"Simon didn't become Peter until he'd been severely tried and tested," Jessie offered, softly.

"Yes. I believe that trials serve multiple purposes. But I think that the greatest purpose is to offer us an opportunity to prove that we love Him more than anything else."

"Like Job did."

"Yes, like Job did."

"So I've failed, then."

"No! Absolutely not, Jessie. Heck, I haven't even failed, and that's what took so long to realize."

"But nothing's changed since my miracle, Ryan."

Ryan smiled and took her hands in his. Jessie tried gently to nudge them free. "We're back to that, are we? Don't push me away, Jessie. I know you don't want to. It's time you let go of that as well and let me in. You have to begin making a commitment to something other than your belief that you can do everything yourself."

Jessie stared at him, then finally said, "I need some time, Ryan." They sat in silence a few moments, then she took a deep breath, smiled, and said, "I'm not sure what time it is, but we probably ought to be getting things under the tree."

# CHAPTER 18

Beth's eyes were glazing over again as she stared at Kenny's computer screen. *What on earth would he use for a password?* She tried thinking like a teenager, but it had been too long. She typed in all of his friends' names. She even tried *Thornton.* She tried the names of the planets, rock stars, movie stars, birth dates, favorite numbers, favorite colors, favorite animals . . . *Wait a second!* She had a thought. A second after she typed in the name, before her appeared what looked like a diary. *Hallelujah! He's always wanted to name a dog Goliath!* She scrolled to the end of the document. *One hundred and twenty-one pages! I can hardly get him to complete a sentence when I try to talk to him.* She read the last entry when he told of leaving earlier than he had planned.

Beth scrolled up to the beginning of the document. The first entry was on Christmas Day when he was nine.

> Wow, Patrick and I got this cool computer!
> He's been on it most of the time, but now it's
> my turn! I wanna have a secret diary like
> Andy. He says he writes things, then puts a
> password in so nobody can read his stuff. I
> need to think of a cool password!

Beth wondered how many passwords had been used over the years. She'd never once thought of him keeping a diary on a computer. She skimmed through the few pages from his ninth and tenth years, and rested on the one dated a week after Patrick's death.

> Won't be writing in here anymore. Nothing to talk about. Patrick's dead. Mom and Dad are fighting again. You'd think they'd stop since that's what made Patrick kill himself.

Beth flinched as tears welled in her eyes. *Is that why?* She continued reading.

> Found him in our room. There was so much blood. I wish we'd move. I don't like being in here alone. His blood's still on the carpet. They're supposed to replace it, but they'll forget.

Beth looked down at the carpet beneath her feet. While she couldn't necessarily see the stains, Kenny was right. In the end they had decided that they couldn't afford to change the carpet at the time, so they'd masked the blood with hours of scrubbing it and later a throw rug. *Why haven't we changed this carpet?*

It was two years before the next entry, the day Michael had left.

> Dad's a jerk. He's leaving us cuz he says he doesn't love Mom anymore. Mom's trying to hide it, but I can hear her crying. First

Patrick, and now Dad's leaving. Mom might as
well give up too. Nothing to stay around for
anymore. I'm obviously not worth it.

Beth retreated to the bathroom for some tissue and to
splash water on her face. *Kenny was never visibly upset,* she
realized with an aching heart. *He's shown no signs—just like
with Patrick.* Then she stopped in her tracks, realization
hitting her. *I was so consumed with the loss of Patrick and
Michael's leaving. Maybe I didn't see what he was going
through.*

She returned to the computer and continued her
reading. The next few entries were more of the same, but
one caught her attention:

That stupid nightmare's back. The one where
Patrick is chasing me with a bloody sword.
What's he so mad at me for, anyway? I didn't
do anything. He didn't kill himself because of
me, did he? He hated when my part of the
room was a mess, and that I stole his T-shirt
to make a flag for the clubhouse, and that I
told Mom and Dad that he liked that girl
Sarah. He got really mad at me the day he
caught me playing with his battle figures. I
thought he was going to rip my head off. But
that was a long time ago. Did I make him
mad enough to kill himself?

Anguish rolled through Beth in waves. She remembered
it was about that time Kenny became fanatical about his
room being clean. He would throw a fit if he didn't get an

"A" on everything he did at school. Regardless of her prodding, he would never talk about what happened with Patrick or his father leaving. That's when she'd decided he needed therapy. The first couple sessions she was included, and then after that he went on his own. She hoped he'd feel comfortable talking to a stranger, although now she suspected he released his frustrations only to himself through the computer.

The next ten entries were dated a day apart, with only one message: *Nightmare again.*

*My poor son, I had no idea.* Beth had experienced a few nightmares of her own through the past five years. Why hadn't she ever asked Kenny about whether he was having them too? *It had to have been worse for him, since he was the one who found Patrick. Why hadn't the therapist ever mentioned it? Kenny was probably unwilling to share his real concerns with the therapist too. This must be why he turned to Greg. He needed acceptance from somewhere—to feel valued . . .*

* * *

"I don't know how you managed to get all these gifts for Ken. It's not like we were expecting him," said Ryan, placing the third present for Ken under the tree.

"I simply took some things that I planned on giving you and Gramps," Jessie said heartily.

"Whoa, wait a minute. That kid's getting *my* presents?"

Jessie smiled as she inched past him on her hands and knees, stuffing smaller gifts in front of bigger ones. "Well, not all of them, but yeah, a couple."

"Maybe I just ought to give him *your* present, and see what you think of that," Ryan threatened good-naturedly.

"Thought I heard tinkerin' down here," Gramps called. He was in his typical jeans and suspenders but had added a festive red sweatshirt to the ensemble, and he was holding a few gifts of his own for the tree.

"Santa here is givin' Ken the gifts she'd planned for you and me," Ryan jested, now standing back, out of Jessie's way.

"Is that so? Well, I suppose he needs them worse than we do."

Ryan jabbed him. "Speak for yourself!"

"Oh, for crying out loud. You keep this up and Santa isn't going to leave you anything at all!" Jessie said to Ryan as he headed into the kitchen.

"Got room for a few more?" Gramps asked, bending over to find an open space.

"Of course. Hand them over and I'll nestle them in here," Jessie replied. She finished rearranging the various brightly covered packages under the tree, then plugged the lights in. She stood back admiringly.

"Not a bad job, little lady, all things considered," Gramps said.

"Yeah, I think it turned out fine. Hope we didn't wake you."

"Nah. Wasn't sleepin' much. Gotta stop takin' those darn naps so late in the day."

"Gramps?"

"Yes, ma'am?"

"Thanks."

"For what?" he asked.

"Everything."

Gramps scooted next to Jessie and placed his arm around her shoulders. She found herself relaxing to accept the tenderness the moment offered.

"Been good havin' you around. Gonna be sad to see it end," Gramps said. "I believe you're headed out tomorrow?" Gramps turned her toward him and rested his hands on both her shoulders. "If you want my opinion, I think you're makin' a mistake."

"But, how did you . . . ?"

"Doesn't matter. The point is, that kid in there's in love with you." He motioned his head toward the kitchen. "And you're in love with him. Ought to stay put and do somethin' 'bout it, rather than runnin' off. As educated as you are, young lady, you're missin' what life's got to offer."

Gramps moved toward the couch and motioned for her to join him. For some unknown reason, she didn't feel upset with Gramps for expressing how he felt about things. He had never forced his opinion on her before; in fact, he had rarely shared it at all. She respected him for that, so hearing him out now seemed a natural thing. She hoped whatever Ryan was doing in the kitchen would last long enough for Gramps to finish saying his peace.

"All right, Gramps. Tell me what life's all about."

"When I first laid eyes on Ellen, I knew she was the only one for me. I wanted to grow old with her. It was a feelin' no words in any language could relay. I had aspirations, like any young kid, to be successful and wealthy, you know, to really make somethin' of myself in the world. After Ellen got ahold of me, things changed. Those things didn't seem to matter anymore. Only thing mattered was being with her. She made me feel like I *was* the richest man in the world. Love, young lady—that's what life's about."

"But . . ." Jessie paused, unsure if she should say what was on her mind.

"Go ahead."

"It's nothing."

"It's something or you wouldn't have said 'but.'"

"Well, her complications from having lupus meant that you weren't going to grow old together."

"No, we weren't. But that doesn't change a thing. I still love her, and the time we had together makes up for the pain of losing her. Nothin' has ever been more important than that."

"But don't you miss your son?"

Gramps's eyes blinked quickly. She was certain she'd just crossed the line of hospitality.

"I'm sorry, Gramps. That's none of my business. I was just caught up in processing what you're saying to me."

"Of course I miss him. He's a piece of his mother, and I would like nothin' more than to know what he's doin' and see him. But that's not in the cards, I'm afraid. He's got to be the one makin' the first move, 'cause I haven't got any idea where he's at. I could hire one of those fancy detectives, I suppose, but I figure since he's the one who left, he ought to be the one makin' his way back—on his terms, when he's ready. No use forcin' somethin' that ain't right yet."

Ryan returned holding a plate of fudge. Gramps and Jessie instantly stopped their conversation. "Hmm, could we make the fact that I'm interrupting any more obvious?"

"You're not interrupting. I only got one more thing to say," Gramps responded, though still looking at Jessie. "Stop thinkin' with that brilliant mind of yours, and start feelin' with that beautiful, warm heart. Now with that, I'm off to get a couple hours of shut-eye before that kid in there wakes up wonderin' if Santa has actually left him anything."

# CHAPTER 19

Christmas morning found Beth wide-eyed at her son's computer. She had found several entries painting the picture she'd been searching for. She had discovered why Kenny planned to leave long before the Thornton mess, and she understood why he longed to belong to something—even if it meant breaking the law. All that remained was to tell Michael and make sure that the problems were solved before they lost another son.

Beth turned off the computer, picked up the phone, and dialed the number. "Hello, Janice. I was wondering if all of you were planning on coming over this morning, or if it was just going to be Michael." Her voice was forcibly sweet. "You're all coming? Good, see you at ten, then. Good-bye."

Beth did a quick once-over through the house. She picked up miscellaneous items and found homes for them. She wiped down counters and ran the vacuum. Then she plugged in a small Crock Pot that was full of cinnamon-scented liquid potpourri. Before hitting the shower she looked out the front window—no black sedan was visible.

A loud noise caused Beth to hurry her shower. *Has Michael arrived early?* she wondered. "Hello? Michael is that you?" Beth called, dressing quickly. She grabbed the wet towels and reached for the door. It wouldn't open. "Oh no, you've got to be kidding," she said out loud.

"I know I checked that lock." Beth continued to chastise herself for not having listened to Michael. He had repeatedly told her to turn the lock back around after the boys grew out of their tantrum years and the need for a safe place to throw a fit was no longer a necessity.

"Great. Well, I hope Michael has his key."

\* \* \*

Jessie waited until she was sure Gramps and Ryan were asleep, then she crept silently out into the cold of the early morning. There was just one more thing she had to finish in the barn for Ryan. She promised herself she wouldn't peek at Gramps's present if it was still there.

This time as she trudged through the snow there wasn't the glow of light from the barn to lead her there, and the moon offered little illumination. She instantly chastised herself for not having brought a flashlight. Jessie hated the dark, and more than that she hated being *alone* in the dark.

She kept to the path that had been shoveled. She shivered—not because of the cold but because her surroundings seemed creepy and her imagination wasn't helping any. Every now and then she'd jerk her head, positive she'd seen a shadow move. She heard rustling sounds, but the wind was still. *Just get to the barn, Jessie, and quit doing this to yourself.*

The last movement was too much. She turned quickly. *There's something there, I know it!* "Blake? If that's you trying to scare me, I swear I'll give *all* your presents to Ken and you won't get a single thing," she whispered loudly. No response came. "Okay, Jessie, chill!" she said out loud. Hesitatingly she began to hum a familiar Christmas carol as she entered the barn.

Once inside, she quickly set about finding a piece of wood with which to create Ryan's last gift. The piece did not appear quickly, and a second carol soon filled the silence of her search. She'd finally found a suitable scrap when a cold breeze hit her face with a suddenness that made her bolt upright. The door was not open but seemed to be unlatched. She stood there like a statue. *Didn't I shut that?*

"Ryan?" she called. Nothing. "Ken? Gramps?" Jessie forced herself to move toward the door. Although the present wasn't yet finished, she was. She wanted out of there. Something wasn't right and she wanted to be back in the safety of the cabin. She carried the large piece of wood in her hands, ready to strike anything that got in her way.

She closed the barn door behind her just as something growled in front of her. After a quick scream, Jessie looked down as Nelly relaxed and rubbed her nose on Jessie's leg. "Nelly? Good gracious, dog, you scared me to death! That's the second time since we've been introduced you've had me convinced you were an intruder." She leaned over and rubbed the back of the dog's ears. "At least this time I'm not holding a priceless vase over my head. How on earth did you get out of the cabin? Did I leave the door ajar? It'll be freezing in there. C'mon girl, let's get back inside."

As Jessie and Nelly headed back to the cabin, Jessie's eyes focused on a shadowy line of prints leading into the woods. For one moment the hair on her neck rose, but as she looked down at the dog, she considered all the animals in the area. Taking a step forward, a prayer for calmness on her lips, she let Nelly lead the way back.

* * *

"Can I be Santa and pass around the gifts?" Jessie asked gleefully to the three men sitting sleepily on the couch.

"Don't think any of us are up to arguin' the point," Gramps replied.

"Great! Okay, Gramps, here you go. You're first." Jessie set a small, simply wrapped gift in his lap.

"Well, go on, open it," Jessie said eagerly.

"I can wait till everyone's got theirs."

"We're taking turns, so it's okay. Go ahead."

"Taking turns?" Ryan piped up, leaning forward and rubbing his eyes.

"Uh-huh. One present at a time."

"Jessie, by the looks of that pile there, we could be here a week."

Jessie scowled. "It'll take less time if we just bypass all the ones that are addressed to you."

Ryan laughed, leaned back, and looked at Gramps. "You better get started. I want mine next."

Half an hour went by as each person unwrapped various gifts. Gramps and Ryan smiled at each other while Jessie opened a few with her name on it. It became obvious that since neither Ryan nor Gramps had bought those things, Jessie had bought them for herself. Everyone had received new socks, razors, cologne or perfume of choice, and their favorite treat. Jessie had crocheted Gramps a scarf, and he also received new suspenders and five crossword-puzzle books.

"Okay . . . let's see. Ken, these two are for you," Jessie said.

"I already got enough, ma'am—I mean, Jessie." The words might have been a little more convincing if his eyes weren't wide and his arms already outstretched.

"These are from me, so you *have* to take them." She placed two snowmen-papered packages in his arms.

"Thank you." Ken opened the first one slowly and read the label to himself. Then, looking bewildered, he turned it over to read the instructions on the back.

Gramps and Ryan chuckled when they saw what it was—a product used to restore hair to its natural color.

"I picked that up a few months ago," Jessie began, "along with some dye to color my hair. I wanted to have it on hand in case I felt like a change. Since I'm sure now that I'll never get up the courage to go through with it, I thought you might want to put that to use. You'll make a much better blond than me. I'm certainly not telling you to change, but it's there if you choose to."

Ken smiled as he put it down and picked up the book that was still in the box. He read the title out loud: *The White Company* by Sir Arthur Conan Doyle."

"Don't sound too thrilled," said Ryan, grinning.

"Oh no, it's great. Thanks, Jessie."

"Take the time to read it. I think you'll like it. It's a knightly tale of honor and chivalry. That other box there ought to be more to your immediate liking, though."

Ken unwrapped—faster this time—the tiny box. Inside he discovered a big, red pocketknife of the variety that included everything but the kitchen sink.

Ryan glanced at Jessie with raised eyebrows. He realized that most likely the book was originally intended for *his* library and that the knife was also supposed to go to him.

"Now after we're done, Gramps will give his 'appropriate times to use a knife' speech, okay?" Jessie said.

"Sure." The knife was a hit. Ken ignored everything going on around him and began fiddling with all its gadgets.

Ryan unwrapped a scarf like Gramps's, and some white work shirts, and new CDs from Gramps. Then he leaned under the tree and pulled out a small box he had hidden earlier. "Here. This is for you, Jessie."

"Thanks," Jessie replied kindly. She chuckled as she unwrapped her cherished snowflake scarf, which had recently doubled as a flag. "So when did you go find this?"

"A couple nights ago. I replaced it with a red bandana."

"That was uncharacteristically thoughtful of you," she replied teasingly.

"Here's another one for you, Ken," Jessie said handing him a larger gift.

Kenny unwrapped the book on horses that he'd been lost in for hours previous. "Oh. I wouldn't want to take your book," he said hesitantly to Gramps.

"It's yours now," Gramps replied. "We can always get another one. Besides, we have more books on horses than the town library."

Jessie leaned over and quickly pushed Ryan's lower jaw closed. At least he wasn't yelling that it was *his* book and not Gramps's.

"Oh, here's one for me," Jessie said excitedly. She noticed the effort Gramps had taken in decorating the heavy package. She gently undid the ribbon and slowly pulled the lid off the box. She simply stared, then tears began to swell. *How could he have known?*

"Hope you don't mind. Those were Ruth's. She'd been needing a new set pretty bad and ordered those a week before her stroke. They got here a couple weeks later. They're brand new, and, well, I thought you could put them to good use."

Stillness filled the room. Ken had no idea what the big deal was, but he was in tune enough to know it was a moment for silence.

Jessie carefully pulled out the green, leather-bound set of scriptures. They were larger than Brecca's Book of Mormon; she had no idea they came in this size. She stroked them softly and cleared her throat before saying, "Thank you, Gramps. This is more than I could have hoped for."

"She'd be happy you're usin' them."

Ryan handed Ken an envelope with a red bow attached. "Ken, I'm afraid I wasn't as inventive as these two. You only get money from me. But I figure there's probably something you want that you're not going to get, so hopefully this will help."

Ken happily opened it and coughed when he saw the bill. "I can't accept this, sir. It's far too much."

"I appreciate your manners, but it's yours." Then he turned to Gramps. "Okay, Gramps, yours was too big for under the tree, so you're going to have to follow me." Gramps, a bit stunned, followed Ryan to his room with Jessie and Ken close behind. Ryan reached under his bed and slowly pulled out a large item wrapped in several pieces of wrapping paper.

"So that's where all that paper went. I wondered what happened to it," Jessie said jovially.

Gramps's curiosity was piqued. "What in the Sam Hill?"

"Go on, open it," Ryan said, motioning him toward the box.

"Well, you all better get in here and help me, or it'll be hours before we eat!"

Ken, Jessie, and Gramps tore away the paper to find a new flat-panel TV. "It's to hang on your wall so you can get rid of that old, boxy, wood thing of Aunt Ruth's."

"Ryan, you outdid yourself this time," Gramps announced. They spent the next few minutes locating the manual and getting rid of all the paper and the box.

"Okay, Jessie, let's go find yours," Ryan said.

All three went back to the tree. Gramps was buried in the TV's manual as he plopped down in his chair.

Jessie took her spot back on the couch, and Ryan pulled out a long cardboard tube from the side of the tree and handed it to her.

"This wasn't here last night," she mused. Again, she unwrapped slowly and pulled out the lightweight canvas from its container. She unrolled it, and her eyes filled with tears again.

"Always a good sign when they do that," Gramps whispered to Ryan.

"Ryan, it's . . . it's . . ."

"I know you're the real artist, but I couldn't get the vision out of my mind. It had to go somewhere."

"This is what you were hiding in the barn? It wasn't a present for Gramps at all!"

"There's a frame for it still out there. I put the last coat of finish on it, so it should be ready for use by tomorrow." Jessie turned the canvas around to show Gramps and Kenny.

"Hey, that's the big horse in the barn—the one that had a foal. Is that supposed to be *you* next to the horse?" Ken asked Jessie.

"Oh, all right, it's not the best portrait of her. But hey, you try doing people!" Ryan said in his defense.

Ken burst out with laughter, as did Gramps and Jessie. "I was just kidding. It looks just like her."

"Ryan," Jessie said. "It's . . . it's . . ."

"Are you still stuck on those words? It's . . . *what*, exactly?"

Jessie wiped her eyes, and without saying anything else, lifted the tree skirt to reveal a small package. She walked over to Ryan and placed it in his lap. "It's this," she said softly, retreating back to her seat.

Ryan took the lid off the tiny box to reveal a sprig of mistletoe. He grinned from ear to ear. Not caring that Gramps and Ken were staring, he walked over to Jessie, held the sprig over her head, and slowly leaned in.

Jessie took his face in her hands and readily accepted the soft and tender kiss. Ryan pulled away gently with the realization he had most assuredly been kissed back. "Now *that* was worth waiting for," he said. On impulse, he leaned in again.

"Okay, okay, that's enough. Got a kid and an old man close to a heart attack sittin' here," Gramps humphed.

Ryan forced himself to lean back. "Well, now that I've got my kiss, I guess there's no need to give you your last present."

Jessie looked at him thoughtfully. "There's more?"

"There's something in the bottom of the tube there." He pointed to the tube her painting had been in.

"I didn't see anything."

"Look again."

Jessie found a piece of paper taped to the inside rim near the bottom. She pulled it free and read out loud, "'Buddy would be happier if his mother was near.'" It took a moment for the words to sink in. "You're *not* selling Joanie!" Jessie leaped in the air and threw her arms around his neck and squeezed tightly.

"She's yours," Ryan whispered in her ear.

Jessie pulled her chin off his shoulder and looked directly at him. "What?"

"She's yours, if you want her."

This kiss was given without thought and fully from the heart, no greenery necessary.

"Oh, man, is that all they're gonna do?" Ken asked Gramps in annoyance.

"Reckon so. Been a long time comin', kid."

# CHAPTER 20

"Beth? You here?" Michael called after Janice and the girls filed through the front door.

"Michael? I'm up here. Locked myself in the bathroom. And since this is Christmas, you'll not say a word about it!"

Janice rolled her eyes in disgust and began taking her coat off. Michael concealed a smile as he walked up the stairs.

"Thanks," Beth said to Michael after he'd opened the door. "I'll be down in just a minute."

Beth came down the stairs to find Janice, Diana, Andrea, and Allyson wearing the best artificial smiles they could muster. "Sorry about the wait. Merry Christmas to all of you," Beth said.

"Merry Christmas," Michael said. "You doin' okay?"

"Fine, Michael. Girls? You'll find a gift under the tree for each of you. Your mom and Mike and I are going to be in the kitchen. I have some things I need to talk to them about. If you get bored with your gifts, you know where the TV is, okay?"

"Can we, Mother? Huh, can we?" asked Allyson, dancing around.

"Well, I—"

"It's all right girls, go ahead," Michael interrupted. The girls were gone before Janice had finished the sentence.

Janice's scowl followed Michael and Beth into the kitchen. Beth sat down and waited for Michael and Janice to join her at the table before she began. "Have you talked with Ken this morning?" she asked. Michael's expression clearly showed his surprise at Beth's reference to their son as *Ken.* "No, thought we could do that together. But I did talk with Mr. Blake, and all is well."

"Good. I've checked and I know the roads were started on last night. They'll get back to it later tonight. So I'm headed to get him later this afternoon."

"Now hold on there, Beth. I'm not sayin' you can't go, but we brought the boys in that Jennifer saw Kenny hanging with."

"I already know everything," Beth informed him.

"You know about the deal going bad, and that he kept some money?"

"He didn't take any money, Michael. Well, I mean he didn't take *their* money. He only has the money he earned—illegally, but earned. Before he left, he recorded every job and mentioned seeing Thornton with that accountant whose body was found. And they think he witnessed Greg's murder. We *have* to get him, Michael."

"How do you know all this?"

"I've been reading his diary."

"You read someone's diary?" Janice asked, appalled.

"Not *someone's,* Janice, my son's."

Janice folded her arms, crossed her legs, and with a stern look of disapproval said, "It's still wrong." Michael's glare quieted Janice, at least for the moment.

Beth continued, slowly. "I knew his running away this time was due to Thornton, but I also knew that his habitual running and moodiness was from something different, so I investigated his journal when I came across it. Anyway, when I was staring at Patrick's old battle figurines, I noticed that the soldiers were arranged on one side of the sandbox, all except for one. He was placed on the other side. That probably doesn't seem like such a big deal, except for the fact that he had no weapon. Somehow Ken broke it off."

Michael tightened his brow. "Why are you suddenly calling him Ken?"

"One of his entries stated that he wished we'd realize he's not a little boy anymore. He wants to be called Ken."

"Fine. But I'm not following this sandbox stuff," Michael said, bewildered.

"He feels all alone," Janice jumped in.

"Very good, Janice," Beth said, surprised. "Yes, that's part of it. But the bigger picture reveals that he feels defenseless."

"Defenseless against Thornton?" Michael asked.

"No, Michael. Defenseless against *you*."

"Me? I'm not the one after him!"

Beth let out a huge sigh. "Okay, let me try this again. This isn't about who's after him. There's something bigger going on."

"Bigger than being targeted by the local drug cartel?" Michael spat.

"Yes, as off the wall as that must sound to a cop. And it's time you took responsibility for your part in all of this. Ever since Ken was young, he wanted to be like Patrick. *You* idolized Patrick, Michael. He was the perfect child.

You took him everywhere. Ken usually had to stay behind because he wasn't old enough. He couldn't wait to grow up so that he could go with you too. Then, when he finally was old enough—"

"Patrick died," Michael finished.

"Yes. During those long months when we were trying to make sense of it all, Ken got lost in the shuffle. When you went places, you didn't think to take Ken with you like you had Patrick. You went alone."

"So he feels neglected, chooses drugs, and it's all *my* fault?" Michael exclaimed.

"No, there's plenty of blame to go around. We were so worried about having lost our *perfect* son that we ignored our *normal* one. We didn't consider what Ken was going through for several months. The brother he idolized kills himself in their room, and Ken finds him." Beth's voice cracked before she continued. "And all we did was argue, fight, stop communicating, ignore him, and then you left us."

"I understand what you're sayin', but I'm not seein' the defenseless part."

"He feels like he can't win, and he wants to. He wants to understand why Patrick killed himself, and none of us ever will. He's tried for several years to be a perfect child, like Patrick was. He tried to fill Patrick's shoes so it'd be like we never lost Patrick. He's been trying to be something or someone he's not to please us, and he thinks he failed because you left. And now, well, now . . ." Beth stalled, this was the most difficult part.

"And now?" Michael inquired impatiently.

"Michael, the reason he planned on running away before this mess with Thornton came along was because—"

"Because we're going to have a baby," Janice readily pointed out.

"No, because you're *not* having a baby." There, she'd said it.

"What?" Michael asked, confused.

"I don't have any idea what you're—" Janice started.

"I know the truth, Janice. You can continue to deny it all you want. It won't take but a phone call to settle it, though. Ken's left the name in his diary."

"He eavesdropped?" Janice demanded explosively.

"What? It's true? You're *not* pregnant?" gasped Michael.

"Michael," Beth interrupted. "Ken heard the conversation between you and Janice when you told her that you . . . well, that you—"

"Might leave," Michael finished softly.

"Yes."

Michael looked directly at Janice. "That's when you told me you were pregnant. You told me that just so I'd stay?"

Janice glared back at him defiantly. Michael shoved the chair back and stood, his face as red as the Christmas-tree lights. "Of all the—"

"Michael, sit back down, please. Now's not the time for that conversation. You can do that when I'm not around. Please." Michael sat back down, but his glacial stare remained aimed at Janice. "In his teenage mind, Ken figured if you were leaving Janice, it meant you were coming home to us. Then with the news of the baby, he lost you all over again."

The expression on Michael's face changed slowly, and he finally broke off his glare. "But I thought you said he knew there wasn't a baby."

"Yes, that's right. Just be patient. It was right after that birthday weekend that he found out about the baby, and that is when his temperament changed. He started becoming sloppy, skipping school, not doing chores, not wanting to be with me or you, and just wanting to be alone. Remember?"

"Yeah."

"Well, Michael, while we thought he was falling apart, he was actually pulling himself together!"

"How can *that* be construed as pulling yourself together?" Janice asked.

Beth ignored Janice and continued looking at Michael. "Ken was finally coming to terms with who he was and who he wasn't. He was trying to stop being Patrick, because you were having another son in Patrick's place. He didn't have to fill that need for you anymore. And still confused as to what you would do, he decided it was time he could just be Kenny—Ken. The way he went about it may be a bit odd, but it was *his* way. He was finally letting go of Patrick, while we thought he was becoming suicidal *like* Patrick! Then, just as he's feeling comfortable finding who he is, he overhears Janice and finds out that you *aren't* pregnant after all, and the pressure was back on. It was too much. He couldn't go back to being someone he wasn't. He couldn't fight the battle inside himself any longer. So he retreated."

"It sounds a bit out there, Beth," said Janice.

"Please, be quiet," Michael said as gently as he could muster. "So he becomes involved with drug dealers?"

"He got involved with that a long time ago, Michael. He's been trying to get out of it. This last escapade was to be his final job."

"So I know how to take care of the Thornton thing, but how do we fix the other stuff?"

"First, you and I need to apologize for ignoring him before, during, and after Patrick's death. We need to let him know that we love *him* for who he is, regardless of the choices he's made. Obviously we need to encourage him to make better choices, but he has to know that we love him no matter what. And then he has to know exactly how you and Janice are doing. He needs to see you stand up for what you truly want or what's right—not what you feel forced into doing. He needs that example *especially* from you."

"How dare you!" demanded Janice.

"Doesn't matter how you sugarcoat it, Janice," stated Beth.

"I can do all that," Michael interrupted. "We'll leave tonight to get Kenny—Ken."

\* \* \*

"What do you mean you can't get to him?" Thornton screamed into the phone. "A woman and a dog and a few cameras? You're joking, right? Forget it! I'll take care of this myself." He slammed the phone down and grabbed his coat.

\* \* \*

"Thanks for your help, Ken," Jessie said as Ken retrieved the last garbage bag full of wrapping paper and boxes to take outside.

"Sure. Those two ever gonna get that TV working?" Ken asked, heading toward the back door.

"Even if it takes all night, I guarantee they'll get it working!" Jessie set about putting everyone's gifts into separate piles on the great-room floor. She picked up the painting Ryan had made and took a longer look at it. *It's not bad, not bad at all,* she thought. There were a few techniques she could teach him, but she could do that without referring to his mistakes in the gift.

"Um, Jessie?" Ken had returned and stood behind her with his hands in his pockets.

Jessie put the painting back into its packaging. "Yeah?" she replied enthusiastically.

"I just wanted to thank you for everything. You guys didn't have to do all that."

"Sounds like a good-bye speech. Planning on going somewhere tonight?"

"Where would I go?"

"Ken, the weather has cleared and you know you were planning on leaving just as soon as we all crashed tonight."

"I can't let you take me home."

Jessie sat on the couch and motioned for Ken to sit in the recliner. He did so reluctantly. "We have to take you home, Ken. Unless we would be placing you in harm's way? If you can convince us that your home situation is abusive, then we would consider doing something different."

"It's nothing they did. It's what I've done."

"Can you tell me?"

The room fell silent. Had she gained his trust yet? "Look, Ken, I've been running for a long time too. I can assure you, it doesn't help. Sooner or later we're forced to face the situation we're in, unless we want to spend the bulk of our lives looking over our shoulder or pushing people away."

"I'm not a coward."

"I'm not saying you are."

"I just want to keep my mother safe, that's all."

"Safe from what?"

"You're a religious person, right? I mean, since you were excited about your new Bible. That means you're religious, right?"

*Where on earth is this coming from?* wondered Jessie. "I believe in God, if that's what you're asking, although I haven't always agreed with how He runs things."

"I've been told that if you kill yourself, you don't go to heaven," Ken said hesitantly.

"Okay. I'm not avoiding the question, but I want to ask you something before I answer it. What's the real reason you read *The Giver* while you were here? There are thousands of books in there, from fantasy to science fiction to westerns, and you chose that one—one you've already read too. I'd like to know why."

"You're going to dissect it, right?"

"Yep." Jessie suddenly felt like Ryan. It was a nice change being on the other side of the couch again.

"I was trying to get the ending."

"And did you?"

"I think the ending was that there *wasn't* an ending."

Jessie watched his slouching body language. "And that depresses you?"

"I think it stinks."

"Why?"

"Jonas goes through all that just to die."

"But I thought it didn't have an ending?"

Kenny rolled his eyes and said nothing.

"I believe Lowry didn't give a specific ending because she wanted the reader to decide for themselves how the story ended. *The Giver* is different things to different people. People bring to the ending their individual sense of hopes and fears. And to you, Jonas died."

"So what does that say about me?"

"I don't know enough about you to say for sure, but I feel it safe to say that you're afraid of something. Maybe your family, maybe yourself—*I* don't know, exactly. But I'm betting *you* do." Jessie watched Ryan walk toward the family room with a childish grin—the TV was no doubt working, she surmised. As Ken looked down at the floor, Jessie shook her head slowly back and forth, indicating to Ryan that he should postpone his entrance. His presence would certainly bring the conversation to an end. Ryan stopped midstep and retreated quietly.

"I don't like my dad much."

"Is he abusive?"

"No. He just likes my brother better than me."

"How come?"

"'Cause he was perfect—" Ken began to look around the room.

"How old was he when he died?"

Ken, a little shocked at her perceptiveness, answered, "Fifteen."

"So he was the age you are now."

"Yeah. And my dad still likes him better, and he's been dead for five years!"

"Have you talked to your dad about that?"

"Are you kidding? No way. He'd think I was a sissy or something."

"So you tell all this to a therapist, then?"

"Not really, no. Started to, but then he looked at his watch and I figured he wasn't really listening anyway. Therapy wasn't for me."

"Therapists make mistakes too, Ken."

"Yeah, whatever."

"How did your brother die?"

"What difference does that make? I don't want to talk about that anyway."

"Did you and he get along okay?"

"He was perfect, remember? He got along with everybody."

This was the part of talking with people that always amazed Jessie—the verbal commitment to one stance and the body language reflecting something totally different.

"What was it about your brother that you didn't like?"

"I didn't say I didn't like him! Are you going to answer my question or not?" It was clear that he was ready to walk out.

"Yes." Jessie knew she had to be careful. It was obvious from his reluctance to talk about his brother's death, along with Ken's earlier comment and discomfort, that he had probably taken his life. What she was not *absolutely* positive of was whether or not Kenny was considering the same. "Suicide has become the third leading cause of death for fifteen- to twenty-four-year-olds. Typical reasons include stress, self-doubt, pressures to succeed, parents' divorce, abuse, feelings of seclusion—not belonging, if you will. The list goes on. What's easy for one person to handle may be an incredible burden to the next. Suicide is too often a result when the pain and despair a person is feeling is bigger than their ability to cope."

"So you're saying suicide is a sickness?"

"A sickness that can be treated."

"But what happens if it's too late? Do you go to heaven or not?"

"Well, suicide is a tragedy because it leaves many victims, not just the one who dies, but also the family and friends who are left behind to face the years of confusion, anger, guilt, rejection, et cetera. Again, the list goes on. I've learned just recently that one purpose for our lives is to prove ourselves to the God who created us. If this is true, then I would say that we have no right to destroy what we didn't create, which is why murder is part of the Ten Commandments. I would also submit that in doing so, we possibly subject ourselves to a severe penalty. But I have to believe that a merciful and perfect God would temper any such penalty with love and justice, and with a deep understanding of what the person was going through and how aware and in control of themselves they were at the time."

She paused to let that sink in. "I talked earlier about how stresses can overload people. Are they deeply depressed? Emotionally traumatized? Was their cry for help unheeded too long? In my opinion, when these things happen, many people lose control and their minds become clouded. They can no longer rationalize between right and wrong. In a way they're no longer accountable for their acts—and would not be condemned for doing what, in their minds, was not a choice but a necessity."

Kenny was meeting her eyes now. "Don't misunderstand me, I believe suicide is wrong, but I don't think God will judge the person who does so *strictly* by the act itself. He will look at all the circumstances surrounding it, for He knows our thoughts, intents, and abilities. He has all the facts, while mortals are simply left with confusion."

Kenny was still quiet, so she finished her thoughts. "So, having said all that . . . would a person who took their own life go to heaven? I can only answer based on what I know *here.* I'm not God, I don't have the big picture, and I certainly don't have the right to pass judgment. The peace that I hold to is the belief in a kind, loving Father who takes care of us when we're sick." The moment the words fell off Jessie's lips, she felt a wave of calming peace sweep through her body. It nearly choked her up, but she continued, "Like I said before, as a loving and caring Father, He will certainly do everything possible to help each of His children to achieve happiness, especially if they are sick." Jessie stopped, momentarily distracted by a scripture she had read earlier.

"Ken, hand me my new Bible, there, would you please?" Using the tabs that marked each book in the Bible, she flipped open to John chapter fourteen and began reading: "Let not your heart be troubled; ye believe in God, believe also in me. In my Father's house are many mansions: if it were not so, I would have told you. I go to prepare a place for you."

Jessie's eyes immediately fell to the twenty-seventh verse on the next page. She continued to read: "Peace I leave with you, my peace I give unto you; not as the world giveth, give I unto you: Let not your heart be troubled, neither let it be afraid."

She paused to savor the beauty and comfort in the words. "I believe, Ken, that the reason it's difficult for the world to offer peace is that true peace can only be found in trusting in the God who created us—putting our faith completely in Him. And we each do that in our own way. You have to find your way. For me, these scriptures have become a guide to peace and to an understanding that God has a unique message for each of us, but we won't know what that is if we don't seek for it."

"So, you think Patrick's in heaven, then? Even though he killed himself?" Ken asked.

"I would think from that scripture that there is a place prepared for him, and since Jesus has prepared it, it must be a wonderful place to be."

"My family's pretty messed up," Ken said, trying to remain in control of his emotions.

"I'm sorry."

"Can I, maybe, talk to you if we want, sometime, like at your office?"

"Absolutely." *What did I just say? I don't have an office!*

"There's something I haven't told you all. I don't think you're in danger or anything, but there is a chance some guys are looking for me."

Jessie was immensely grateful as Ken found the courage to relay his side of the Thornton situation in its entirety. She didn't mention that she was already aware of what was going on or what had happened to his friend. "Well, I think we better talk with Ryan and Gramps and call your parents and get this mess you're in taken care of. Are you ready to do that?"

# CHAPTER 21

Ken found Gramps and Ryan watching a football game on the new TV. "Ryan, sir? My mom wants to talk to you. Good luck understanding her. She's done nothing but cry ever since I said hello." Ryan took the phone, and Gramps waved at Ken to join him.

As he talked to Beth Moon, Ryan also went in search of Jessie to share the conversation he was having. As his knuckles hung motionless inches from her bedroom door, he realized that there was a conversation coming from within. She couldn't be on the phone, he thought, because *he* was. She was talking with someone, though, and rather loudly, and he thought he'd heard crying. Was she asleep and having another nightmare? He checked her door; true to Jessie's nature, it was locked.

Beth was talking nonstop through her sobbing, and not really saying much of substance, so he figured he had a couple more seconds before he'd have to respond. He put the phone down and pressed his ear against the door. Finally understanding, he pulled the phone back to his ear.

* * *

A quiet Christmas afternoon at the cabin found Jessie sipping hot chocolate by the fire, her new set of scriptures on her lap. Gramps, Ryan, Ken, and Nelly were all piled in Gramps's room watching the new TV. It had been an exhausting day, and it wasn't over yet. The Moons and other police personnel would be in town within the hour.

She flipped through the Book of Mormon and felt the smoothness of its pages. She peeked at the Doctrine and Covenants and the Pearl of Great Price, skimming their introductions. While she was curious about the Doctrine and Covenants, she had promised the missionaries she'd continue reading the Book of Mormon until she had finished. She placed the triple combination next to her and picked up the Bible. She opened to John again, and with a red pen underlined the passages she had shared with Ken. She put his name and the date in the margin. Her mind went back to that discussion. There was so much more to what Ken was going through. For the first time in months she wanted desperately to help him, not for her own selfish reasons, but because she truly wanted to help him find peace. Suicide was an unbearable heartache to those left behind. She had just brushed the surface of his feelings, and she found herself hoping that he honestly wanted to continue therapy.

Her thoughts turned to the prayer she'd had after her talk with Ken. That petition for peace was a long time in coming. She had taken all her struggles to the Lord, completely trusting and open to His guidance. In that hour she had begged Him to take the horror of Katie's dying face from her dreams and that she was willing to do whatever He asked of her.

She mourned her mother's suffering from cancer—alone. She decided she would look for support groups that might help her understand more about her mother's last days.

She agonized over her father's bitterness, anger, and abuse, and vowed to find out more about him and what drove him to drink. And then there was the meaning of the items he had left behind in his military ammo can.

She forgave her brothers for their part, knowing that they were young and just doing as their father had taught them. She would find out where their lives had taken them and try to find her half sister.

She forgave herself for not allowing others in, and thanked God for Ryan, Ruth, and Gramps, who had brought so much into her life.

And finally, she asked God to forgive her for having hated Him. After her prayer had finished, she was drawn again to her scriptures. Allowing the book to guide her, she had flipped through the pages. The first book of Corinthians caught her eye and she stopped. She had always liked the writings of Paul. As she skimmed the pages, her eyes fell to the thirteenth verse in chapter ten:

> *There hath no temptation taken you but such as is common to man: but God is faithful, who will not suffer you to be tempted above that ye are able; but will with the temptation also make a way to escape, that ye may be able to bear it.*

The tears of that hour were no longer a result of anger, hurt, or frustration, but ones of gratitude and peace.

"Hey."

The sound of Ryan's voice broke Jessie's concentration. "Hey yourself."

"You up for tonight?" Ryan asked leaning completely into the recliner.

"You bet. Think he'll end up in juvenile detention?"

"Hard to say. Depends on what they want from him. I noticed you were staring at the fire."

"Yes, I was. And yes, you were right. The flames are very hypnotizing."

Ryan grinned. "Can I ask you something?"

"Sure."

"I'm just wondering what brought out the change."

"What change?"

"Feel free to correct me, but wasn't it during the early hours of this morning when you told me that *nothing* had changed. That you were still miserable and confused?"

"Yes."

"So that conversation with Ken that you relayed to me—was everything you said to him entirely motivated to pacify him?"

"No. I meant what I said."

"Then, I repeat, what brought about the change?"

Jessie stood and stretched. Taking a deep breath, she meandered slowly to the fireplace, losing herself again in the flickering flames. "I merely trained the horse."

"You broke a horse?"

"No, I *trained* a horse. While I was staring at the fire after our talk, a memory came back to me. I was seventeen and living with the couple who had horses. For a while they were working a typical Paint—until they tried to train him. You know how it goes, the poor thing fought and fought and fought. The Ericksons were training him like all the rest, only this guy seemed to know he was different—stronger, bigger, and faster. After a couple days of the same routine, they didn't bring him in with the rest of the horses but left him alone in the pasture. They repeated this process for several days, when suddenly, Hunter, the Paint, began mirroring the simple commands he'd been given for days. I tried for a long time to figure out why Hunter gave in, what had happened that made his spirit conform.

"It was later this morning that I realized that Hunter and I aren't very different. My spirit wasn't *broke,* it was *trained.* All I've known how to do, until we met, was to protect myself by fighting and resisting, like Hunter in the beginning. I thought that was the source for my freedom and control. And for a while, it was. I needed to fight and resist to survive, like you've reminded me. I think Hunter did the same thing until he realized *he* was the one causing himself pain and torment—not the Ericksons. Allowing Mr. Erickson to teach him, offering him a more peaceful life, wasn't *losing* control. It was *taking* control. Bottom line—Hunter couldn't survive without his trainer's help. He needed food and water and wasn't going to get very far unless he changed his behavior.

"I understand this all sounds bizarre coming from me, given my stubborn streak. But I've simply realized that most of the pain I deal with these days is, like you suggested, self-inflicted. I don't know much scripture, but along with Job, my mother spoke a bit about the Apostle Paul. So while skimming Corinthians this morning, I found a scripture where the Lord tells Paul, 'My grace is sufficient for thee: for my strength is made perfect in weakness.' I know we all have weaknesses and limitations and that they act as a reminder of our dependence on God, so today I remembered what you said and I took my weaknesses to God, sincerely and humbly, hoping that He'd grant me His grace—and help me move beyond what my natural abilities have allowed.

"So, having said all that, I think I understand the need for 'the test.' I understand that what happened to me, Katie, and our mother wasn't a punishment. And I understand that, although I'm sure He wanted to, God couldn't interfere, either. He couldn't take away my father's freedom of choice . . . or He would cease to be God. He had to allow him to do the things he did, no matter how awful. But what I think God did do, that I hadn't seen before, was take Katie and my mother out of their misery quickly. Neither suffered very long nor were in much pain. Or at least I hope my mother wasn't.

"And as for me, well, while my childhood was a nightmare, I survived. I'm okay. I feel like I've broken the cycle and I've been able to help others. And God brought me . . . you. As little as that may seem," she added with a grin.

Before Ryan could respond, she went on. "It could be much, much worse. Part of my test I think has been to see if I would love God no matter what, and while I failed miserably at that for a long time, He never stopped loving me. I can look back now and see just how good He was to me, even though I was quite indifferent. I didn't want to be trained. I didn't want to learn His ways. I wanted things my way. But I was being trained all along, and by letting go and recognizing that . . ." Jessie let out a huge sigh, "I'm at peace."

Ryan was a little in awe and sat quietly for a moment. Then he looked Jessie in the eye. "You know, even with this tremendous insight, you're going to have difficult times. There are still things to sort out," he said carefully.

"Yes. I know. There are unanswered questions and misunderstood things in my past, but I hope with time and effort I'll find those answers. For now, if only the nightmares ceased, I would consider myself blessed."

"And if they don't?"

"We both know the nightmares were because I was holding it all in and wouldn't let go. But if there *is* more to them, then we'll just have to figure out if they mean anything." Jessie turned toward him and winked.

"We?"

"Sure. Wait here. I'll be right back." Jessie darted up the stairs and ducked inside her room. Before retreating down the stairs, she stole a glance at Gramps and Ken to make sure they were still glued to the TV. She placed a long, wrapped gift in Ryan's arms.

"I thought we were all done with this," he chuckled.

"Last one, I promise."

Ryan stared at the heavy package.

"Go on! Open it. It's not entirely finished. It needs a little work, but I didn't think of it until earlier this morning."

Ryan could see excitement dancing in her eyes. He sat down by the dying fire, crossing his legs. He pulled the paper off to expose a piece of an old log with "Crystal Peaks Ranch" painted on it in calligraphy. "Wow, this is cool."

"You like it, really?"

"Yeah, I do. What is it?"

"You mean, with all that massed intellect, you're not able to figure this one out on your own?"

"Okay, I have an idea, but I want to hear it from you." Ryan set the sign down and leaned closer to Jessie.

"It's the new name for our summer program. I thought since your cabin is at the base of 'Crystal Peak' Mountain, it was a good idea. I know that's not the mountain's true name, but that's what everyone around here refers to it as."

"*Our* summer program?" Ryan grinned.

"Yes, *our*. It'll be sixty-forty, with you being the sixty, of course, since it's your property and your money. So that means you'll have the final say in matters, although I can promise you that if I disagree with anything, I'll put up a good fight."

"As if there was any doubt."

"And I have two conditions."

"Why am I not surprised?"

"First, we can't charge an unrealistic fee."

"I agree. My reason for doing this in the first place is to help those that can't afford it."

"Good."

"And number two?"

"I want Ken to be our first enrollee, and we'll also need to help his family . . . I'm not sure how all that will work. But in Ken's case they all need counseling."

"Yes, they probably do. So you'll sign a five-year contract?"

Jessie smiled sincerely. "No contracts. We're going to do that trust thing you're so big on."

"Hmm, remember the one that goes something like 'you shouldn't go into business with family'?"

"I'm not family, I'm . . . I'm not sure what I am, exactly, but I'm not family." Jessie's heart began to skip beats as Ryan moved closer.

"How about . . . *girlfriend?*" Ryan suggested, spurred on by the fact that she still remained close to his side.

"*Girlfriend* doesn't sound very professional. I'd prefer just *partners,* all around."

Ryan leaned in for a kiss. "Of course you would."

# CHAPTER 22

Beth was breathing hard as she pushed Ken's dresser into the hallway. It was a good thing she had already cleaned his room and hers, she thought to herself. It made the move go smoother. The only piece of furniture that she couldn't handle alone would be her log bed. She would call Trudy's husband for that. She wasn't sure exactly when Ken would be coming home, but the switch would be accomplished just the same.

She had already packed a suitcase for her and Ken. Michael had asked her to pack enough things for a month. Since everything had already been organized, the task was accomplished quickly.

Trudy and her husband Ben came by after everything had been crammed into the hallway. It didn't take long for him and Trudy to help take it apart and put it back together again.

"You could have brought the boys over," said Beth. "I wouldn't have minded."

Trudy carried her end of one log to Ken's old room. "If we'd have brought the little brutes, I would be of no help whatsoever! Besides, they're busy with all their new toys. I don't even think they know we left."

"As long as Pete doesn't try out his new chemistry set, we'll be fine," Ben added.

"The worst that will happen is that Benny will use his new pastels to decorate the walls," Trudy finished.

Ben and Beth carried the last of the bed into the room. It took another thirty minutes to complete the bedroom ensemble and say their good-byes.

Beth promptly situated Ken's things around his new room, then it hit her. *The computer! It's not here!* "Wait a minute, that's ridiculous. It has to be here somewhere."

After making a thorough search of the hall, her old and new room, she called Trudy and Ben. Neither one of them remembered having seen it. Hanging up the phone, she realized she hadn't imagined that noise in the shower and she didn't lock herself in the bathroom. She was locked in on purpose!

* * *

"Tucker Hansen's plowin' like mad out there," shouted Gramps from the kitchen table. He was as eager for the plow's arrival as anyone. He'd asked Tucker Hansen to bring him all the newspapers he'd missed; he was anxious to catch up on the daily crossword puzzles.

"I'm all set," Jessie called, coming down the stairs. "Where are Ryan and Ken?"

"Don't know. That's why I was yelling."

"I bet they're getting the horses ready. Ken's pack is there by the door, and their coats are gone. Are you going to be all right here by yourself for a while? I'm not sure what time Ryan and I'll be back."

"You betcha. Lookin' forward to some peace and quiet."

"You just want that TV all to yourself!" Jessie found an apple in the fridge and was washing it when the front door opened.

Gramps stood to greet their visitor. "Hey there, Tucker. How long'd it take you to get through that mess?"

"Not as long as you'd think. You guys got a couple vehicles stickin' out not too far from here. You want me to dig them out before it gets any darker?"

"Grateful for anything you can do, but tomorrow would be fine given it's Christmas."

"Gotcha." Tucker was in his late fifties, but his height and muscle made Gramps feel short and out of shape. He was the type of man you wanted on hand in a major disaster. "Who's the kid?" Tucker watched as Ryan and Ken brought three horses down the path that Gramps and Ken had shoveled from the cabin to the barn.

"Long story. I'll fill you in later," Gramps answered.

"Hello, Mr. Hansen. Thanks for coming to our aid," said Jessie, reaching for Ken's backpack. "All right, Gramps. I'm headed out. We'll call as soon as we're through tonight and on our way home."

"It's gonna be black out there when you do return. Won't mind if you stay in town for the night."

"Well, *I'd* mind! I want to be *here* for the rest of the holiday week."

\* \* \*

The air was crisp as Beth opened her front door to Michael, Smoot, and Reynolds. Two other uniformed officers followed them in. Each wiped their feet on the rug, removed their coats, and set about their duties.

"You okay?" Michael asked.

"Yes, Michael. I'm fine. I'm sure that's why I was locked in the bathroom."

"Ma'am, while we're waiting for the officers to make their search, I'd like to get your statement," Smoot said.

"I'm gonna look around," Michael said as Beth and Smoot sat down on the couch.

It was only a matter of minutes until Michael returned with news. "Seems they got in through the hall window. The lock was broke."

"It's been broke for about a year," Beth said.

"A year! Why didn't you tell me it needed fixin'?"

Beth remained quiet. She remembered having mentioned it on several occasions. But with all eyes on her and Michael, she wasn't going to bring that up. "What's that?" she said, pointing to a few small devices that one of the police personnel was holding.

"Phone's been tapped and most of the house has been bugged," the officer replied.

"They heard me!" Beth gasped. "Then they would know where Kenny is for sure."

"I know. Are you ready to go?"

* * *

"Michael, what on earth is that?" Beth asked, looking over the passenger seat onto the backseat floor of the car. A large brown box began to shift position.

"Well now, it's my gift for Ken. Neighbors been watchin' it for me for the past week or so, but it's been drivin' them crazy."

Beth leaned over and popped off the lid. Bent on immediate escape, the brown ball of fur jumped up, knocked the box onto its side, and scrambled out. The puppy took two steps before trying to mark its territory. "Oh, no you don't! Michael, pull over!"

Beth reached over quickly and picked up the pup and scurried him out the door. She set him in the snow and watched him disappear in the drifts. "Michael! You got this without consulting me? I know Janice wouldn't allow it, so you must think it's coming to my house. Are you out of your cotton-picking mind?"

Michael smiled as he put on his coat and radioed Smoot and Reynolds that all was well; they had just needed to stop for a few minutes.

"What am I supposed to do with that?" Beth asked.

"Well, let's see—you feed it, water it, play with it, and watch it grow. Besides, I thought you *wanted* a dog! That's all you and Kenny—I mean, Ken—have talked about for years."

"Yes, but—" She had no idea how to argue with that. "Well, it's just that—planning is one thing, but having one show up on your doorstep—and there's the cleaning up of puppy messes and the chewing of things. I hadn't worked myself up to this." As the pup rolled around in the snow, Beth's countenance softened. "Ken *will* adore him, but I wouldn't want him to think you did this just to keep him here."

"Kid only wanted two things for Christmas. And by the looks of that box in the middle of his room, I'd say he got them both. So what if he considers it bribery?"

A patch of snow began making its way toward them. As it closed in, the puppy began to bounce and shake about in an attempt to extricate itself from the wintry quicksand. Michael picked up the pup and brushed him off. "Wonder what he'll name him."

"Most likely Goliath."

"Goliath? Not sure this thing's gonna get *that* big."

"Wouldn't matter if it was a poodle. It'll be Goliath." Beth looked around anxiously. "I want to go, Michael. We need to get to Ken."

\* \* \*

"Hey, you're not doing too badly there, Ken. You been on a horse before?" Ryan called, nudging Steel closer to Ken, who was riding Tawny. Jessie was in the lead on Joanie.

"No, sir. Just did a lot of reading."

"Well, it's paid off. Stay in the center of the path Hansen made for us. Tawny's likely to wander if you hold those reins too loose. She's gentle, but adventurous."

"Yes, sir."

It wasn't long before the small country town came into view. "Would it be okay if I went on ahead?" Ken asked over his shoulder to Ryan.

"You know how to stop her if she gets going too fast?" Ryan asked.

"I think so."

"Okay. Keep a close watch on the path and meet us at the sheriff's office. It's on the south side of the street about half a mile in once you get into town."

"Got it!" Ken was off. He maneuvered past Jessie and didn't even bother waving.

"Well, he's a bit enthusiastic, considering where we're headed," Jessie said as Ryan pulled in alongside her.

"Think he'll run off?"

"No. If he does, I'll hang up my license for good," Jessie said. "But we better keep up. There's always the possibility Thornton's in town waiting."

"Look at him go!" Ryan said. "He's feeling it, Jessie."

Jessie knew exactly what Ryan was talking about. Ken had become one with Tawny, experiencing that surge of exhilaration and freedom that comes from sharing, however briefly, the power and grace of an animal that you have truly come to care for.

* * *

The sun was setting before Ken as he flew down the path toward town. The wind had picked up, gusting through his hair as well as Tawny's mane as bits of snow were thrown into the mix by the rhythmic beat of her lengthening stride. Ken felt an intensifying sense of control and invulnerability. Tawny, he knew, would do whatever he wanted. It was almost as if he had only to think it and she would respond—an outgrowth of his own will. The euphoria grew ever stronger within him. *This is better than any drug.* Suddenly he felt his mind peeling like an onion. Deadened layers were stripped away, his inner thoughts exposed to the warmth and brilliance of the sun. Things that seemed clouded before, he now saw clearly. He realized intuitively that in general, things had not changed, but that it was his relationship to them—his choices regarding them—that was the freeing agent. He suddenly perceived that yielding to the love of those around him, and more importantly to what he felt intrinsically within him to be right and true, would somehow solve the problems he faced.

* * *

"Kenny!" Beth threw her arms around her son's neck and held on tight, the intensity of a mother's love in full bloom.

"Mom, Mom, I can't breathe! Okay, Mom, it's okay now, you can let go."

"Let the boy breathe," Michael's voice came softly from behind her, understanding woven into his tone.

"Okay, okay," replied the now-sobbing mother. She forced herself back from him and busied herself with the removal of her coat. Smoot and Reynolds shut the door to the sheriff's office after they trailed in.

Ken made the introductions. "Mom, Dad, this is Ryan and Jessie. Gramps didn't come. He was the one that found me. Ryan's his grandson." They all took turns shaking hands.

"Ken, your hair!" exclaimed Beth. "It's normal! I mean . . . not that orange was so bad. It's just that . . ."

Kenny's cheeks flushed a pale pink as he shoved his hands into his pockets. "It's fine, Mom, no big deal."

"We want to thank you for taking care of our son," Michael began. "We can pay for anything that he used, or any expenses that you incurred."

"That's not necessary," Jessie graciously replied.

"Hate to interrupt this reunion, but we'd better get started. We've got lots of work to do," Sheriff Jensen said. He'd been pulled away from his family on Christmas and quite obviously wasn't too thrilled about it.

"Right," said Michael. "Suppose we better get the official stuff out of the way, first. Ken, Officer Reynolds here is going to show you some pictures. We want you to point to anybody you talked with or encountered since this business started." Beth, Ryan, and Jessie removed themselves from the circle and seated themselves in a small grouping of chairs away from the unfolding police business.

Michael continued, "Tell us all you know. Afterwards, Officer Smoot will take some information about you and you'll make a formal statement. We're taping this for the record, okay? Any questions?"

Ken sat down at the sheriff's desk. "No, sir."

Reynolds pulled out several photos from a manila envelope. He laid them neatly in front of Ken, and everyone waited anxiously.

"This guy I'm guessing is Thornton. Only I've never really met him. Just heard him talked about a lot. He was in the backseat of the car with him," Ken said, pointing to the photo of a dead man's face.

"Ken, let me verify. You saw this man, Alan Phillips, in a car with this man, Randolf Thornton?" asked Officer Reynolds.

"Yes, sir. This guy, Phillips, had his hands tied behind his back, and his mouth was duct-taped. Thornton was sitting next to him, blowing cigar smoke out the window."

"And when was that, exactly?"

"It was just before Christmas break. Don't know the exact date, but I think I have it on my computer."

"Fine. Do you recognize anybody else?" asked Reynolds.

"These two guys were standing around the car that last day. That was my last run, I swear." The room fell silent.

"Go on, son," Michael urged.

"These guys never said anything to me. This guy here is the one I talked to." Ken pointed to a large-faced man with a head full of black, curly hair. Ken spent the next few minutes replaying the entire events of that day.

"So, Kenny, it wasn't a bust gone bad. We think they want you because you witnessed Greg's murder and can place Thornton in the car with Phillips."

"It's Ken," Michael quickly corrected Officer Smoot.

Ken looked up at his father, surprised. "But I didn't actually see Greg get shot. I mean the last I saw was him waving his hands at me. Then I heard shots and ran like crazy toward town. I didn't think to wait for Greg. I just figured he was running too. Am I going to jail?"

Sheriff Jensen's response was to Michael. "I'm sure the D.A.'s office will be lenient, maybe even give him immunity if he testifies against Thornton."

"I have to go to court?" Ken asked, looking at his dad.

"It won't be that bad, son. But we can't take you home right now. They'll be watching the house. Thornton's going down if you testify, and he knows it. The chief pulled some strings and has gotten some help from Denver, since the safehouse is within their jurisdiction. They'll also be placing some uniforms nearby at our request."

"How come he waited so long to come after me?" Ken asked no one in particular.

"Who knows how this guy thinks. It may have been because he'd already ordered two murders back-to-back and a third would have resulted in a lot more pressure to bring him down," said Reynolds. "Once you ran away, you made it easier for him to come after you."

"Whether you testify is up to you, son. You're old enough to make this decision," Michael said.

Ken didn't need any time to think it over.

# CHAPTER 23

Before the sheriff's office completely cleared out, Jessie spoke to Michael and Beth. "We understand you're on a tight schedule, but Ryan and I were wondering if we could have a few minutes of your time."

"Of course," Beth said. The four of them walked to an adjacent room where they could have a little more privacy.

Once behind closed doors, Ryan pulled out the gun Ken had carried and handed it to Michael, along with the bullets.

"Do you think he intended to use it on himself?" Beth asked.

"At first, I have to admit, I wasn't sure. But now I'm convinced he brought it along in case he needed to protect himself from Thornton's men," Ryan said.

"He talked to you?" Beth was genuinely surprised.

"Not to me. He connected with Jessie."

"So you don't think he's suicidal?" Michael asked Jessie.

Pausing before her response, Jessie said, "I think he's looking for a way to break free from an incredible amount of guilt he's placed on himself, but no, I don't believe he will take his own life. It's going to take a lot to work through his feelings, and we were hoping you'd let us help—as soon as this ordeal with Thornton is over."

"I think that should be up to Ken," Beth replied.

There was a knock at the door, and Reynolds walked in. "Better get going, Lieutenant."

"Yeah, okay," Michael said. Then he turned to Jessie and Ryan. "We'll be in contact with you later. But thanks so much for everything you've done." Then all four of them left the room, and Ryan and Jessie watched as both cars pulled away. The town was quiet. It felt eerie, like an abandoned ghost town. The only voices were those echoing from the local bar; a few intoxicated people were taking turns walking down the narrowly shoveled walkways.

Jessie shivered, and Ryan put his arm around her waist. "He's going to be okay."

* * *

Michael watched Ken through his rearview mirror. "You look exhausted, son."

"It's been a long day," Ken replied.

"It's been a long *week*," Beth added.

"You guys mad?" Ken asked tensely.

"Mad doesn't even begin to express our feelings, Ken," Beth quickly responded.

"And how come you're calling me Ken?"

Beth's eyes shot a look of helplessness at Michael. She didn't want Ken to know she'd read his journal.

"Does it bother you?" Michael asked.

"No. Just wondering. And how'd you guys find out about Thornton, anyway?"

"Actually, Jen told me," Beth said.

"Jen?"

"Yes. She told me about you and Greg. She was threatened at gunpoint by Thornton's men. They wanted to know where you were. She came to warn me about them."

"Is she okay?" Ken asked.

"She's fine, son," Michael answered. He noticed Beth hadn't mentioned the incident in their home. "I told her that you'd call when this was all over. Can't be talkin' to her before then. By the way, it's bad manners to listen in on other people's phone conversations. That's how you found out Jan wasn't really pregnant the weekend you came for your birthday."

Beth's eyes narrowed as they focused on Michael.

"And it's bad manners to read someone else's diary!" retorted Ken. "How did you guess my password?"

"It was me, Ken, not your father," Beth tried softly. "And it took hours before I figured it out."

"I can't believe you read my diary!"

"And *I* can't believe you got mixed up with drug dealers!" Michael boomed.

"Okay, okay, that's enough. We've all made mistakes," Beth said. "The important thing is that nothing has happened that can't be fixed."

"Patrick can't be fixed," Ken said.

"No. You're right there. That can't be fixed," Beth said.

"You guys never even tried!"

"Ken, there weren't *any* signs of Patrick's unhappiness, or depression, or whatever it was he was feeling, at least that we could see. There wasn't anything out of the ordinary that led us to even consider the possibility that he would kill himself. He didn't take our gun and run away. Ken, if we would've had any reason to believe Patrick was suffering, we would have tried to help him."

"Dad should have known!" There, he'd said it after all these years.

"What?" Michael boomed.

"You guys did everything together. If you were so close, you should have known! I heard you that day in your room, talking with Mom. You said you wished God had taken me instead of Patrick!"

Beth motioned for Michael to pull off to the side of the road. Smoot was immediately on the radio asking what was wrong. Michael relayed that they were just tired and needing a short break. Then he turned to face his son. "I never said that."

Ken had forced himself to calm down. His voice low and shaky, he said, "Yes, you did."

"Look, Ken, I don't remember ever saying something like that. But if I did, well, I was messed up when your brother died."

"So that's it? That's your apology? 'I was messed up when your brother died'? News flash—so was I! And so was Mom. But hey, we at least tried to face it. You, well, you just left us!"

Michael put both hands on the steering wheel and put the car back in gear. "Now's not a good time, son."

"That's not surprising. There's never a *good* time."

"Look, right now I gotta concentrate on keeping you physically safe. I gotta be a step ahead of Thornton. I can't talk about Patrick the way we all need to. I've already promised your mom that we'd all get some help from professionals as soon as we can. That's gonna have to do for now. Okay?"

"You going to stay with Jan?"

"I'm not ready to answer that either, son. I have decided, however, that as soon as I get back, I'm packing my things and heading to Uncle Bill's."

The silence was thick. Finally Ken asked, "Can we go to Jessie and Ryan for help?"

"If that's what you want," Michael replied. "Your mom and I will discuss it later."

A slight whimper broke what had been several minutes of silence. "What's that?" Ken asked, looking down at the now-undulating blanket on the floor opposite him.

"That would be your Christmas present from your father. He picked it out over a week ago," Beth answered, surprised the puppy had slept this long.

The possibilities were written all over Ken's face. He threw his seat belt off and leaned across the seat. He turned the cardboard box around and was met with paws and a wagging tail. "No way! This is really for me?"

Michael was relieved to have a diversion. "It really is."

"What kind is he?"

"He's part shepherd and part whatever-jumped-over-the-fence. He's a mutt, son, but a good-lookin' one."

"Do I get to keep him inside, Mom?"

"Yes, he can stay in the house," Beth surrendered. "But you're responsible for all his puppy needs, which we'll go over later. I hope we're headed someplace he can have a dog."

\* \* \*

It was late when Ryan and Jessie arrived at the cabin. Gramps was snoring in the great room, Nelly at his feet. "Should we wake him?" asked Jessie.

"No. He'll sleep fine there. I'm headed to the loft to unwind. You want to join me?"

"Sure."

Refreshment in hand, Ryan and Jessie headed to the loft. Nelly followed them and laid her bulk at Ryan's feet.

Barkley made a quick exit from off the back of the couch and lunged toward the safety of Jessie's room.

"What a Christmas, huh?" Ryan said, pushing the recliner to its fullest potential with Nelly perturbed at having been shoved out of the way.

"I'll say."

"Tired?"

Jessie yawned. "Exhausted is more like it."

"Are you headed to your house tomorrow, since the path is clear?" Ryan asked.

"Yeah. But I'm coming back at dinner for leftovers and a movie. Unless of course you have other plans?"

Ryan smiled. "No other plans. Dinner and a movie sound great. I have something for you."

"What? I thought we were all done with the gift giving!"

Ryan stood and leaned on the staircase before heading to his office. "I wanted us to be alone when I gave this to you. I'll be right back."

Jessie suddenly became anxious. *Oh no, what if it's a ring? He wouldn't ask me to marry him. Not now. Please don't be a ring, please—*

"Here," Ryan said simply as he handed Jessie a large manila envelope.

"What's this?" she asked, relieved.

"Open it."

Jessie slowly opened the envelope and pulled out a file folder. It was marked *Samantha LeAnn Borne.* "Ryan! This is my file from Family Services. How in the world did you get this?"

Ryan winked. "It pays to be the best in your field. All kinds of people can owe you favors."

"How long have you had this?"

"A couple weeks."

"But Ryan, you had to have broken several laws to get this."

"Hmm. If it's going to bother you—" Ryan reached for the envelope.

"No, no, no! *You* stole it—not me!"

"That's harsh." Ryan yawned and stretched. "Well, I'll give you and your past some time to yourselves. Don't stay up too late."

"Ryan?"

"Yeah?"

"Merry Christmas." She grinned, tilted her head, and gave her lashes a flit.

Ryan leaned forward and gave her a gentle kiss on the cheek. "Merry Christmas."

\* \* \*

Ken was asleep when Michael pulled in the driveway of the safehouse. Visibility had been unobstructed, and the roads were clear enough to make travel comfortable. As far as they could tell, they hadn't been followed. It was in the middle of the night, and there had only been a few cars on the road, none of which had looked suspicious.

The house was a large, secluded rambler set on four acres, Michael had been informed, equipped with six bedrooms, three baths, and a large fenced-in yard that was currently buried under snow. After the suitcases were carried in and everybody chose a room for themselves, Michael woke Ken and Goliath in the backseat.

Ken rubbed his eyes and picked up the puppy. "We're there?"

"Yes, son. Everyone is settled in. Gave you and the mutt the largest room. Don't plan on getting too much sleep, though. Looks like he's ready to play." Goliath was squirming his way out of Ken's grasp.

Ken put him down in the driveway and watched his new friend explore his surroundings. It seemed as if Goliath knew he had a lot of territory to cover and was determined to do so, but Ken was exhausted and finally picked up the little guy and carried him into the house. He took the next hour to get settled in his room. He gave Goliath the attention the dog was so adamant about being given, then he settled himself into bed with the puppy curled up next to him.

Early the next morning, Michael found Beth removing dustcovers and tarps from the living room and dining room furniture. The only information she got out of Michael was that the homeowners were on a sabbatical and wouldn't return until spring. "Sleep okay?" he asked.

"No. How about you?"

"Not at all. Think I got the smallest bed in the house. It's a twin."

Beth smiled. "Okay. Compared to you, I slept all right."

Michael reached over to help pull a tarp off the dining room table. "Smoot and Reynolds?"

"Up an hour ago. Smoot is making a check of the neighborhood, or something like that, and Reynolds was working on some kind of alarm system."

"Sounds about right. I'm going to need to head out by noon."

"I was hoping you could stay, Michael."

"You know I can't, Beth. I need to be closer to Thornton and the case. You'll be safe here. I wouldn't leave if I didn't think you were in good hands. Smoot makes lousy coffee, but she's the fastest and most accurate shot around. Reynolds's instincts have always been right on, so if you do what he says, you'll be fine."

"I know. It's just that I'd feel better having you here, and so would Ken, I think."

"I'll call every day. We need to set up a code word for both you and Ken before I leave. Only you will know yours, and Ken his. Not even Smoot and Reynolds can know. Understand?"

If Beth had been uneasy about Michael leaving before, she was even more so now. She moved to the kitchen and began pulling things out of drawers to put in the dishwasher. "I thought you trusted them."

"I do. It's standard procedure. There are a number of reasons for the code words to be kept silent. I don't want to get into all that right now, but just trust me on this. I may have been a lousy husband and a terrible father, but I'm a good cop, okay?"

Beth bent over to load the dishwasher. "Okay. And, you weren't a lousy husband, you just stopped trying."

Ken walked into the kitchen carrying Goliath. "Okay, I don't know about you guys, but I didn't sleep at all. Anyway, we can take turns at night with him, right?" Goliath began chewing on his forepaw.

* * *

It was still dark outside, but the clock read 7:00 A.M. when Ryan entered the kitchen. Jessie was sitting at the table, sorting through a pile of papers from her file.

"Are you *still* awake or just getting up?" Ryan asked.

"Yeah, well, you know. I think I fell asleep for a couple of hours."

Ryan poured two glasses of eggnog, setting one in front of Jessie. "How far have you gotten?"

"I stared at it for a long time before I opened it. I came across a copy of the letter that my mother left. The state must have made a copy of the original and kept it with all the other copies they made. Amazing. I could have had access to this once I turned eighteen—all those years of wondering why my mother left might have been avoided. Here, look at these." Jessie shuffled through the papers to reveal a few black-and-white photographs. "This is my mother, and that's Katie."

"And who's the adorable little redhead?"

"Yeah, yeah, yeah. Look. There are the lilacs!" She pointed to the bushes growing wildly behind her mother, sister, and herself.

"Wow. Those *were* huge. What's this?" Ryan picked up a sealed envelope.

"I'm not sure. There's nothing written on the outside."

"You haven't opened it?"

Jessie took a deep breath. "No."

"Okaaaay. Who's this?" Ryan picked up a picture of a woman sitting in a porch swing.

"That's Loretta Pine."

"The sunbather you could see from your basement window?"

"Yes. I'm still embarrassed at that thank-you letter I wrote."

"Like I told you before, you thanked the one person who provided you, however remote, with a sense of security during the bleakest time of your life."

"I suppose."

"Ah, your profile."

"Yeah, I read that. There are some leads I'll look into after the holidays. My mother's lawyer is listed. That's where I'll start. Since I'm an adult now and my mother is deceased, I'm hoping he won't see the harm in divulging any information he may remember.

"My stepmother's last known address is also there. I'll look her up and see if she'll talk about anything she knows regarding my father's past. It'll give me the opportunity to find out about my stepbrothers and half sister too."

Ryan looked at Nelly, who had sauntered in and lain down by her food bowl. "Nelly's going through withdrawal."

"I think she misses Ken. She wandered the cabin all night, sniffing at all the doors."

"I'm going into Denver today to pick up some supplies. You want to come along? I'm taking one of Gramps's trucks."

"He's letting you drive one of his trucks?"

"Well, the roads will be cleaner once we get out of the valley. They've been out there since the storm broke."

Jessie closed her file folder and sipped at her eggnog. "You know, I think I'm going to head home and do a few things there."

Ryan reached over and rubbed her hands. "You're going to make me drive there and back all alone?"

She smiled. "Yep."

* * *

Ken walked into the room his mother was staying in next to his. He watched as she pulled the sheets off the bed. The washing machine had been running all morning. "TV only has one good channel."

"As long as it's not one of those music-video channels, we'll be just fine."

"No, it's a lousy news channel."

"Where's the puppy?"

"He's still sleeping."

"Don't let him sleep too long this afternoon. And wear him out before bed, then maybe you'll get a little better sleep tonight." Beth carried the sheets to the laundry room and put the washer to use one final time. "Here, help me fold these towels," Beth said to Ken. "Then it'll be time to make everyone some lunch."

"How come I haven't seen Officers Smoot or Reynolds?"

"Oh, they're around, trust me. Simply say their names loud enough and they'll jump out from wherever they are."

"How long do we have to stay here?"

"We stay until your dad tells us otherwise. I'm certain he's meeting with the D.A. today. They've probably picked up Thornton and his buddies and are setting things in motion. With any luck at all, Thornton will plead guilty, you won't have to testify, and we can all go home."

"I don't think he's the type to just give in," said Ken.

"You're right. I'm not." The throaty voice sent chills through Beth.

# CHAPTER 24

Gramps came in the back door of the cabin carrying firewood. "Hey, look what I found outside," he said to Jessie.

"Well, hello," Jessie said to Michael.

"I was on my way to the city and had a couple things on my mind—if you've got a few minutes?"

"You bet. Here, let me take your coat. We can talk in Ryan's office."

"No need if you wanna stay here where it's warmer," Gramps offered. "I'm headed down to the Gas N Go, to see if Cal needs any help. I'm just gonna grab my coat and I'll be off."

"All right, then. Please, Michael, have a seat. Can I get you anything to drink?"

"No, nothing, thanks."

Jessie sat down in the recliner as Michael's large frame seemed to take up the entire couch. "Ken's reference to Ryan's *cabin* was a bit off the mark," Michael said as his eyes wandered around the expanse before him.

"It's how Ryan's always referred to it. It's certainly not descriptively accurate, but the phrase seems to have a way of sticking. So how is Ken?" she asked.

"Doin' okay for now. But that's why I'm here. Seems he wants to talk to you and Ryan when this is all over. Next time I see him, I want him to know I'm taking all this seriously. I wanted to know how much you guys charge and when you're available and all that." His eyes strayed again to his surroundings. *I hope I can afford this,* he thought.

"I'm glad he wants to see us. He's a good kid, Michael—bright for his age. Confused and hurt, too."

"Yeah, well, he hasn't had a great childhood. Guess that's mostly my fault."

"Placing blame isn't going to do any of you any good. What's done is done, and it can't be changed. But what can change is how you're all communicating *now* and what you want for your futures."

"So you'll meet with us, then?"

"Absolutely. In fact, Ryan and I have an idea—for Ken, especially. We were going to wait till this Thornton thing was over to discuss it with you, but since you're here, I might as well give you something to think about. What we'd like to do, with your approval, is have Ken come for a six-week stay this summer. He would earn his keep by working with the horses, in the gardens, and helping with some remodeling we need to do—so no monetary fee. After Ken's been with us for a few weeks, we would meet with you and Beth, and your current wife, if you wished."

"Beth and I would be able to see him, then, when we came out?"

Jessie made a mental note that Michael was not including his current wife in his plans for Kenny. "It would be better to meet with you and Beth away from the cabin. The purpose of the separation would be to isolate him for a time from relationships of reliance so he has a better opportunity to face and deal with his issues on his own. From the discussions I've had with him, I feel he wants to talk things through, he just doesn't know how or where to begin. He starts, but then changes the subject. Somehow he has gotten the idea that he shouldn't have the need to talk about feelings and that he should be able to easily deal with what's happened on his own. But suicide is huge, and now this episode with Thornton—he's not going to get over it by simply ignoring it." She wondered if Michael would realize *he* was the major contributor to Ken's conflicts regarding communication.

"The bottom line is that you can't fix this for Ken. He has to do it on his own, but if the three of you want to find some sense of peace in all this, Ryan and I can hopefully show you how. Ultimately it will be up to you to make certain choices, but we can help get you on the right path. He'd be allowed a phone call every two weeks, and of course he can write as much as he wants. We can't *force* you to stay away from your son," Jessie continued, "but please understand that it could jeopardize his progress, or at the very least slow it down."

"That would be hard for Beth but it makes sense, I guess. We'd have to look into it more. You got a license for this place?" the cop in Michael asked.

"We're both licensed therapists, but our summer program is still in embryo. One of the reasons there wouldn't be a fee for Ken is because not everything is officially completed yet. We're hoping to have everything in order by spring, but there's so much to do it may take longer."

Michael's eyes narrowed in concern. "So my kid's your first client?"

"He would be our first client together, yes. But we've each had many years of experience. Michael, I know we can help him," Jessie said tenderly. "And we'd meet with the three of you together before the summer. Ryan and I haven't solidified our rates, but I promise you, it'll be only a nominal fee for those sessions. What we want for our future is to be able to help kids. It isn't about money."

Michael stood and gathered his coat. "I know how much you people make, so I appreciate the offer. I'll talk it over with Beth and Ken and get back to you." Michael stopped short. "That's it!" He frantically pulled out his cell phone.

* * *

Ken instinctively moved in front of his mother. "Get out." His voice wasn't even shaking. Beth had no idea where his courage came from. She wanted to run.

"Bold words from such a boy," Thornton said as he pointed his .09 millimeter toward them. "Why don't we move across the way, maybe get away from these big, open windows?"

"I think we're fine right here," insisted Ken, folding his arms across his chest. Beth's heart rate intensified. She knew this man wouldn't take the back-talking, and they could be dead within seconds. She looked around cautiously, trying to come up with some kind of plan. The laundry room had an outside entrance. Maybe she could run toward Thornton and push him to the outside. Surely Smoot and Reynolds would hear the commotion?

Thornton watched Beth's eyes fix on the door. "Oh, in case you're wondering, Mrs. Moon, your officers ran into some 'technical' difficulties working on the alarm system. I'm afraid they won't be joining us. Now move." Thornton motioned Ken to go first, then Beth. He held the gun at Beth's temple to ensure Ken's cooperation as they worked their way up the stairs.

*This can't be happening,* Beth thought. *All these years with Michael on the force and nothing has ever happened. Why now? I can't lose another son.* The tiny sound of a familiar tune brought Beth back into focus.

Thornton waited until the three of them were in Ken's room before he answered what must have been Reynolds's cell phone. "Reynolds," Thornton said into the tiny phone.

Beth gasped. Thornton sounded *exactly* like Reynolds. *We're dead. We're dead,* she kept repeating over and over in her mind. She was becoming dizzy. Ken saw the beads of perspiration forming on her forehead. He leaned over and whispered, "It's going to be okay, Mom."

"Alarm system is up and going," Thornton continued in Reynolds's voice. He never once took his eyes off Ken and Beth.

Beth considered screaming but knew her son's life would definitely end at that moment. He hadn't killed them yet, and she hadn't seen any other men around, so maybe, just maybe she could save her son's life, regardless of whether it meant losing hers.

"She's right here." Thornton handed Beth the phone and moved directly behind Ken with his gun pointed at the boy's head.

Beth drew in a deep breath and tried to calm her nerves. "Hello, Michael. Yes, we're doing just fine. Working on the laundry still. You did? How did that go?"

Beth listened for a couple minutes while Michael rehearsed his conversation with Jessie. Every now and then she nodded and said, "uh-huh." She waited for the question. She wanted so desperately to give the code word. Would he forget? No, she told herself. *He's a good cop. He's a good cop.* "What?" There it was. She tried not to show her anxiety. "No, Mac's been sleeping most of the day. He likes it under the dining room table."

Ken knew exactly what was going on. *Mac* must have been her code word. Now they would have to stall. Help would be on its way. Would he have enough time? Thornton signaled to Beth to end the conversation.

"Well, okay then, we'll talk to you tomorrow," she said, her whole body visibly shaking. "Okay. Bye."

Thornton walked around and took the phone from Beth, keeping his eyes on them the whole time. "Nicely done, Mrs. Moon."

"You're not going to kill my son," she said, grabbing Ken and throwing him behind her. She couldn't believe her own strength and will.

"You watch far too many movies. The bad guys get things done and get away a great deal more in real life."

"Someone else saw you with the man you murdered, and they saw you kill him and Greg." Ken stepped out slowly from behind Beth.

Thornton eyed Ken carefully, scrutinizing him for signs of a stall. "Well, they would have seen a vision, then, as I didn't personally kill Greg and Phillips. You'll never find forensic evidence connecting me with the murder weapon."

"So why are you so worried, then? Your high-priced lawyers can't get you off?"

Who was this boy beside her? Beth wondered. She was so frightened that she could feel sweat gather and run between her shoulder blades. She tried to put her mind to better use. *Look around, Beth, look around. What is in here that I can use to my advantage?*

"Oh, they can get me off. But you know how it is, loose ends and all that. With you dead, they can't put me at the crime scene. I can open shop somewhere else. I'm ready for warmer weather, anyway. This winter stuff is chaffing my skin. So kid, as I assume you're just stalling, let's get this over with."

*I need more time—* Beth's thoughts were interrupted as Goliath rounded the corner and entered Ken's room.

Thornton's attention was distracted for a split second. That's when Ken made his move. He lowered his head and plunged into Thornton's stomach, forcing him to the wall and knocking the gun from his grip. Beth got a hold of her senses in time to lunge for it. Thornton and Ken were wrestling when a shot sounded. Ken broke free of Thornton's hold and staggered backward. He righted himself, then lifted the gun from his mother's trembling hands. "She's not afraid to use this, but I'm a much better shot. 'Course, I'd be more likely to shoot you in both legs and hands just to make you miserable. Either way, it isn't gonna bother me any."

Thornton slid to the floor and looked around. "My men heard that shot, and this place will be flooded any second."

"Nope. Afraid not," said Smoot. She entered the room quickly, followed by three other police officers. "You know, if you're going to shoot a cop, you ought to do it in the head." She took the gun out of Ken's hands. "We wear vests, you know."

"See, it pays to watch movies," Ken added snidely.

"Cuff him," said Smoot. "And this time, make sure his rights are read correctly, loud and clear."

Thornton spit at Ken. "I'll get out soon."

"Yeah, whatever."

The officer cuffing Thornton took the opportunity to push his face toward the door so that he couldn't respond. Then he read Thornton his rights—correctly.

Beth was sitting on Ken's bed, shaking. Ken walked over with a glass of water. "Here, Mom." He sat next to her and started rubbing her back. "It's all over. See, I told you it would be okay."

Beth started to bawl. She didn't care that the room was filled with people. She just let it all out. It wasn't just Thornton, it was Patrick, and Michael, and Ken all rolled up into one long cry.

"The lieutenant's on his way, Mrs. Moon," Smoot said softly.

"How did you . . . I mean . . . how did the officers get here . . .?" Beth said in between shallow breaths.

"When I came to, I realized none of Thornton's men were watching me. They figured I was dead, so I started making my way up here. The officers the lieutenant stationed next door took care of them after they were alerted. Sorry it took us so long to get to you."

"How did he find us?" Beth asked.

"No way to know for sure, ma'am. There were only a handful of police personnel who knew where you were. I'm sure that will be investigated."

Ken looked out his bedroom window as another car arrived. "Dad's here. I'm going out to meet him, okay?"

Beth nodded as she blew into the tissue Ken had brought her from the bathroom.

Ken ran outside in time to see his dad lifting the white sheet off Reynolds's face. Ken had assumed that since Smoot had made it, Reynolds had too. He stopped in his tracks, then steeled himself and moved on. As he passed the police cars, he saw Thornton and his men handcuffed in the backseats. "Dad!" Ken yelled.

Michael placed the sheet back over the dead officer's face and ran to his son. "Ken!" Ken threw himself into his father's chest and breathed deeply. "You okay?" Michael asked.

"Yeah, Dad, I'm fine."

"Mom?"

"She's fine too. She keeps crying, though."

"Yeah, women do that. Especially mothers. Let's go see her."

Ken looked over at the silent ambulance as it left. "Reynolds died because of me."

"It was his job, son. It's what we do. We all know the risks. Now, you're going to need to fill me in on the whole story."

# CHAPTER 25

Jessie rose from her couch to answer the knock at the door. "Hey, Ryan. Looks like you finally got your truck! Does that mean you wrecked Gramps's?"

Ryan leaned in and kissed her on the cheek. "I missed you too."

Jessie closed the door as Ryan walked to the fireplace rubbing his hands together. "I did miss you," she replied tenderly.

"Uh-huh. So how are things?" He began removing his parka and boots.

Jessie pointed to the tabby sitting on top of the couch like a statue. "Barkley is clearly happy to be back home."

"And you?"

Jessie curled herself into the recliner. "Well, I like having my space. But I must admit, I do miss being around . . . Gramps."

"Oh, you miss being around Gramps, huh?" Ryan sat in the wooden rocking chair across from her.

"Yes, I do. Would you like some warm apple cider?"

"Absolutely."

Within a minute Jessie was back with the cider. She leaned over Ryan's shoulder and handed him Rebecca's Book of Mormon. "Here. And, thank you."

Ryan rubbed it gently, then slipped it under the rocker. "Must feel good to finally have your own."

Jessie returned to the recliner. "Actually it feels odd letting go of that one."

"I'm in no hurry to get it back if you want to keep it."

"No, it belongs with you. I'll get used to my new one."

"I stopped in and saw Ken on my way back."

"Really? So, how is he?"

"They're all going to be fine. They need time and tools . . . time will come naturally, and the tools we can help with."

"So, they said he could come then, for sure?" Jessie asked excitedly.

"Yeah. And the kid got a dog for Christmas."

"No kidding. What kind?"

"Shepherd mix." Ryan grinned. "Lots of energy—I don't think Ken's getting a whole lot of sleep. He asked if he could bring him along this summer."

"And you said . . . ?"

"Why not? It'll be good for Nelly to have a friend."

Jessie sighed as she looked over at her cat, which was pawing at something in the air. "Two dogs? Poor Barkley. Hey, I've actually been keeping up on the news. I heard Thornton took a plea bargain, so no trial."

"Yep. He pled guilty to all the drug-trafficking charges, accessory to murder, and conspiracy to commit murder. Turns out his men weren't as loyal as he had hoped. He should have been charged with at least two counts of first-degree murder, too, but those were dropped in exchange for the other. Thornton also named Reynolds's shooter. Someone was going down for killing a cop. Thornton got a thirty-year-to-life sentence, as opposed to the death penalty. He'll be close to eighty when and if he lives long enough to get out."

"Good." Jessie's face turned sullen. "You think he'll try to hurt Ken anyway? The man still has contacts."

"He'd be stupid to do that. Even if he made it an accident, Michael would spend the rest of his life making sure he paid for it. I don't think Ken's worried about it. But we'll explore that when he comes." Ryan slid his hands through his hair. "Hey, you up for a sleigh ride tomorrow night around five o'clock? Afterward we could head back to the cabin with Gramps for dinner and a movie."

Jessie's cheeks reddened quickly. "That sounds like a date."

"Well, yes, it would be our first official date. What do you say?"

"Hmm. I don't know, Ryan. Sadly it's my day to clean baseboards and trash cans, and the floor needs mopping—"

"All right, all right. A simple *no* would suffice."

Jessie smiled. "Well, I don't suppose the dirt's going anywhere. Okay, you're on."

"Well, miracles never cease!"

"Funny you mentioned that. I've been thinking a great deal lately about miracles. Do you have a few minutes? Or do you need to leave?"

Ryan winked. "I'm yours for as long as you'll have me."

"All right, Romeo. Focus." Jessie leaned over and picked up her Book of Mormon. "We're talking religion now. I was researching miracles using the Book of Mormon's index, and I came upon an interesting scripture."

"Yeah?"

"Well?" Jessie pointed toward Rebecca's Book of Mormon.

Ryan smiled and picked it up.

"Good. Open to Ether. It's chapter twelve, verse twelve." Jessie waited till he was there and then she read out loud. "'For if there be no faith among the children of men, God can do no miracle among them; wherefore, he showed not himself until after their faith.'"

"I think God wanted to tell me all along about that letter in the lilacs. I just wasn't ready. I was bitter, resentful, and faithless. I wasn't ready to accept everything that would come as a result of that letter. But what I still don't understand is why some people get miracles and others don't. Gramps wanted Ruth to live, and I'm sure my mother prayed to get better." She paused thoughtfully. "Change of subject for just a minute. I was wondering if you would join me in my discussions with the missionaries? I mean, if you're ready that is?"

"I'd be glad to."

"Sometimes we meet at the church . . ."

Ryan's eyebrows rose and he rubbed his chin. "Is this an attempt to get me back into that building?"

Jessie spoke quickly, not wanting to ruin the moment. "Actually no, it isn't. If you're not ready for that, we can just take turns between your place and mine."

"Let's begin at your place and see what happens from there, okay?"

"Fair enough. Okay, back to the miracle thing. What do you think?"

"There's a lot to say on the subject, Jessie." Ryan settled back into the rocking chair, closing the Book of Mormon. "How much do you want to hear?"

"Start talking and I'll tell you when my brain is fried, okay?"

"The first thing that comes to mind is a scripture from Proverbs. 'Trust in the Lord with all thine heart; and lean not unto thine own understanding.' We have to remember who it is that's in charge, Jessie."

"But aren't miracles connected to faith? There are a lot of times I remember in the Book of Mormon where individuals prayed for the masses and because of their faith miracles took place. How are they any better than Ruth, my mother, or Katie?"

"They're not. Nothing is too hard for the Lord. But it *is* His plan, and our presence here on earth indicates that we accepted this plan. We proved faithful in premortality and are now subject to the test of mortality. That test, like we discussed before, entails doing *all things* whatsoever the Lord requires. Not just the good things, *all* things. The best gift we can give to the Lord is to willingly trust Him in everything, including those areas we don't understand. That's why I'm going to come to those missionary discussions with you—yes, even if it does mean going to the church building. Now, you said that you told Ken he needed to have a personal relationship with the Savior?"

"Yes."

"Well, I believe when you have fully accomplished that yourself, you won't question—as often—who gets a miracle and who doesn't."

"I just miss my mother and Ruth."

"I know." Ryan moved to the couch and reached out for Jessie's hands. "But remember, there is a great deal of work to do on the other side of the veil. Their lives go on." Ryan looked around her home and marveled how only six months previous it was a complete disaster, ready to be condemned. "You know, you're a lot like this house."

"Okay. Is there a compliment in there somewhere?"

"Remember when I first came out here with you?"

"How can I forget? You were terrified to enter. The front door fell off when you touched it. You feared for your life." Jessie chuckled at the memory.

"That's exactly how you were the first day we met. You were terrified. You thought your whole world had come crashing down. And look what you've accomplished. You created something wonderful out of this mess. And you also saw something wonderful in you and made it happen."

"No. *You* made it happen."

"Jessie, I was simply a tool. No different than all the tools we used on this place."

The crackling fire imbued the atmosphere with calm, and they both realized how much they appreciated the shared moment. "Hey, what's hanging in the doorway to the kitchen?" Ryan asked.

"Oh, that's just some greenery I found in the stable," Jessie teased.

"Hmm. Think we ought to go get some fresh cider?"

"Sure, why not?"

* * *

Beth knocked on Ken's door. "Come in, Mom." Beth opened the door to find the room amazingly cluttered again. She sighed happily. It was good to see the mess. "Hey, son, how's it going?"

"Great. I can't believe how fast this computer is."

"That was your dad calling. Turns out the hunch he had at the Blakes'—the one that got him to call us—*was* right after all. Those bugs were placed during the time he and some officers came out to investigate the shooting. Apparently one of the recently hired officers was on Thornton's payroll." Ken's attention was completely on the screen before him. "Ken? Yo, Ken!"

"Oh, yeah. Sorry, Mom."

"Did you hear me?"

"Yeah, Mom. I got it." Ken continued to plunk away at the keyboard.

"Either you give me a hundred percent or I pull the plug," Beth said, trying to remain patient.

"Okay." Ken clicked on SAVE, then shut the computer down.

"Ken, I'm worried about you. We've only been home a couple of days, and since the events of the day after Christmas are still quite vivid in my mind, I'm certain they are in yours too. You haven't said much about how you're doing."

"I'm not sure what you want me to say, Mom."

"You were so calm when Thornton was threatening us. It was like you weren't afraid to die."

"You're still worried I'm going to kill myself. I'm not going to kill myself. I *was* afraid to die, but I was more afraid that *you* were going to die. I just tried to think of what Dad would do if he was there. I don't know what else to say."

Beth knew there was more to it but that she wouldn't be the one to get it out of him. "Your dad and I have decided to let you go to the Blake place for the summer."

"Yes! Can I take Goliath?"

"They've agreed to that also, yes."

"Awesome."

"Until then, we do plan on meeting with them once a month together."

"Dad too?"

"Yes."

"Wow. He said he was going to be at Uncle Bill's for a while."

"That's what he said. He has some things he has to work through. He's coming over tonight to go over finances."

"Things okay?"

"Things are fine. But I'm going to be looking for different work because I want to move." She waited for his reaction.

"You mean, move out of this house?"

"Yes. What do you think?"

"Are we going into hiding because you're worried Thornton will send someone after us?"

"Well, I can't say that hasn't occurred to me—I don't want to spend the rest of our lives looking over our shoulders. But no, I want to leave because I think that in the process of therapy and with you going away for six weeks, well, we'll want a change. I think we're ready to move on physically as well as emotionally. This home holds too many memories that I just don't think are healthy to hang on to."

"I wouldn't mind moving as long as I can have a yard for Goliath."

"Oh, don't worry. We'll find a place with a yard, fence, and garden for him to dig in."

Ken's eyes swept across his dresser and fixed upon the lone gift sitting on its top. "Oh, Mom—I can't believe you haven't opened this yet!" Ken reached up and grabbed the present he'd wrapped days earlier. He tossed it in her lap. "Here."

"Thanks, son." Beth began to open it slowly as her son watched from the corner of his eye, seemingly uninterested. She didn't care what was inside. Her son was home. She watched as he grabbed Goliath, tossing him gently in the air. His elbow knocked over the lone pewter soldier in the sandbox. He reached in, picked him up, and slowly placed him on the side with the rest of the army. It was a beginning.

# ABOUT THE AUTHOR

Cherrann Kaye Bailey was born and raised in South Bend, Indiana, and joined the LDS Church when she was seventeen. She moved to Utah after serving a mission in Japan. Her writing career began at age seven, and while her teachers cringed at her attempts, she never stopped trying.

Cherrann and her husband own and operate a full-time daycare in their home. This career allows her time with her husband and two children on a regular basis. She enjoys writing and sharing stories with the children in her care and learning from them. She's active in the LDS Church and thrives when kept busy.

Cherrann enjoys corresponding with her readers, who can write to her in care of Covenant Communications, P.O. Box 416, American Fork, Utah 84003-0416, or e-mail her via Covenant at info@covenant-lds.com.